FAERY FORGED

Book Two in the War Faery Trilogy

D1104692

43522676

Lush Publications

PERTH

East Baton Rouge Parish Library
Baton Rouge, Louisiana

Published in Perth, Australia by Lush Publications.

First Published in Australia 2014

Copyright © Donna Joy Usher 2014

Cover Design: Derek Murphy, www.creativindie.com

Editor: Felicity Kay

The right of Donna Joy Usher to be identified as the Author of the Work has been asserted in accordance with the Copyright, Design and Patents Act of 1988.

This book is a work of fiction. Any similarities to that of people living or dead are purely coincidental.

All rights reserved. No part of this publication may be reproduced, stored in a retrieval system, or transmitted, in any form or by any means without the prior written permission of the publisher, nor be otherwise circulated in any form or binding or cover other than that in which it was published and without a similar condition being imposed on the purchaser.

Usher, Donna Joy

Faery Forged

ISBN: 978-0-9925999-1-1

Pp 361

Acknowledgements

I would like to take this opportunity to thank all of my loyal fans for your emails, tweets and Facebook messages. Your kind words make the late nights and hard work worth it.

Thanks also go to my editor, Felicity Kay, for her tireless work, her in-depth grammar lessons and her sparkling company, and to my cover designer, Derek Murphy, for another amazing cover.

Last but not least, I would like to thank you for buying *Faery Forged*. I truly hope you enjoy it.

Previously in *Faery Born*...

In Book One of the War Faery Trilogy, Isadora Scrumpleton (Izzy) is finally found by her familiar. The only problem is that he is a dog, an unprecedented event in the witching world. But even though his presence gives her access to her magic, she is unable to control her powers.

When the Faery Queen, Eloise, comes knocking on her door, Izzy learns that not only is she half-witch, half-faery, but that she is a dream-walker who roams the dreamland Trillania while she sleeps. In Trillania, she has been dating the scrumptious Aethan, a Faery Prince, and son of Eloise.

Unlike other faery dream-walkers, she has no memory of this because her witch-half, which is dominant in her waking hours, allows for no memory of these night-time dalliances.

After goblins crash her eighteenth birthday party, she joins the faery Border Guard and starts officially courting Aethan. Galanta, the evil goblin Queen, takes a personal interest in her and her relationship with Aethan. Izzy eventually realises that Aethan has been trapped into courting her by his Border Guard binding, a spell that prevents them from talking to others about Trillania.

Humiliated, Izzy runs away from him during an expedition into Trillania and calls Emerald, a dragon, to her. She rides Emerald into battle against the goblins, but is overcome and captured. Galanta tortures her, but an unexpected effect of the torture enables her to access her powers and escape.

After she has healed, Aethan reveals his true feelings for her, but is immediately kidnapped by Galanta. Izzy rides with the Border Guard to the Black Mountains in their bid to save him. There, they encounter a barrier that only she and her arch-nemesis, Isgranelda, are able to pass.

She and Isgranelda traverse the mountain and find Aethan unconscious, but alive. Isgranelda sheds her shape-shifting guise to reveal she has been Galanta all along. A vicious battle erupts between the two, but Galanta escapes before Izzy can kill her.

Izzy drips blood onto the rock where Aethan sleeps, releasing him from Galanta's spell. The rock splits in two and, as a strange wind blows around her, her two sides merge and her memories of Aethan return. He wakes as she kisses him, but when he opens his eyes and looks at her he has no memory of *her*.

The rest of the Border Guard arrives as goblin drums begin beating. They all flee down the mountain and back to Isilvitania. Izzy returns to her home, quickly falling asleep so that she can access Trillania to see what Galanta is up to. She is horrified to see Galanta weaving a spell over the rock on which Aethan lay.

While Izzy watches, Galanta sacrifices a little girl, releasing her blood onto the rock. A shape begins to emerge, flowing out of the rock until a man has formed. As the man speaks, Izzy is horrified to realise that Galanta has released Santanas Gabrielle, the mad War Faery, from the stone he was imprisoned in 12 years ago.

Now... read on to find out what fate has in store for Izzy in *Faery Forged*.

Chapter One

The Bad News Is, There Is No Good News

Silent screams sounded in my head as I struggled against the bed sheets. Wet with sweat, the material wrapped my legs like a cocoon. I tore and pulled until first one leg and then the other escaped their silky prison. Then I collapsed back on the bed, my breath coming in hoarse rasps and my heart thundering as if about to burst from my chest and race around the room.

I stared at the ceiling without seeing it. Instead, what I had just witnessed played through my mind like a horror movie stuck on loop.

Do something.

I blinked until my vision returned and forcibly relaxed my hands. One-by-one my fingers released their death grip on my sheets.

You have to do something.

Scrubbing tears from my cheeks, I threw the covers back, clawing through my wardrobe for fresh jeans and a t-shirt.

You have to tell Rako.

I threw my clothes on and shoved my feet into sneakers, giving up on the laces the third time my shaking hands failed to tie a bow.

He'll know what to do.

I took the stairs two at a time and burst into the kitchen. Grams sat at the kitchen table, a cup of tea in one hand and a spoon in the other. My familiar, Scruffy, sat at her feet, staring hopefully at her lunch.

'Who died?' she asked.

I pawed through the contents of my bag searching for my car keys.

She put her spoon down and peered at me. 'Izzy, what's going on?'

I turned my bag upside down and shook it. The contents rained onto the floor. The keys were not amongst them.

'Isadora Scrumpleton.' Grams' voice would normally have stopped me in my tracks.

The fruit bowl!

Throwing the bag on the floor, I pushed past her to the fruit bowl and snagged my keys out from under a bunch of bananas.

I bent to retrieve the bag, whacking my head on the corner of the kitchen table. Black clouded my vision, but the pain was nothing; nothing compared to what I knew.

Grams stopped me as I was shovelling my things back into my bag. 'You can't drive like that.'

'Santanas is back.' I wrenched open the front door and sprinted to the car. Scruffy jumped onto my lap and over to the passenger side while I fumbled with the keys.

The third time I dropped them onto the floor I had to concede that perhaps she had a point. My hands were shaking too much to turn on the ignition, how was I going to drive safely?

Grams wrenched open the car door. 'Move over,' she ordered. She waited while I slithered to the other side of the car and then slipped behind the wheel. Plucking the keys off the floor she deftly inserted one into the ignition.

'Show off,' I said as the car roared to life.

'You know this for sure?' She drove out the driveway and headed up the main road, her foot flat to the floor.

'Yes.' I put my head in my hands. 'It's all my fault.'

'You can't blame yourself for not being able to stop Galanta.' Grams pulled into the other lane and raced around a car doing the legal speed limit.

'Oh, yes I can.' I shook my head vehemently, fighting the nausea that crawled up my throat. 'Last night, while I was saving Aethan, I released Santanas's soul.'

We were silent for the rest of the drive to the Border Guard barracks.

***

'You're early.' Rako looked as if he could do with another few hours' sleep. 'I said sixteen hundred.'

'Galanta resurrected Santanas.' I yanked the seat out from the other side of his desk and perched on the edge.

All signs of weariness disappeared. 'In Trillania?'

I nodded my head. 'She sacrificed a little girl.'

He slumped back into his seat. 'You actually saw him?'

'I don't know what he looks like but I'm pretty sure it was him.'

He ran his fingertips down the long scar on his cheek while he stared at the space above my head. 'But how?'

I squirmed on the edge of the hard stool. 'It's my fault.' I leant forward and put my head in my hands. 'I released his soul from the stone.'

'That's not possible.'

'Aethan was lying on it. I read the poem and gave blood.'

'Do you remember the poem?'

I looked up at him through my fingers. 'Only blood can let me live. Only blood can set me free. Blood of my own one true love, or of a descendant born of me.'

Air hissed through his teeth. 'That's the stone all right. But you shouldn't have been able to activate that spell.'

'I'm his niece.'

He shook his head. 'Had to be offspring from his loins. He didn't have any. That's why we chose that. His one true love was dead and he had no kids. It was a no-brainer.'

'Why did you have to choose anything? Why couldn't you have just locked him up in that rock forever?' Petulance rode my voice like a bull rider.

'A spell that powerful had to have an out. A relief valve of sorts. We knew he'd be fighting it from the inside so we couldn't risk the pressure blowing the whole thing apart.'

It made sense in a weird way. There was still a lot (nearly everything) I didn't know about faery magic.

'We *all* need to hear the whole story. Wait here.' He hopped up.

'Wait,' I said. There was something I needed to know. 'This thing with Aethan, is it the same as it was with me?'

'His memory loss?'

I nodded my head.

The look on his face softened. 'I would assume so.'

'So if he gets told anything about me?'

He nodded. 'He may not get those memories back.' He stared at me for a second longer before he turned and strode from the room. Ten minutes later he returned. 'Not enough room in here,' he said. 'Come on.'

Scruffy and I followed him up the sandstone stairs to the top floor of the barracks. I'd never been into this part of the building before. Down the end of the corridor was a large conference room. Several of the Border Guard were there already. Wilfred grinned and gestured to the empty seat next to him.

Aethan sat on the other side of Wilfred. He glanced at me as I sat, but returned to his conversation without even a smile. I did a valiant job of ignoring the knife stabbing into my chest.

More men filed into the room over the next few minutes, but Rako didn't close the door until Wolfgang, my one-time faery tutor, arrived. He gave me a small wave and took the seat at the opposite end from Rako.

'Isadora has some disturbing news,' Rako said. He waved a hand in my direction.

I cleared my throat and told them about how Isgranelda had really been Galanta, the Goblin Queen. I told them about the stone, and how I had woken Aethan. And finally, I told them about what I had seen in Trillania.

There was a deathly silence when I had finished. Even Wilfred seemed lost for words. And then Rako said, 'A *shape-shifter*? Wolfgang, is that possible?'

Wolfgang tapped his fingertips on the table. 'Years ago I heard rumours that a shape-shifter had emerged in the west. I didn't give them much credence.' He sighed. 'Looks like I should have.'

'You can't blame yourself,' Aethan said. 'There hasn't been a shape-shifter in a thousand years. Besides,' he let out a laugh, 'how can we believe this, this,' he waved a hand in my direction, '*girl* about something this important.'

The knife in my chest twisted painfully.

'If Izzy said that's what happened, then I believe her.' At least I could still count on Wilfred.

'As do I,' Rako said.

'And I,' Wolfgang said.

Aethan stared at me, distrust etched into the lines of his perfect face. Then he shrugged. 'Seems like I'm outnumbered.'

'It's not a total disaster – yet,' Wolfgang said.

'How is this not a disaster?' I wanted to scream with frustration. Why were we still sitting here? We needed to be doing something. Anything.

'He still doesn't have a body.'

'But I saw him.'

'You saw his spirit reforming. That's why Galanta had to do it in Trillania. If she reforms him here, without a body ready, his soul will fragment. But a spirit can live in Trillania forever.'

'So she still needs to join him to a body,' Wilfred looked thoughtful. 'Why wouldn't she have put him into one of her warriors?'

'She needs an empty shell with a beating heart,' Wolfgang said. 'So his spirit can enter uncontested. And it would have to be compatible with his spirit.'

'A faery.' Aethan leant back and put his hands behind his head. 'She needs a faery. What can we do to stop her?'

'Only she can join his soul to a body, so it's very simple. We kill her.'

I liked the sound of that a lot.

'First we have to catch her,' Rako said.

From there the conversation turned to one on tactics. Emissaries would need to be sent to warn and unify the magical lands. The Heads of State and other Border Guard units would have to be notified of the threat. And a rotating roster of Border Guards would be organised so the hunt for Galanta was continuous.

'You three,' Rako pointed at Wilfred, Aethan and me, 'why don't you go in and look at the site. See if you can find anything useful.'

Wilfred got an armband for himself and then the three of us trooped down to the sleep room. I tried not to notice the rippling of Aethan's muscles as he vaulted onto the bed next to mine. Thoughts like that would just get me into trouble.

The adrenaline rush I had been operating on had vanished, leaving only exhaustion in its wake. I needed no sleep spell to get to Trillania today.

While I waited for Aethan and Wilfred to join me on the other side, I clothed myself in battle gear. Fitted leather pants with daggers strapped to my thighs and ankles, and a fur vest which left my arms free for movement. I added a dagger to the outside of my left bicep, a sword across my back, and a quiver and bow. Then I sent out a mental call to Emerald. There was no answer.

Before I could start to worry, Wilfred and Aethan shimmered into view.

'The A Team is back in business.' Wilfred held up his hand for a high five.

I ignored it and cut my eyes to Aethan. He didn't know we were *any* sort of team let alone the *A team*.

'Oh yeah, right.' Wilfred's arm fell limply to his side.

'So, umm, Isadora,' Aethan said my name awkwardly, 'where did the resurrection happen?'

'Edge of the Black Forest. I'll take you there.' I reached out and grabbed Wilfred's hand, leaving him to connect to Aethan, and then I pictured the thicket I had hidden in earlier that day.

'Owwwwww.' Wilfred let out a screech as I landed us inside the thicket I had crouched in. He vanished from my side and re-appeared standing on the other side of the bush. What I could see of his face through his bushy, orange beard was covered in little cuts.

'Oops,' I said, trying to suppress my grin. The big man had done far worse to me over the years.

Aethan seemed oblivious to Wilfred and me as he combed the clearing for evidence. I think the broken stone covered in dark, dried blood was all the evidence he needed. The little girl was gone and I tried not to think of her parents' grief when they found her lifeless body.

I crawled out from the thicket.

'So that's where you hid?' Aethan pointed at the bush.

I nodded my head. 'Galanta stood there.' I pointed at the area next to the stone.

'You were lucky not to be seen.'

I moved to where he was standing and looked at my hiding spot. The side of the bush was patchy in places. I *had* been lucky.

'Describe what happened.'

Was he asking because he didn't trust me? I took a deep breath and repeated what I had told them earlier.

When I had finished he nodded his head and said, 'So as the blood touched the stone, the figure appeared?'

I felt a surge of power pulling me to the left. 'Watch out,' I shrieked, diving at Aethan. I hit him hard in the middle and carried him to the ground. A long spear sliced through the air where he had been standing and thudded into the trunk of a tree. We stared at the quivering shank for a second before leaping back to our feet. I pulled my sword from its sheath.

'Orcs,' Wilfred hissed.

But it wasn't orcs that surrounded us. A score of mudmen crouched in the trees. Their grotesque smiles showed rows of needle-sharp teeth. Although they were smaller than goblins, about half the size, they made up for that with sheer ferocity. Their green skin and squishy faces had birthed a series of jokes about mudmen and frogs, but I didn't feel like laughing as they surrounded us. Their eyes glowed maniacally as they raised their spears and shook them at us.

'Are we hunting?' I said out of the corner of my mouth. If we tried to take them all on, there was a very good chance one of us would get hurt.

'Don't like our chances,' Wilfred murmured.

One of the mudmen stepped forward and pointed his spear at us. 'We serve the War Faery,' he croaked. 'Hail the War Faery.' He thrust his spear towards the sky and the others followed suit.

'Let's go,' Aethan said.

I reached back and laid a hand on his arm and the mudmen disappeared from view. A quick glance at where we had entered Trillania, then I was opening my eyes to a view of the sleep room ceiling. Scruffy hopped up from his position at my feet and proceeded to lick my face.

'That was weird,' Wilfred said as he unclipped the armband. 'I wonder why they didn't attack.'

'They tried to skewer me,' Aethan said. 'I'm guessing they didn't attack any further because they'd lost the element of surprise.'

I wasn't so sure, but I didn't voice my opinion. It didn't hold much weight with Aethan at the moment. I mean the man hadn't even thanked me for saving his life.

Rako entered the room as I was climbing off the bed.

'It all checks out,' Aethan said. 'The stone, the blood, it's all there.'

As if there had ever been any doubt.

'And we encountered a band of mudmen.' Wilfred moved to stand next to Aethan. 'They pretty much told us Santanas was back.'

'You need to go talk to your father,' Rako said to Aethan. 'And Orion. They need to know.'

Aethan nodded his head and moved towards the door. 'Not alone,' Rako said. 'You three stay together from now on. Consider yourselves a unit.'

I felt a thrum of pleasure at the thought of staying near Aethan. That faded when he gestured towards me and said, 'She'll just slow us down.'

'You are a high profile target. All pure faeries of royal blood will have guards with them at all times.'

I shuddered as I realised what Rako meant.

Galanta needed a body. A *faery* body.

Aethan pulled a face. 'Well give me a *proper* guard. Wilfred and Brent.'

The twisty knife was back. Damn him and his amnesia. I was going to enjoy killing Galanta when I caught up with her again.

'I saved your life once already tonight and I'll do it again if need be.' I met his gaze and held it.

He stared deep into my eyes and for one brief second I thought I saw a flicker of recognition. 'Fine,' he said, pushing past me, 'but if you can't keep up, I'm leaving you behind.'

I spluttered as I followed him. *Can't keep up?* I'd show him a thing or two about keeping up.

Wilfred grinned and rubbed his hands together. 'Excellent.'

***

'Get what you need,' Aethan said when we reached the landing that led to the second years' accommodation. 'We'll meet you downstairs.'

I raced to my room, changing into my uniform and strapping on my weapons in record time. Then I bolted down the stairs two at a time, meeting Aethan and Wilfred at the entrance to the car park. My car was nowhere to be seen so I made a mental note to contact Grams. I was going to need to get it back at some stage.

'Finally,' Aethan said, gesturing towards Wilfred's red sports car.

I rolled my eyes at Will and climbed into the back. Scruffy jumped in beside me and stretched out onto the rest of the bench seat.

'We have to be back in time to take our turn tonight,' Aethan said, as if to explain his impatience.

I had a feeling his bad mood was more to do with the hole in his memory than my tardiness. He had never liked being in the dark about anything and having me there as a walking-talking reminder that Galanta had played with his mind would make him clench his teeth in frustration.

Well, he was just going to have to get used to it because I wasn't going anywhere, *especially* not if he were in danger.

Wilfred made record time through the country lanes back to Eynsford. He pulled up at the entry to the castle ruins and met my eyes in the rear view mirror. 'You want to help Aethan with the veil?'

I'd only ever done it once but I didn't want Aethan thinking I was more of a hindrance than he already did. 'Sure.'

I wiggled out through the passenger side door and went to stand next to Aethan. The last time we had been here, doing this, he had almost kissed me.

Great.

The last thing I needed was to get distracted by the thought of his hard body pressing into mine. I shook my head and pushed the memory to the back of my mind.

Then I closed my eyes till I could feel the weight of the veil settle over me. I could feel a weakness in it where Aethan was preparing the opening. I reached for that weakness with my mind and my hands, then I grasped the edge and pulled.

The veil gathered in my hands like the fabric of a heavy curtain as I moved it to the side. I opened my eyes and stared through the hole Aethan and I had rent in the fabric of the veil. We held it like that as Wilfred drove the car through, and then we moved through to the other side and let go of the edges. They flowed back together, overlaying the view of the village with that of a forest of tall oaks.

I clambered into the back of the car for the short drive to the castle, stifling a yawn as I stared out the windows at the garden faeries that flitted through the branches.

'Perhaps you should stay in the car and catch up on some sleep,' Aethan said.

'I don't think so.' Even though my blood boiled I managed to smile sweetly at him. 'Goodness knows what trouble you might get into without me there to watch over you.'

Wilfred chuckled as Aethan shook his head and climbed out of the car. I crawled out and trotted to catch up. When he got his memory back I was going to make him pay for every single time he doubted me. And the currency for that payment was going to be in kisses.

I followed them into the castle, up a flight of stairs and down a long hall. Aethan knocked on an ornately carved door.

'Enter.' I recognised King Arwyn's voice.

As we entered, he looked up from a piece of paper he had been reading. His face broke into a huge grin and he rose to clasp Aethan's arm. Another faery with his back to us studied a piece of parchment. Piles of paperwork sat on the table between them.

I was happy to see that Queen Eloise was absent. If she had found out that I was there against Aethan's wishes, I doubted even Rako would have been able to stop her from exiling me.

King Arwyn beckoned Wilfred and me toward the table. 'Orion, say hello to your cousin, Isadora.'

The other faery started as if only just realising we were there. 'I'm so sorry,' he said, standing and turning to face us, 'I was reading a report on this year's crops.' He reached out and swept my hand up in his. 'It's a pleasure to meet you Isadora. I've heard a lot about you.'

'All of it positive I'm sure,' I said, staring at him. It was like looking at a blonde version of Aethan: same height; same broad stature; and same dreamy, midnight-blue eyes. Even his hair had the rumpled, just-got-out-of-bed look. The main difference, apart from the colour of his hair, was that where Aethan always had a delicious amount of stubble on his cheeks, Orion's face was shaved smooth.

'Father,' Aethan said, 'we bring grave news.' We took seats at the table while Aethan filled them in. He managed to do a remarkable job considering he couldn't mention Trillania.

'And you're absolutely certain of this?' King Arwyn directed the question to me.

'Absolutely certain.' I nodded my head.

King Arwyn pushed back from the table. 'This *is* grave news.' His eyes were sad. 'Nothing good will come from this day.'

Orion drummed his fingers on the table. 'But what to do about it? What does Rako recommend?'

'That we kill her before she finishes the resurrection. Other than that we need to start uniting the lands,' Aethan said.

Orion nodded his head. 'We need the night faeries.'

'We will need them all, son.'

'Yes, we will. We're not going to win over the goblins or the orcs, but the night faeries have always been fence sitters. With the right enticement we could win them to our cause. At last count their population rivalled our own. Their allegiance could make or break us.'

King Arwyn was silent while he contemplated Orion's words. Finally he nodded his head. 'You are right, as usual. If we get to them first, we might sway them to our side. What sort of enticement were you thinking?'

'A marriage.'

It took a few seconds for me to understand what he meant.

Aethan got there before I did. 'Orion, no. You don't need to sacrifice yourself. Tell him father.'

Rather than agree though, King Arwyn stared at the ceiling. Those sad eyes were back. He sighed and shifted his gaze to Orion's. 'It might work,' he said.

'You can't,' Aethan said.

Orion chuckled lightly. 'You were always the romantic.' He reached over and touched Aethan's arm lightly. 'I always knew it would come to this.'

Aethan shook his head, 'It doesn't have to. You could marry someone you love.'

'Perhaps I will,' Orion said. 'If I am lucky, love will blossom from the union.'

'But a *night faery*.' Abhorrence dripped through Aethan's words.

'It will be what it will be.' King Arwyn pushed his chair back from the table. 'Will you go son? On behalf of your brother?'

'You want me to choose his bride?'

'I doubt there will be much choice in it,' Orion said. 'But yes, you must present the offer. As next-in-line to the throne, it is only proper.'

Aethan looked between his father and his brother. His eyes held the anguish he felt for his brother. I resisted the urge to reach out a hand to comfort him. He would not appreciate it.

'Fine,' he said. 'I will do this thing for you.'

'You will need to take an entourage.' Orion reached for a piece of paper to start making a list. I got the feeling he was very good at list making.

'No.' Aethan shook his head. 'We will traverse goblin country. We need to travel light and fast. That's no place for an entourage. The fewer people we have with us, the less chance our path will be detected.'

I waited till we were back in Wilfred's car, speeding towards the barracks before I voiced my main concern. 'Do you think this is very wise?'

'Of course not. Night faeries are treacherous creatures.'

'Not that. Do you think going through goblin country is wise? What with Galanta after a body and everything.'

'It's the most direct route. To avoid it would add weeks onto our trip for no real gain. Besides, the other options are just as dangerous.'

Our trip? Well at least he wasn't trying to exclude me any more.

I made a non-committal grunt in my throat and settled back into the seat. We'd see what Rako had to say about it.

Chapter Two

We're Off To See The Wizard

'It just might work.' Rako scratched his chin while he contemplated Aethan's plan.

So much for the voice of reason.

'With the night faeries as firm allies, the goblins would be less likely to raid the country between their lands and ours. We could crush them between us if they did.'

'And the whole Galanta-wanting-a-faery-body thing?' I raised my eyebrows and pointed at Aethan.

'You don't think you're up to guarding me?' A faint smile matched the mocking tone in Aethan's voice.

'Oh, I can guard you.' I put my hands on my hips and stared him in the eye. 'It's stopping you from doing something stupid that may be the problem.'

He met me stare-for-stare and I felt the old chemistry zing between us.

'I'll make you a deal,' his voice was a low murmur. '*I'll* only do stupid stuff if *you* do.'

'There will be no *stupid* stuff.' Rako's voice caused me to jump.

For a second I'd forgotten he and Wilfred were there. I felt a blush creep up my cheeks.

Aethan smirked and turned to Rako. 'No stupid stuff,' he reiterated.

Rako shook his head as he looked at Wilfred. 'I'd ask you to keep them out of trouble but that's like asking a bear to stay away from the honeypot.'

Wilfred fixed an expression of wide-eyed innocence on his face and spread his hands. 'I don't know what you're talking about.'

Rako took a seat behind his table and turned back to Aethan. 'So who are you going to take with you to Emstillia?'

Emstillia. I'd seen the name on a huge map hanging in the second years' recreation room. It was a long way from Isilvitania.

'I want to be able to travel fast, but I need enough people so that we can fight our way out of any chance goblin encounters.'

'You'll want to go the long way round, skirt along the edge of Galanta's lands.'

Aethan nodded. 'If we're lucky we can make it there and back without her realising we've even been.'

'So no more than ten.'

'I was thinking six.'

Rako let out a low whistle. 'And if you run into a band of them?'

'Ride really, really fast.' Aethan grinned. 'Let's face it, if we run into a band of them, six or ten's not going to make much difference.'

Rako nodded his head. 'Take Brent and Luke.'

'And I was thinking Wolfgang.'

'You don't want another sword?'

'It would be good to have some magic on our side.'

I wanted to tell him that *I* could handle the magic side of it, but the problem was, I couldn't. Even with my faery and witch sides aligned I still had no idea how to control my powers. But on the bright side, if I were going to spend time with Wolfgang he might be able to help me.

'You leaving tomorrow?'

'First thing. I want to make it to the edge of the goblin lands before we stop.'

Wilfred rubbed his hands together. 'Road trip. Awesome.'

Rako stood and walked towards the door. 'Pack light, don't forget your dream-catchers, and you two,' he pointed at Aethan and me, 'no visits to Trillania while you're away.'

Not go after Galanta? Was he kidding?

I put what I hoped was a meek expression on my face and kept my eyes downcast. If I didn't vocalise a response then I wouldn't be breaking any promises.

I left the conference room and headed back to the second years' dormitory to start packing for the 'road trip'.

'You're back.'

I stopped in the process of folding my camouflage pants and turned to Jared. 'Not for long.' I gestured towards the saddlebags I had found in the back corner of my wardrobe. Where we were going, cars wouldn't cut it. Apart from the notorious terrain, there were no fuel supplies in any of the magical lands.

Jared's feline familiar Tinka extended her nose to Scruffy. She stretched out her tongue, licked him on the nose, and proceeded to groom him.

'Always the mother.' Jared shook his head and opened his own wardrobe. He dug around and pulled out saddlebags identical to mine. 'Where are you off to?'

'Night faeries. You?'

'Peace mission to the gnomes.' He was silent for a moment while he checked the pockets on the bag. 'So, is it true?' He looked up at me through his shaggy, brown fringe. 'Is he really back?'

I sighed and sat down on the edge of my bed. 'Yep.'

'And you saw it?'

'Saw the whole thing. It was....' How best to describe the horror of what I had witnessed? 'Disturbing.'

'Man, that's the pits.' His face scrunched up and for a second I thought he was going to cry.

Tinka finished grooming Scruffy and jumped up onto Jared's bed. She circled a few times, pawing at the blankets before settling into a ball pressed up against Jared's thigh. He reached a hand down and rubbed behind her ears.

'You okay?'

He dashed the back of his arm across his eyes (whizbang, he *had* been about to cry) and said, 'My sister was one of the 'Taken'.'

My breath escaped my body in a loud whoosh. Taken. One of the children sacrificed by Santanas.

'That's why I got into this gig.' He waved a hand at his Border Guard uniform. 'When they brought her body home, I swore I would avenge her.'

'We will stop this.' I reached a hand towards him. 'And you will have your revenge.'

A wry grin came over his face. 'You, me and the rest of the army.'

'Indeed.' I returned his smile.

We were silent while he packed the rest of his stuff. 'Gotta go. They'll be waiting.'

'Good luck,' I said.

'I'm about to meet a group of gnomes. How much luck do I need?'

'Don't make any bargains with them and you won't need any.' Gnomes were notorious deal makers. No matter how well you thought you'd managed to broker, you always ended up with the short end of the stick.

'Try to stay out of trouble.' He patted Scruffy on the head, picked up his saddlebags and waved goodbye over his shoulder.

After Jared had gone I used my mirror to contact Sabby. I told her I was going on a peace-making expedition, but didn't mention why we needed the peace making. It was probably best not to start a world-wide panic if we could help it. If Wolfgang were correct, we still had a chance of stopping Santanas's full return.

Then I tried home, but neither Mum nor Grams were there, so instead I finished packing, had a shower and headed down to the mess for dinner.

I filled my plate and took a seat next to Wilfred. 'Where's amnesia boy?'

Wilfred snorted. 'That's the pot calling the kettle black.'

'Mine wasn't amnesia. Mine was schizophrenia.'

He barked out a laugh. 'He's organising provisions for the trip.'

'So what's the plan for tomorrow?'

'We ride as far as we can.' He stuffed a piece of roast pork into his mouth, chewed twice, then swallowed.

I rolled my eyes and handed a chunk of roast beef down to Scruffy. Wilfred had never been a planner. He preferred to wade into battle and fight his way back out. 'We hunting tonight?' There were some first years sitting near us so I couldn't mention Trillania.

'Nah,' Wilfred said with his mouth full. 'Rako wants us fully rested.'

'How are they going to hunt successfully with so many of us off on other missions?' I was guessing none of us would be allowed to dream-walk whilst away from the barracks.

Brent pulled the seat next to me out and put his plate on the table. 'The Australians and South Africans are spreading their shifts to help us out.'

I smiled at him around a mouthful of food. I hadn't had all that much to do with him while my fae side had been dream-walking but I liked and respected the man.

Luke pulled a seat out from the opposite side of the table and plonked into it. 'Have you heard? Larkson and

Bobbington are having none of it.' He took a long swig from his mug of coffee and then banged it back onto the table. 'Dark Sky save us from pompous fools.'

Mark Larkson and Ralf Bobbington were the human and witch Prime Ministers. It didn't bode well if they didn't believe us. The Border Guard may have been a faery-derived body, but it strived to protect *all* the different races – magical and non-magical alike.

I ate my dinner while listening to the easy banter of the three men. Then I dilly-dallied over dessert, and then a cup of tea, but it soon became apparent that Aethan wouldn't be joining us. I squished my disappointment into a little ball and tossed it at the waste-paper basket in my mind. I missed, of course, and instead had to live with the dull ache around my heart.

When I could no longer pretend there was any reason for me to still be there, I headed up to bed. The room was empty but for one exception. Aethan's sister, Isla, was curled up like a cat on the middle of my bed. She stretched when she saw me, her long limbs slender and toned, and then she pushed herself up until she was sitting cross legged. As usual, I felt like a pimply adolescent in her presence.

'I came to see how you are.' Her glorious eyes bored into mine.

I ignored my sudden urge to cry. 'I'm fine, why?'

'A little birdy told me what happened.'

I sighed and plopped onto Jared's bed, pulling my legs up underneath myself till I was mimicking her cross-legged pose. 'It'll work out.'

'Hmmmm.' She held her hands out in front of her, inspecting her nails. 'Well for your sake I hope so.' She frowned and pulled her left hand in for closer inspection. 'Oh phooey. I've chipped one.'

'Don't you hate that.' I stared down at my dirty, torn nails. I couldn't remember the last time I'd taken a file to them.

'So what time do you leave in the morning?'

'First light.' They really were disgusting. If I were to win Aethan again perhaps I should consider at least *cleaning* them.

'Off to get Orion a bride. Who would have thought?' She pulled a file from her hair and began to reshape her nail.

Maybe I should try some polish. The bright-red lacquer Isla had on hers looked nice.

She finished with her nail and tossed the file to me. I set to work making mine presentable. It was going to take a while. 'Yes,' I said, 'and a night faery too.'

Isla hissed and jumped off my bed. All urges to make my nails pretty fled from my head. 'A night faery?' Her face held muted rage.

'You didn't know?' I looked at the nailfile in my hand and snorted in disgust. 'You *thralled* me?' I threw the file at her.

She whipped her hand out and plucked it from the air. 'I did what I needed to do to find out what I needed to know.'

'You could have just asked me.' I stood up and glared into her eyes.

'You wouldn't have told me.'

'No,' I said. 'But I might still trust you.'

For a second her eyes held a trace of sorrow, but then she stiffened her spine and the look in her eyes hardened. 'Well, it sure has been nice chatting.'

'Lovely,' I said.

'Perhaps we can do it again sometime.' A small smile tugged the corners of her mouth up. 'Next time you can choose the conversation.'

'I look forward to it.'

As she sauntered off, I realised the crazy thing was, that even though I didn't know her, and I sure as hell didn't trust her, I couldn't help but like her.

***

My alarm woke me while it was still dark. I dressed quickly in my camouflage pants and black t-shirt, trying hard not to wake the students still asleep in my dorm, then I carried my saddlebags and weapons down to the entry hall. Brent, Luke and Aethan were already there.

'Here.' Aethan handed me a package containing dried meat and biscuits. 'The rest of it is on the packhorses but I thought you two might be hungry.'

Scruffy let out a little bark and stared up at me with his big, brown eyes. I shook my head and passed the majority of the meat down to him. 'Thanks.' I tried to say it casually, but of course my voice caught halfway through and, instead, I sounded like a pubescent boy.

For a few seconds everything had been perfect. I had known that I loved him and he loved me, and then Galanta's spell had hit, and now I felt like a love-sick girl, crushing on her teacher – again.

I bustled Scruffy outside to where the horses were waiting. The same white mare I had ridden the other night was the only horse without bags already in place. I placed mine onto the blanket on her back and then went over the saddle, checking the girth strap and adjusting the stirrup length. When I was happy with everything, I hooked my quiver full of arrows and my unstrung bow over the pommel.

The rest of the group emerged from the building while I was settling my sword onto my back. They went over their horses while I picked up my mare's hooves one-by-one to check for stones. Then I ran my hands over her ankles and legs, checking for tender spots.

'Never fear, I am here.' Wilfred bounded down the front stairs and slapped Luke on the back.

'Wonderful,' Luke said, giving Wilfred a dirty look.

'On time as never,' Brent said, looking up from his horse's foot.

'We're meeting Wolfgang in Isilvitania.' Aethan swung up into his saddle.

Brent and Luke reached out together, each grasping an edge of the veil. They pulled open a large enough gap for man and horse to enter.

'You're late.'

I groaned inwardly as Isla's voice chimed from the other side of the veil.

'And you're not invited.' Aethan used his knees to direct his horse through the break in the veil.

'Now, now, brother, don't be like that.'

I leapt up onto my horse's back and dug my heels in so that she leapt in front of Wilfred's horse. Ignoring his jibe of 'young love' I urged her towards the veil. I had to stop Isla from dropping me in the poo.

'How did you even know we would be here?'

'I have my ways.' She laughed gently.

I resisted the urge to mention the word thrall. If I did, they would know I was the mole for sure.

'Well, ways or not, you're not coming.'

She was dressed in black from head-to-toe and looked every inch the warrior. A bow and quiver hung over the pommel of her horse, and a large broad sword was strapped to her back. I was impressed that she could handle such a large blade. 'You need me.'

Aethan burst out laughing. 'Why would we need you?'

'A little thing called etiquette.'

Aethan didn't say anything but she had his full attention.

'It would be unseemly for the future bride of the heir to the faery throne to be escorted by a group of men and only one female. Are you trying to cement a union,' she looked ill as she said the word, 'or start a war? You need an entourage of fae women to keep her company and protect her virtue.' She sniffed as if she didn't believe that a night faery might have any virtue to protect. 'At the very least, two females of the blood of the throne may appease them enough to allow this mission to be successful.'

Silence followed her words and then Brent, who had brought his horse through and mounted, said, 'She's right, damn it.'

She buffed her nails on her shirt and shot me a coy smile. I pretended to ignore it while I bit into one of the hard biscuits.

'But...,' Aethan started.

'I'm your only option. Which other female of the blood would you risk taking?'

He stared at her for a long moment while he weighed her words. 'If we tell mother,' Aethan said, 'she will insist we take the entourage.'

'Best to keep this our little secret till we are far enough away that they can't do anything about it.'

'Day's a wasting.' Wilfred was the only one who didn't seem upset by the idea of Isla coming.

'Fine,' Aethan said. 'We'll send a thought bubble when we get to goblin territory.'

Isla clapped her hands together and then turned the head of her mare and trotted off.

'Let's get one thing clear,' Aethan said as he rode after her, 'I'm the leader.'

Isla laughed her tinkly laugh as she let him take the lead. Instead she dropped back till she was riding next to Wilfred.

'What's a good-looking gal like you doing in a dump like this?' Will said.

'Looking for some fun. You look like fun. Are you?'

'I'm more fun than the lovechild of a circus and a fun-park.'

But I couldn't help but feel that with this one, he might have met his match.

***

We skirted around the woods surrounding the castle until we came to the road that ran towards goblin territory. Wolfgang was waiting for us there. He raised his bushy, grey eyebrows when he saw Isla riding beside Wilfred, and looked at Aethan.

'Isla thinks we're going to need her help with the etiquette side of things.' Aethan shrugged a shoulder. It seemed he'd come to terms with his sister's presence.

Wolfgang scratched at his beard. 'I was going to ask how she found out.'

I squirmed in my saddle, waiting for them all to look at me with accusation in their eyes.

'You know Isla,' Aethan said.

Wolfgang flicked his bridle and his mare trotted towards us, falling in beside me. 'And how have you been Isadora?' he asked me.

'Busy,' I replied. 'You heard that I'm whole?' It was the best way I could describe what had happened to me when my witch and faery sides had joined.

'Yes Rako told me. He also told me about....' He nodded his head towards Aethan.

I sighed. I didn't want to talk about that. There was, however, something else I did want to talk to him about. 'Wolfgang.' I cleared my throat nervously – I mean what if he refused me? 'Will you help me?'

'With that?' He nodded his head toward Aethan again.

'No.' My voice came out as a strangled yelp. 'With my powers.'

'Oh, well yes *that* I can help you with.'

A vision of Wolfgang trying to match-make Aethan and me popped into my head and I pressed my lips together so the resulting laugh could not escape.

'What in particular are you having trouble with?'

'Everything.'

Normally, when witches' powers came in, the witch was almost fluent in the field of their talent straight away. The hard part was discovering exactly what their talent extended to. The generic spells, that all witches could do, were taught well before our 17th birthdays when our familiars might find us.

It didn't seem to be working that way for me. I had a blend of faery and witch powers that sometimes worked together, but mostly competed for dominance. The results were only occasionally predictable. The best that could be said of them were that they were strong. But what were the use of strong, unpredictable powers?

Wolfgang rubbed his hands together. 'We'll start tonight. It will give us something to do while we travel.'

'How long will it take to reach Emstillia?'

'Well, if we encounter no difficulties, a little over a week.'

I didn't ask what those difficulties might be. Sometimes it's better not to know. That way the fear doesn't cripple you.

We didn't encounter any 'difficulties' that first day, arriving at the edge of the goblin territory as the sun was setting. I was happy to hand Scruffy down and clamber out of the saddle. My bottom had progressed from sore to numb and I felt like I had left it behind a few hours ago.

After we had groomed and fed the horses, we set up our small tents. I watched as Brent dug a hole and built a fire in it. 'Last chance for a hot meal till we get to Emstillia,' he said as he placed a pot over the flames. I watched him add water, dried meat and some herbs to the pot.

'Gotta love the smell of a campfire,' Wilfred said as he plonked onto a log next to me.

'There's something very romantic about it.' Isla's voice came from right behind us.

I was happy to see that Wilfred appeared as startled as I was.

She slid into view and perched on the log next to Wilfred, her waterfall of midnight hair shimmering in the light from the fire. 'Don't you think?'

I saw Wolfgang emerge from his tent and look in my direction.

'Don't normally have time for romance.' Will sounded out of his depth.

Wolfgang raised a hand and beckoned me.

'No time for romance?' Isla's voice had taken on a sultry edge.

I really wanted to stay and hear how this played out. It wasn't often that someone flummoxed Wilfred. But *I* had asked Wolfgang for the lessons; it would be rude to make him wait.

Wilfred made a grab for my arm as I hopped up off the log. 'Wolfgang needs me.' I shook his hand off and gave him a Cheshire-cat grin.

I followed Wolfgang into his tent. A small ball of light hovered in the air, casting a soft glow.

'Sit, sit,' Wolfgang said, lowering himself into a cross-legged position on a rug.

I made myself comfortable and then said, 'So how are we going to do this?'

'I want to see the extent of what you can do.'

'That's just it,' I tried unsuccessfully to keep the frustration out of my voice, 'I can't do *anything* predictably.'

'You can make a shield.'

'About ninety percent of the time.'

'Well let's start with that.'

Make a shield. I'd never consciously done it before. Where to start?

I threw my arms out in front of me, imagining the air hardening till it solidified. Nothing happened. I willed the air to obey me, I wished it with all my might. I closed my eyes and threw my arms out and prayed to the Dark Sky, but nothing that I did worked.

'Excellent,' Wolfgang said, rubbing his hands together. He took a rock from a pile beside him and placed it on the floor in front of me. 'Try levitating this.'

I wasn't sure what had been so excellent about my last effort but I shrugged and pulled my wand out of my braid. Pointing it at the rock I said, 'Risius rockius.' The rock quivered. 'Risius rockius,' I raised my voice. The rock hopped up and down as if there were something stopping it. There was no *way* I was failing at this as well as the shield.

The next time I flicked my wand and cried out the spell, Wolfgang threw another rock at my head. I shrieked and threw my hands up in front of me. A shield of air sliced through the tent in a perfect line, the material fluttering to the ground around us. I could see Aethan, Brent and Luke staring in our direction, their hands resting on their swords.

'Very interesting.' Wolfgang wiggled his fingers and the tent fabric danced back into the air, sliding up the tent poles till the two sides met. The edges seemed to bleed into each other until once again, the tent was whole.

I put my head into my hands. 'I'm useless.'

'On the contrary,' Wolfgang said, 'your use of magic is instinctual.'

I lowered my hands a little and peered up at him through my fingers. 'My magic is what?'

'You use magic without thinking about it. That's what we need to work on.'

'But… how am I meant to work on it without thinking about it.'

Wolfgang let out a laugh. 'Well that's what *I* have to think about. We will continue this tomorrow night.' His mouth widened into a yawn. 'I don't know about you but I think I am not long from my blankets. Let's get some grub.'

I put my hands over my face as I yawned as well.

'They really are contagious,' Wolfgang said as he pulled back the flap of his tent.

Brent had served up the stew while I had been having my lesson, leaving two bowls close to the fire to stay warm. Scruffy sat near the bowls, staring at them as if he could magically summon the food to himself.

'I've already fed him,' Brent said, 'but he licked that one.' He pointed at one of the bowls.

'Well,' Wolfgang picked up the other one, 'I guess this one's mine.'

'You licked it?' I said to Scruffy.

He seemed unconcerned by his lack of manners, instead continuing his staring.

Wolfgang finished before me. He rinsed off his bowl and headed back into his tent, leaving me sitting on a log by myself.

Isla and Wilfred were still sitting where I had left them and the other three were deep in their own conversation. Before Galanta's spell I would have quite happily joined them, but tonight I was too tired to resist the pain from being treated like a stranger, so instead I headed for my tent. I had things I needed to do.

I didn't bother to light my candle, unbraiding and brushing my hair in the dark. Then I took off my boots, lay down and pulled the blanket over me. Tonight was the last night I would have the luxury of even partially undressing. Once we were in goblin territory, what sleep we got we would get fully clothed and fully armed.

I heard low murmurs and scuffing boots as the others kicked dirt onto the fire and made their way to their tents. Material rustled and then a few minutes later, silence. I wanted to get to sleep as fast as I could; I was betting Wilfred was a snorer. And besides, I had work to do.

A few minutes later I was standing in Trillania. I sent my mind out to Emerald, searching north, west, east and south. She was nowhere to be found.

Where could she have gone? Was it possible she was hurt?

I was pushing my mind out to hunt for her again when an arm grabbed me from behind. I shrieked and ripped myself out of the grip, lashing out with my right arm as I turned around. I felt my fist connect, heard a crunching sound, and then Aethan was clutching his face. Blood dribbled through his fingers from his nose.

'That's going to hurt tomorrow,' Wilfred said.

We both spun towards him and said in unison, 'What are *you* doing here?'

He was wearing one of the armbands from the sleep room.

'You stole an armband?' I wasn't sure if the tone in Aethan's voice was for the armband or his broken nose.

'Not all of us are dream-walkers.' Wilfred's contrite voice was ruined by the big grin on his face.

'Yes, well, *none* of us are going to stay here.' Aethan put his head back and pinched the bridge of his nose. 'You both heard what Rako said.'

'Well, what are *you* doing here?' I put my hands on my hips and tried to stare him in the eyes. It was a bit hard though, what with him trying to stop the bleeding, and I had to be content with peering up his nose.

'I came because I knew *you* would.' He pointed his free hand at me.

'Such devotion,' Wilfred said in a dreamy voice.

I kicked him in the shin and said, 'Shut up Will.'

'None of us will be entering Trillania while we are away from the barracks.'

'Ahhh,' I said, turning to Will. 'And here I was thinking Galanta had only taken his memories. Looks like she stole his balls as well.'

I heard Wilfred laughing as I willed myself back awake. 'None of us will be going into Trillania,' I mimicked Aethan as I dug through my saddlebags, searching for the dream-catcher. Finally, I felt the edges of it digging into my palm. I pulled it out and shoved it under my pillow.

A groan from the tent off to my right put a smile on my face. That'd teach him for sneaking up on me.

My anger at Aethan and Galanta and the world in general coursed through me, making sleep impossible to find. Then my thoughts turned to my training session with Wolfgang and that did *nothing* to improve my mood.

Finally I thought about Emerald. My concern for her was enough to soothe the fire in my veins.

Was she sick? Was she in trouble? There hadn't been a time since we'd bonded that I'd not been able to contact her. I had to go back to Trillania to find her. I had to.

Decision made, I reached a hand up under my pillow and pulled out the dream-catcher.

Chapter Three

They Seek Us Here, They Seek Us There

I'd only been in Trillania for a couple of seconds before Aethan reappeared.

'Ahah,' he said. 'I knew it.'

I really wasn't in the mood for his goody-two-shoes act. 'If you want to spend more time with me I have a few hours free tomorrow.' I turned away from him and sent my mind out to Emerald.

'Rako said....'

'Oh shut up.' I'd had enough of him parroting Rako. I mean honestly, like I didn't know what Rako had said.

I closed my eyes and pushed my mind out further than I had ever had to. Where was she?

'What are you doing?'

'Trying to find my dragon.' I snapped my eyes open and glared at him. Practically ignores me all day and now, when I need him to be quiet, he turns into a regular little chatty-cat. What was it with men?

'I'm sorry.' He shook his head and grinned. 'It sounded like you said you were trying to find your dragon.'

I was going to have to go looking for her. 'Well, at least we don't need to get your hearing checked.' I closed my eyes and willed myself to a cave located high in the mountains rising out of the Black Forest. It was where I had found her after the fight with the goblins.

The soft, white sand carpeting the floor glowed gently. It was enough for me to see the smooth indentation made by her body, and the drag marks from her talons, but the cave itself was empty.

'What are you doing?'

'Whizbang.' I jumped at the sound of Aethan's voice and cracked my head on a stalactite. 'Didn't your mum ever tell you it's rude to sneak up on people? Oh wait...,' I snorted out a laugh, 'I forgot who your mother is.'

The look on his face hardened. 'I don't appreciate your cracking jokes at my mother's expense.'

'Oh really.' I wasn't quite sure what had gotten into me. I could only assume it was the stress of the last few days. 'So what are you going to do about it? Ask me politely to take it back.' I put my hands on my hips and stared him in the eyes.

'I was going to try that,' he said, matching me stare-for-stare, 'but I'm not sure if you could do *anything* politely.'

'Ouch. If I gave a damn, that would have really, really hurt.' I raised an eyebrow.

'Yes, well, I can't expect a girl of your calibre to care about anything.'

Now *that* was punching below the belt. I launched myself at him and crash tackled him to the ground, making sure that I pinned his arms with my legs. 'I would have thought one broken nose for the night was enough.'

He struggled beneath me, trying to free his arms. 'Bring it on witch.'

'Don't say you didn't ask for it.' I balled my fist and slammed it into his cheekbone. It made a satisfying crunch.

He roared and flipped his body up, throwing me backward off him. I rolled over and scrambled away, but he grabbed my ankle and dragged me back. 'How... do... you... like... it?' he grunted as he struggled to contain me.

I fought him like a wildcat, punching and kicking but he used his weight superiority to pin me down.

'Get off,' I gasped, as he wrestled my arms to my side.

'Not unless you say pretty please.'

'Never.' I twisted my body from side-to-side, using the momentum to try to roll. If I could get onto my belly with my arms under me....

He tightened his grip till it was painful. 'Pretty please,' he hissed.

I snarled and renewed my struggle.

'Well if we're going to stay like this for a while I might as well have some fun.' For a wild second I thought he meant to kiss me and I wanted it so badly the yearning was like a tsunami racing through my body. But instead, he mimicked my earlier position and tucked my arms under his knees. 'Ever played typewriter?'

'What?' The absurdity of the question froze my struggles.

'Typewriter.' He began to tap my forehead with his fingers as if typing, and then slapped the side of my head.

I threw my head to the side trying to escape his hands. 'What in the Dark Sky are you doing?'

'Writing a letter.'

Tap, tap, tap, slap.

It was enough to send me into a frenzied struggle, but try as hard as I could, I couldn't break free.

Tap, tap, tap, slap.

'Stop it,' I screeched.

'Say the magic words.'

'Never.'

Tap, tap, tap, slap.

'Preeettyyy pleeeease,' he said in a sing-song voice.

Tap, tap, tap, slap.

I reared up and slammed my forehead into his already broken nose. He let out a yelp and rolled off me, his fingers clutching his face.

'And that,' I said as I stood up and dusted myself off, 'is how we say pretty please where I come from.' And then I willed myself back to the campsite and to my body.

***

It was still dark when I clambered out of my tent the next morning. Brent had a pot of water boiling and Luke was over at the horses. I went to join him, checking them over for any sore areas that may have arisen from yesterday's ride.

My white mare, whom I had named Lily, nickered when she saw me, pressing her soft, pink nose into my hands.

'Oh okay,' I said, offering her the bit of dried biscuit I had brought for that very purpose. Scruffy whined and I laughed and handed him down a piece as well. When Luke and I were sure all the horses were fit to travel, I packed up my tent and then accepted a cup of tea and some dried meat from Brent.

'Here boy.' Brent held out a bowl to Scruffy. It held the remnants of last night's stew and a couple of biscuits.

I sat on a log and watched the sun peeping over the horizon. Isla joined me a few moments later. 'I love watching the sunrise,' she said. 'It always holds such hope for the new day.'

I looked at her to see if she were taking the piss, but her face was radiant as she gazed at the rising sun.

'I must admit,' I said, 'I'm never normally up early enough to see it.'

'Humans and witches always get it wrong,' she said as Wilfred sat on her other side, 'daylight is for achieving things, night time is for sleeping. Well that, and making love.'

Wilfred sprayed a mouthful of tea out and started coughing. I wasn't sure if it were that, or Isla's comment that made his face go bright red.

I saw Aethan moving towards his horse, Adare, with his gear. 'Come on people,' he said, 'we want to get as far today as possible.'

The three of us rose off the log, but while Isla and Wilfred grabbed their bags, I stretched my arms above my head, using the activity to delay having to interact with Aethan. I wasn't looking forward to that after the damage I had done.

Wilfred let out a low laugh and pointed at Aethan. 'She got you a beauty,' he said, making me wish I had gone with them so that I could kick him in the shins again. The man had no sense of secrecy.

'I fell,' Aethan said, casting a quick glance in my direction.

The left side of his face was so swollen his eyelids resembled two grapes jammed together. The bruising extended from the eye, down the side of his face and ran in an angry line along his jaw line. I felt the teeniest weeniest bit guilty.

'I'm thinking you should sleep on two pillows tonight,' Isla said. She turned away from him toward her black stallion and winked at me.

When we had finished placing the gear on the horses, we gathered in a group in front of Aethan. He drew a few squiggles and a triangle in the dirt with a stick.

'We're here,' he said, stabbing his stick into the ground.

'Well obviously,' Isla said.

He rolled his one good eye toward her and she pressed her lips together and mimicked turning a key.

'This is the Black Mountains.' He pointed at the triangle. 'The mountain range extends hundreds of miles, winding towards the goblin territory border.' He pointed towards the dark shadow I could see off to the left. 'That's it there. Today we are going to make our way around the edge of the mountain range, and then as far along the border as we can before nightfall.'

'Why are we staying in goblin territory?' I asked. 'I mean wouldn't it make more sense to cross over the border to get away from them.'

'See these squiggles?' he said. 'This is the Livia River. It runs deep and fast along the border. Crossing it would be dangerous.'

'Yeah,' Wilfred said, 'and if you did make it, you'd be wishing you'd stayed to have tea with the goblins instead.'

'Giants,' Isla said in a low voice. 'Nasty ones.'

I'd only ever seen giants from the air, and that was as close to them as I wanted to get.

'Talk only when necessary,' Aethan said, 'and stay alert. We want to avoid confrontation if we can.'

We mounted our horses and followed Aethan out of the clearing. Scruffy trotted beside Lily for a while, but soon got bored of the exercise. I pulled him up behind me and he tucked himself between the saddle and the bags and promptly fell asleep.

We had been riding for a couple of hours, dodging our way through the small, spread-out trees, when we heard the sound of goblins moving through the woodlands off to our left. They didn't seem to be making any effort to be quiet, and their guttural voices echoed through the trees.

Aethan held his hand up and we stopped. Brent slid from his saddle, and disappeared into the undergrowth. I held my breath, waiting to hear evidence that he had been detected. There was none, and he reappeared a few minutes later.

He held up his hand once and pointed at an angle in the other direction.

Five goblins moving away from us.

We waited till the sound of them had disappeared before we began to move again.

As the day wore on the parties of goblins became larger, until it seemed we were stationary more than we were moving. Brent and Luke handed the reins of their horses to Wilfred and me and ghosted off to the front and sides, reappearing only to send us in another direction. By the afternoon we were tracking backwards and to the sides nearly as much as we were moving forward, and we were still this side of the Black Mountains.

As the sun was beginning to set, Luke and Brent appeared together. I could hear them whispering to Aethan. They mounted up and led us further north until we came to a dense patch of trees.

Aethan dismounted. 'We'll stop here tonight,' he whispered. The trees were too close to slip between and the path in was narrow. It would be an excellent position to defend, as long as there was another way out.

We led our horses along the track for a few minutes before it widened into a small clearing. A wall of rock bordered the right of the clearing, disappearing up into the gloom. A fissure ran in the rock face. I watched as Aethan and Brent disappeared into it. They returned moments later and Aethan beckoned us to follow.

It was just wide enough for Lily to fit and even then, the rock pressed up against her sides in a couple of places. She whinnied with fear until I stroked her withers and coaxed her through. Scruffy, still riding on her back, didn't look thrilled either.

We rubbed down the horses and ate our cold meal in silence. Then Brent and Luke disappeared back through the fissure to take the first watch. Aethan and I were up second, and Wilfred and Isla were last. Wolfgang had wanted to take his turn but after a hushed conversation with Aethan he nodded his head and sought out his blankets. It seemed Aethan wanted his magic maker well rested in case we needed him during the night.

I cleared an area of the floor, balled some clothes up as a pillow and pulled a blanket over me. All my Border Guard training both before and since I had signed up had not prepared me for sleeping on hard ground. I was softer than I had thought and that annoyed me.

I debated with myself whether or not to use the dream-catcher – I mean I was only going to get a couple of hours' sleep before Brent and Luke woke me – but my concern for Emerald's welfare meant I wouldn't sleep easily. If I knew I was going to search for her I would fall asleep quickly and be better rested.

Well, that's how I justified it to myself anyway.

Closing my eyes, I relaxed my mind, trying to dispel the fear instilled in me from a day of creeping around goblins. It took a little while, but finally I was able to cross over to Trillania.

I sighed when Aethan stepped out from behind a bush.

'We may have gotten off to a bad start,' he said.

'You think?' I cocked my head to the side and looked at him. He had left the bruises and swelling behind and was back to his devastatingly-handsome self.

'I may have underestimated you.'

I couldn't help it. I smiled. It was something he'd often said while he'd been training me.

'Why are you smiling?'

'No reason.' There was no way I was telling him the truth. They were memories I didn't want him losing. We had fallen in love during those training sessions. Instead, I held out my hand. 'Truce?'

He took it in his and shook it. 'Truce, but you know we can't stay here long, right?'

'I just want to have a quick look for Emerald.'

'Your pet dragon?'

'Well obviously she's not my *pet*.' I laughed as I thought of the look she would get on her face if she heard herself described as my pet. 'She's my friend.' I didn't bother mentioning the bond we shared.

'I've never heard of a friendly dragon.' He dragged the heel of his boot through the dirt. 'Only a bonded one.'

I looked at him sharply. Was he remembering me?

'Santanas had one. She came out of Trillania to Isilvitania in one of the battles at the end.'

'They can leave Trillania?' *Santanas was bonded to a dragon?*

'They're the only animal that can naturally traverse between all the planes of existence.'

Well that certainly gave me plenty to think about. But right now, I needed to find her. 'Are you coming with me?' I held out my hand.

'Someone's got to watch your back.' He reached out and took it and a zing of energy leapt up my arm. I could tell by the widening of his eyes that he had felt it too. He tilted his head to the side and stared at me questioningly but I wasn't about to explain that *that* sort of thing had been quite normal between us.

I closed my eyes and concentrated on a large, grassy plain I knew had been one of Emerald's favourite hunting grounds. When I opened them, we were staring out over a huge herd of morths. Except for the fact that they had six legs, morths looked remarkably like sheep. They had been her favourite food. If Emerald were around they wouldn't be grazing so peacefully.

I closed my eyes again and thought of the beach she used to help shed her old scales. One end of the bay had grainy sand, perfect for exfoliating dead skin. The other had powder-soft sand for burnishing her new scales till they shone. She had been overly vain about the brilliance of her dark-green scales.

The waves breaking at the base of the sand dunes boomed as they curled on themselves and pounded the shore. High tide. Not the right time for a dragon to come.

'Perhaps she's migrated.' Aethan still held my hand as we stared out over the lonely ocean.

'What?'

'Like a bird. Maybe she moves with the seasons.'

Maybe she did, but that didn't explain why I couldn't contact her.

He tugged on my hand. 'We have to go.'

'I know.' I let him take us back to the cave and woke up as Brent was shaking my shoulder.

'Izzy,' he hissed. He must have been shaking for a while.

'All right, all right,' I mumbled, scrubbing my eyes with my fists. I couldn't believe it had been a couple of hours already.

'Goblins are coming.'

I sat bolt upright. So it hadn't been a couple of hours.

'How far?'

'About a mile. But they're heading straight for this area, and they're moving fast.' He moved on to wake up Wilfred.

Wolfgang and Isla were already up, throwing their saddles onto their horses.

I packed up my stuff and swung my sword into its position on my back. Then I saddled Lily and secured my bags. She snuffled at my hands, looking for a biscuit. 'Not yet lovely,' I murmured.

'We need to get out of the cave,' Aethan said.

If it was their destination, the cave was a death trap. Were they planning on camping here, or did they know we were here? Either way it didn't bode well for us.

We coaxed our tired horses back outside and waited for Luke to come back from his scouting. When he did, he was running hard.

'They're almost at the start of the path,' he said as he swung up into his saddle.

As quietly as we could, we rode the horses further along the path. It twisted and turned and within moments we were out of sight of the cave entry. But we hadn't gone far before the path began to thin. The trees loomed on either side as they pressed closer and closer and then suddenly the path disappeared. We were trapped.

The sounds of goblin feet slapping the hard rock resonated on the cool night air. I held my breath and prayed to the Dark Sky that they would stop at the cave. The marching seemed to go on forever. How many of them were there? Twenty? Fifty?

Finally the marching stopped, and their voices became muffled as they entered the fissure into the cave. Aethan slid off Adare and crept back along the path, disappearing from view round the corner.

He reappeared a few minutes later and jogged back to Wolfgang.

'No sentry. We can sneak back past them,' he whispered. 'What can you do?'

My breath froze and my heart started to pound. *Sneak back past them?* I looked around at the forest. There was no way we would get through it with the horses, and if they realised we were there we would need the horses.

'I can muffle our noise,' Wolfgang whispered back.

He raised his hands and the air around us thickened. It moulded itself to us like a thick blanket. Lily threw her head up and I placed a reassuring hand on her neck. 'Shhh,' I said to Scruffy. I didn't know if the spell would prevent the goblins from hearing us if he started barking.

We moved back towards the cave entry, the strange air clinging to our every move. With each step we took, my heart beat faster, till it felt like it was mimicking a hummingbird. My breath came in short, sharp pants as I reached over my shoulder and loosened my sword in its sheath.

Aethan rode in the lead with Wolfgang right behind him, one hand in the air as he held the spell intact. Isla and I rode in the middle with Brent and Luke behind us and Wilfred in the rear.

I felt like I had a huge spotlight on me as I rode past the entry to the cave. I stared at the crack, unable to blink as I willed it to remain empty. All it would take was one goblin to poke his head out. One goblin to raise the alarm.

The hair on the back of my neck stood on end and my hands sweated onto the reins. I felt like a hundred eyes were boring into my back as I headed for the path leading out. I gritted my teeth and took deep breaths, resisting the urge to kick my heels into Lily's sides.

I'd fought goblins before, I know, but never in such a dire situation, or with such bad odds. If they realised we were here before we were all past the opening, they would split our group in two. There was no way we would win that fight.

We had almost made it when I heard Isla gasp, 'My bow.'

As if on cue, a goblin yelled from inside the cave and the rest of them followed suit. We could hear then heading back down the crack towards us. Isla had left her bow behind, and they had just found it.

'Go,' Aethan yelled.

They knew we were there. Silence was no longer any protection. Now we needed speed.

I kicked Lily's flanks and urged her after Isla down the long and windy path. We had to break free of it to have any speed advantage over the goblins on foot. I heard Wilfred yell, and the clash of metal-on-metal, but didn't dare stop. I would only make things worse. I had to pray the big man would make it out of there.

We burst from the edge of the forest onto a plain, and raced away from the goblins. A look over my shoulder showed me Wilfred, clutching his arm as he leaned low over his horse's neck.

A horn sounded behind us, ringing out in the night, and a band of goblins broke from the trees to our left. Aethan swore and changed direction. I cradled Scruffy between my arms as I leant low, urging Lily on with my hands and my legs.

An arrow buzzed through the air and I threw an arm up. A couple more clattered off the shield that formed in front of my outstretched fingers. I held it to the side as we outdistanced the goblins.

More horns rang out in front of us and to our rear. Aethan shifted course again, away from the horns, heading north towards the border. We had to hope we could outdistance them before we reached the river or we would be trapped.

Lily's breath was coming in laboured pants, froth flying from her mouth before we were able to drop back to a trot. The horns still sounded but from behind us now. It was possible we were going to make it.

I dropped back beside Wilfred but Isla beat me to it. She tut-tutted as she looked at the gash on his arm. Then she dug around in her bag and pulled out a bandage, pulling her horse in close enough to wrap his wound.

'Seems like I'm going to have to keep a closer eye on you,' she said. 'Can't have you getting yourself killed now can I.'

The look on his face was going to keep a smile on mine for a very long time.

We trotted for a while longer before Aethan considered it safe enough to walk.

'What were you thinking?' he hissed at his sister.

'It wasn't me that picked the hidey-hole with only one exit.'

'I knew I should have left you at home.'

A goblin leapt from behind a tree and swung an axe at Isla's head. I screeched, throwing an arm toward him. Lightning burst from my fingertips and hit him square in the chest. He crumpled to the ground with a hole the size of a fist where his heart had been.

It was just like when Emerald and I had fought the goblins, but I still didn't have a clue how I'd done it. A score more goblins appeared from the direction the first had come, loosing arrows in our direction. I threw my hands at them but nothing happened. This instinctual magic thing was starting to get old.

'Wolfgang,' I yelped.

'Got it,' he said and a shield flickered into being.

As we kicked the horses back into a gallop, horns sounded from all directions and drum beats reverberated in the night.

'Great. Drums,' I muttered. 'Always with the freakin' drums.'

Every time we tried to head south, goblins would appear, running towards our tiring horses. Again and again we tried to break through, but instead we were forced further north.

'They're herding us,' Wilfred yelled.

'Towards the river,' Aethan added.

Towards a trap.

The edge of the Livia River cut deep into the earth off to our right, and goblins massed to our left. We were about to be pinched between a rock and a very, very hard place.

The goblins' cries became triumphant as we turned and raced along the river bank. The water roared as it tumbled deep within the ravine it had cut. Faster and faster the horses ran, fear pumping adrenaline into their muscles as the enemy raced to pin us against the cliff edge.

Wolfgang hurled fireballs that smashed into the goblin lines, exploding with enough impact to take out three or four at a time. But the goblins behind clambered over the charred remains and within moments it was as if Wolfgang had done nothing.

'On my call,' Aethan yelled.

I realised that the rest of them, except Isla, had nocked their bows. No mean feat while galloping. I grabbed mine off the pommel of my saddle and notched an arrow.

'Fire,' Aethan yelled once they were within range.

We released volley after volley, most finding marks, but as with the fireballs, within moments the goblins behind surged forwards to fill the gaps. It was as if all the arrows in the world couldn't stop them. We were going to have to rely on our speed to outrun them.

I slung the bow back over the pommel and leant low over Lily's neck. We were almost there, almost free of the head of the goblin line but they were closing the distance fast - fearsome warriors racing each other to kill us. Their battle cries were deafening as they wielded spears and axes.

All my attempts to hurl lightning came to nothing, and my attempts to shield were useless. I swore and pulled my sword from its sheath on my back. I was going to have to do it the old-fashioned way.

A hand grasped my ankle and I hacked at the wrist, severing it with my sword. I screamed with rage and struck out again and again, forcing them away from Lily. But they crowded around us, pushing us back until escape was no longer possible.

Murderous black eyes, lips curled in rage, a sea of arms reaching out to swamp us. Aethan glanced over his shoulder, a look of determination on his face.

There was only one option, one way we might survive.

'The river,' he yelled.

Wolfgang threw another fireball into the goblins. I shoved my sword back into its sheath and swung Lily around. It seemed we all jumped as one. Away from the goblins, away from their weapons, tumbling down, down into the cold, dark waters of the Livia River.

Chapter Four

Out Of The Frying Pan And Into The Fire

Lily plunged into the river beneath me and I gasped as the cold water closed over my head. I could feel her moving, struggling to break free of the river's grasp.

My weight was not helping. Holding Scruffy's collar, I slid free of Lily's back and immediately started to sink. The weight of my sword dragged me towards the bottom of the river. I reached my free hand up to remove it, but my shirt floated over the top of the sheath. I batted at the fabric, but couldn't find the pommel of the sword.

Kicking my legs, I stroked with my free arm, but now I didn't know which way was up. My lungs started to burn and I had a moment to feel rage at the unfairness of it - that I had gone through everything I had, only to drown, that my sweet, naughty familiar was going to die with me, and then the reins jerked tight around my forearm, pulling me up, up, up to the surface of the river.

I shoved Scruffy ahead of me, but when my head broke free his eyes were still closed. 'Scruffy.' I shook him and squeezed him and he took a shuddering breath and vomited up a torrent of water. 'Thatta boy,' I said, stroking his head.

When he had finished, I rolled onto my back and settled him on my chest so that his front paws hooked over my shoulder. Then I looked around.

Lily towed me behind her as she swam. Her nostrils were wide and her ears flicked from side-to-side and I was guessing that this wasn't the best night of her life either.

'Aethan, Wilfred, Isla.' I swivelled my head but couldn't see anyone else. 'Brent, Wolfgang, Luke.' Even though I yelled, my voice was soft over the roar of the river.

'Isla.' Aethan's voice came from behind me. 'Will.'

It was stupid, but even now, when our lives were in danger, I felt chagrin that it wasn't *my* name he was calling.

'Aethan.' I turned and yelled toward him.

'Isadora?'

'Yes.'

I tried to pull Lily back so that we could swim towards him, but the current had us in its grip. We were going to end up where the river wanted us to.

Where were the others? Were they alive? I pushed my concern for them aside and concentrated on swimming.

The cold seeped into my bones and my teeth started to chatter. Scruffy cowered against my body, his ears down as he trembled. He whimpered and I wrapped my arm further around him, trying to give him some warmth. The problem was that I didn't have any left to give. If we didn't get out of the river soon it would be hypothermia that got us, not goblins. But either way, dead was dead.

It felt like we swam for hours before the river took a sharp right bend. The water swirled in an eddy, swinging us round and round in a whirlpool against the left bank of the river. I could feel myself starting to get sucked under again, and then Lily had her legs beneath her. She heaved herself out onto the edge of the river, dragging Scruffy and me behind her.

I slid out of the water onto my belly and lay there panting till I had the strength to pull myself to my knees and stagger to Lily's side. She stood with her head down and her legs wide, sucking in big lungfuls of air. Her eyes were wild as I placed a hand on her head, but she let me pat her until her trembling stopped and her breathing calmed.

We were cold, we were wet and we were totally alone. It was up to me to save us.

'Come on.' I picked up her reins and led her away from the water's edge. We needed fire if we were to survive, and we needed it now.

I had hoped that the walking would warm us, but a cold breeze blew off the river, amplifying my tremors to teeth-chattering proportions. Finally, I found a suitable spot – a large stand of trees that blocked the wind, and would hopefully mask my fire. A clearing, more than large enough for the three of us, lay snug in the middle of the trees.

We were in enemy country – giant country if what Isla had said was correct – but I had to deal with the most imminent problem first. I rummaged through the undergrowth till I had enough kindling to light the fire. A small depression in the middle of the clearing was going to have to suffice as a fire pit. The shovels had been with the packhorses.

Where was everybody? Had they made it out of the river?

I sucked in a big breath and concentrated on not crying. Self-pity would get me nowhere.

I dug through my saddlebags till I found my matches, thanking the Dark Sky that they were still secure in their plastic bag. Wet matches would have been a disaster.

My trembling hands broke the first few without producing a spark. Lily whinnied and pushed her nose into my back.

'I know, I know,' I said, striking another match. This one lit and, holding my breath, I placed it beneath the kindling. Flames licked over the dry leaves and suddenly we had fire.

I placed a few sticks over the top, being careful not to smother it, and went looking for more firewood. We were going to need it to get us all dry. Once I had gathered a large pile, I led Lily over to the fire and took off her saddle and blankets. I rubbed her down the best I could with handfuls of dry leaves, and then did the same to Scruffy. Then I dug through the saddle bags and pulled out the biscuits. Even wet they were still rock hard. I fed a few to Lily and shared some of the dried meat with Scruffy.

After she had finished her pitiful meal, Lily let out a snort and lay down near the flames. Scruffy joined her, pressing up against her body. I perched on a log and unbraided my hair, running my fingers through it to help it dry. The problem was, my clothes were still wet and cold. They were never going to dry on me, and I was already starting to itch.

I pulled my shirt and pants off and hung them over sticks near the fire to dry. Then I pulled everything out of the saddle bags. Before long the clearing looked like a laundry, blankets and clothing hanging over a large, broken branch.

The heat radiating from the fire was wonderful against my skin. I sat on the ground between Lily's legs and lay back against her belly. I knew I should have been more alert, but I had been tired and cold and scared for so long that the warmth wound around me and before long I felt my eyelids drooping.

It wouldn't hurt just to snooze for a minute. Surely...

Scruffy let out a little bark and my eyes snapped back open. A man stood on the other side of the clearing. Wet, black hair plastered his forehead and blood dribbled down his cheek. He took a step towards me before his eyes rolled up and he fell to the ground.

'Aethan.' I jumped up from Lily's side and rushed to him.

Please, oh please don't let him be dead.

'Aethan.' I rolled him onto his back and pressed my ear to his chest. His heart beat was strong. I blinked back tears and ran my hands over his head. Blood coated my fingers. A large gash darkened his scalp.

A nicker made me stare past him into the dark. Aethan's stallion, Adare, stood there with one of the packhorses. I grabbed their reins and moved them closer to the fire but that was the best I could do for them until I had dealt with Aethan.

I lay my blanket, which was almost dry, next to him and rolled him onto it. Then I dragged it back to the fire. I grabbed my dream-catcher and placed it near his head. The last thing we needed was to have him wandering through Trillania unable to wake up. One of my long-sleeved shirts with the arms tied underneath his chin did as a pressure bandage. I undid his fur vest and wiggled it out from behind him, then took off his boots and pants and hung them out to dry.

I took off the horses' saddles and gave them the same treatment I had given Lily. When they were as dry as I could get them, I let them lie down near the fire. We were certainly testing the space limits of my little clearing.

Once I was satisfied that they were happy, I checked Aethan's wound, pleased to see the bleeding was stopping. But his body was still icy cold to the touch. Was it possible that the bleeding was slowing because he had hypothermia and not because of my make-shift bandage?

I lay down next to him and pulled the edge of the blanket over us. Then I chaffed his skin with my hands, encouraging the blood flow to return. Of course running my hands all over his body brought back memories that were only going to get me in trouble. But his skin felt so good brushing up against mine, and his colour seemed to be improving. His lips were no longer the attractive shade of blue they had been. I decided it would be best for him if I kept on going.

Yep - creepy, lecherous, ex-girlfriend present and accounted for.

When I was certain he was warming, I wrapped my arms around him and rested my head on his shoulder. I would watch over him. I wouldn't go to sleep. No matter how good it felt to let my eyelids lower. No matter how nice it felt to let my limbs relax. I would stay awake until…

***

Aethan's movements woke me. I wiggled up against him, entwining my legs through his. Dark Sky, he felt so good. Still half asleep, I wrapped an arm around his neck and pulled his head down.

I sighed as his lips touched mine. I had been hungry when I had woken but now I felt a different hunger entirely. Rolling so that I was on top of him, I intensified the kiss, moving my mouth and my tongue with his.

He ran his hands down the length of my back, stroking my skin. I groaned and he froze beneath me. His lips stopped moving and his hands dropped to his sides. I lifted my head and opened my eyes, staring straight into his. Why did he have my shirt wrapped around his head?

Aggghhhh. It all came racing back. The goblins, the river, him turning up wounded. Great Dark Sky, *this* Aethan didn't know that this sort of behaviour had once been our favourite pastime.

'Why is it,' he said, 'that every time I end up unconscious, I wake to find you kissing me?'

I rolled off him and pushed myself to my knees. His eyes widened and I realised that apart from my bra and undies, I was still undressed.

I cleared my throat and said, 'Our clothes were wet.' *Durhhh.* We fell in a river. *Of course* our clothes were wet.

He looked around the clearing, taking in the sleeping animals, the drying clothing and the raging fire.

'That's a large fire.'

'If we'd died from hypothermia the giants would have missed out on their chance to kill us tomorrow. That didn't seem fair.'

A smile twitched the corners of his mouth as he shook his head. 'No, not fair at all.'

'I like your hat.' Isla staggered into the clearing and collapsed by the fire. 'Dark Sky that feels good. Do you think there's a chance the giants won't see it?' She stripped her wet shirt off and rubbed her hands up and down her arms, leaving bloody smears on her biceps. 'So, are we playing strip poker or a drinking game?'

'Here.' I handed her the blanket Aethan and I had been sleeping on.

'Where have you been?' Aethan pulled her into a rough embrace.

'Got dropped off a few miles downriver. Climbed a hill and could see your fire.'

I felt my clothes. They were toasty warm. I hurriedly pulled on a set and handed another to Isla. 'Where's your horse?'

Isla's face crumpled for a second. She took a deep breath and said, 'He pulled me to shore, but I couldn't get him out of the river.' She held her hands out, her eyes glazed as she stared at bleeding welts on her wrists. It took me a moment to realise what had caused them. Her reins.

Aethan removed his 'bandage' and handed it to me.

'Here.' I ripped a strip off the bottom and gently took one of Isla's hands in mine. I bound the material around the gashes, then repeated the procedure for her other wrist. After that I helped her into my spare set of clothes.

By the time I had finished, Aethan had dressed again. I felt a flash of disappointment. That was probably the last time I would get to see that much of him. And then of course I felt wretched. Four of our party were still missing and here I was lusting after Aethan.

'Can you ride?' Aethan asked Isla.

She moved closer to the fire and then sighed. 'I guess so.'

'Shall we douse the fire?'

'Nah. If they've spotted it they'll think we're still here.' He piled some more wood on it. 'Besides, if the others find it, it just may save their lives.' He picked up his knife and notched a symbol into the bark of a tree. It was the Border Guard symbol for west.

It took a while to encourage the horses back onto their feet. We loaded our gear and gathered their reins, leading them from the shelter. I placed Scruffy on Lily's back, but he was the only one of us that would be riding tonight. The horses had already been through too much.

With one last wistful look at the fire, I followed Aethan and Isla back out into the night.

***

'We need to rest the horses.' Isla sounded half-asleep.

It wasn't only the horses that needed resting. I had lost count of the times I had tripped over non-existent obstacles. My legs felt like lead weights.

'Soon,' Aethan said.

I felt the urgency too. We had to find somewhere safe to hide. The sky had begun to lighten over the last half hour, and we needed to be as far from my bonfire as we could get before the giants decided to investigate. But it wasn't going to do us any good if we killed the horses.

'*Aethan.*' Isla's voice cracked like a whip.

He stopped and turned to look at her and she gestured to the packhorse. It had begun to stumble.

'Right,' he said, shaking his head as if trying to wake up. 'Rest.'

'What about there.' I pointed to an area just visible in the early morning light. Steep hills descended to meet at a junction where the trees grew more densely. 'If we can get in there it might offer some good cover.'

Aethan nodded and started to lead Adare in that direction. Ten minutes later we reached the tree line and pushed through the trunks, hunting for an area to rest.

'Over here,' Isla called.

I led Lily to the left where Isla was pointing. A small area opened amongst the trees.

'It'll do,' Aethan said.

It was going to have to do. With morning upon us we had run out of time.

We unsaddled the horses and brushed them down before tethering them so they couldn't wander while we slept. Apparently the horses were more interested in rest than exploring because they promptly lay down.

I found an area of the forest floor that didn't seem too hard and curled up on it with Scruffy, putting my dreamcatcher under my makeshift pillow and pulling my blanket over me.

When I finally opened my eyes, the light in the clearing had shifted. I must have been asleep for hours. Isla was using one of the saddles as a seat as she combed out her long, dark hair. Aethan and the horses were nowhere to be seen.

If Isla wasn't still with me I might have worried that I'd freaked him out the night before. But there was no way he would leave without her.

'Where's Aethan?' I sat up and pushed my hair back off my face.

'Taken the horses down to drink at the river.'

'They're all okay?'

'Apart from a few scrapes and bruises, yes.' She finished untangling her hair and threw the comb to me.

I caught it and set to work on mine, wishing, as I pulled the comb through a snarl, that I had done it before it dried the night before. I was working on a particularly nasty knot when a tremor ran through the earth.

Birds burst from the safety of the trees flying in a fury of wings as they fled the forest. They left a deathly silence in their wake.

A second tremor shook the surrounding trees, and then a third; each one larger and louder than the last.

Scruffy bounded onto my lap, looking around as he growled.

'Isla,' I said. 'What's that?'

'If I were an optimist, I'd say it was a series of small earthquakes.' The ground shook again forcing her to cling to the edge of the saddle.

'And since you're not an optimist?'

'I'm going to go with giant.' She pointed up at the sky and whispered, 'Don't move.'

A torso protruded above the top of the tallest trees. The gigantic head peered down into the forest as if searching for something. I had an awful feeling I knew what that something was. Us.

I resisted the urge to slap myself in the head. I had been looking for a hiding spot that would keep us safe from somebody our own size, *not* a giant. We should have been searching the hills for caves.

Scruffy let out a low growl. 'Shhhhhh,' I whispered. 'Quiet.' He let out one more little ruffy growl before he stopped.

The torso came closer, each step shaking us till my teeth chattered. Isla and I sat frozen in place. I know *I* was praying to the Great Dark Sky for all I was worth.

Please don't let him see us.

An enormous head peered down into the clearing. I'm not exactly sure what the giant definition of 'good looking' is, but I'm pretty sure this wasn't it. He had a huge misshapen nose squashed asymmetrically onto his face, bulging eyes that looked in different directions and a crowded mouth out of which the tip of a tongue protruded.

One of his eyes alighted on Isla and he squealed, 'Dolly.'

'Oh fuck,' Isla said, without moving her lips.

He shifted one of his gazes to me. 'Two dollies.' Enormous hands descended towards us.

'Stay still.' Isla warned when I glanced toward the surrounding trees.

What? This was our plan? To stay still and let him capture us?

Before I could decide on another plan of action, a hand grasped my waist and yanked me into the air.

'Pretty dollies.' He held us up in front of him and stared at us as a bit of drool tracked from his tongue and onto his chin. Then he grinned with delight. 'Matching.'

He turned away from the forest and walked back the way he had come. Isla and I swung like pendulums with each thundering step.

My little, white familiar chased after us, darting through the trees. 'Get Aethan,' I yelled. 'Aethan.'

Scruffy threw his head back and howled, but he turned and ran in the opposite direction.

It took the giant half an hour to travel what it had taken us all night to do. He strode past the still glowing remnants of my fire and up over the closest hill. There, rising out of the rocky outcrops, was his home. I had practically built my fire on his front doorstep.

He pushed open the front door and entered. The outside of the building had not prepared me for what lay inside. Bowls of flowers lay on the room's two tables. Animal sculptures lined the walls. Woven rugs, scattered across the floors, gave the room a homely feel. But the oddest thing was the birds, darting in and out of the open windows and perching on the edges of the furniture. Some of them alighted on the giant's head and others on his arms.

He placed Isla and me gently onto the table. 'Pretty dollies.' He gazed at us with adoration and smiled a simple smile. Then he clasped his hands and bustled into the kitchen where he filled a pot with water and set it on a wood stove to boil.

'Oh great. Faery soup,' Isla said.

But I had my doubts that he planned to eat us. With the birds and the sculptures I got the feeling this giant was more about love than war. But hey, I wasn't an expert on giants. Perhaps they liked to have their cake and eat it too!

I looked around the room for a possible escape route. The door fit its frame snugly, and even if one of us stood on the other's shoulders we weren't going to reach the handle. The panelling of the walls was secured by nails as big as my daggers. The only way we were going to get out was the windows, and I wasn't sure we would be able to reach the frame from where the table sat.

I looked back at the giant as he took the lid off a canister and threw a handful of something into the pot.

'That's herbs,' Isla hissed as she stalked along the edge of the table.

He waited a few minutes and then poured the brew into a cup. He blew on the surface a few times and then took a sip, grunting in pleasure at the result. I could smell the tea from where I was.

Isla stilled as he approached us again. He reached out a finger and stroked her hair. 'Pretty,' he murmured, collapsing into the chair at the table. He picked her up and put her next to me. 'Sisters,' he said.

He watched us while he sipped his tea, the birds perching on his arms like ants on a log. When he had finished, he picked up a half-finished sculpture and continued his work.

His huge hands deftly worked his tools as chips of wood flew off the log and a squirrel started to emerge.

'When he's finished that it'll be into the pot with us for a nice snack before an afternoon nap.' Isla's voice didn't sound as confident of that as it had.

'Is it just me, or is he large for a giant?' He seemed far bigger than the giants Emerald and I had fought in Trillania.

Isla tucked her legs up till she was sitting cross legged. 'He's a giant giant.' She laughed lightly. 'Bet his nickname's Tiny.'

He looked in our direction and smiled. 'Pretty dollies talk.'

'He doesn't seem… nasty.'

'Nor clever.' She cocked her head to the side as she stared at him. 'He's an anomaly,' she agreed. 'But we still have to get out of here before he eats us.'

I couldn't disagree with that.

We watched Tiny sculpt for a few hours. Once the squirrel's head and shoulders had been freed from the wood, he set it on the floor and moved back to the kitchen.

'Here we go,' Isla said. She picked up a shard of wood and waved it around in the air.

Tiny made himself a cup of tea, which he drank, and then lay down on a bed in the corner of the room. Within minutes, his snores rumbled through the room.

'Right,' Isla said. 'Let's get out of here.'

'Only way I can see is up the curtain and out the window. You found another way?'

'Nope.'

If we jumped, we could just brush the curtain with our fingertips. I looked around for something to climb onto.

Tiny had left his mug on the table. Together, we pushed it towards the curtain and rolled it onto its side and then upside down so that we had a platform to stand on.

Using the finger hold as a step, Isla clambered up the side of the mug. She jumped onto the curtain, wrapping her arms and legs in the fabric to support herself. I followed.

Moving across the curtain was harder than I had envisioned it would be and I was sweating profusely by the time we got to the edge near the window frame.

'Whizbang,' Isla muttered.

'What?' I peered around her to the window. We were still too far away.

'We're going to have to swing and jump.' She clambered around to the inside of the curtain so that I could have the outside edge, and then we began to swing.

It was hard work getting the voluminous material to do what we wanted, but eventually we swayed out towards the edge of the window frame.

'We're going to have to jump at the same time,' I grunted.

'On three,' Isla said. 'One... two... three.'

As the fabric crested the arc, we both let go, flying through the air to land with a thump. I crashed onto my hands and knees, rolling over and skidding towards the open window.

'Eeeek,' I squealed as I felt open air beneath me.

Isla grabbed my arm, but before she could haul me up, the snoring stopped.

'Ahh buzznuckle.' She lowered me instead, dropping me to the ground. I landed on my feet and stepped back to give her room. As she dropped to my side we heard Tiny.

'Dollies?'

'Quick,' she said, squatting behind a gigantic watering can.

I looked around for a hiding spot but there were none within sprinting distance. I pressed myself against the wall underneath the frame, hoping he wouldn't look down.

'Where dollies?'

The ludicrousness of the situation hit me and I bit back a giggle. A giant thought we were his dolls.

'Dolly in here?' His voice moved away from the window and together Isla and I sprinted back the way we had come up. Shale slid beneath our feet, forcing us to slow down or risk a sprained ankle. A quick glance behind me showed that we would be in view of the window until we crested the hill.

The curtains on each side of the window moved as Tiny searched them.

'Hide,' I hissed, diving to the ground behind a rock.

Isla stood behind a tree trunk.

I peeped up over the rock. Tiny had moved away from the window. 'Go,' I whispered, pushing up onto my hands and knees.

We scrambled up the side of the hill, staying as low as possible, but as we crested the hill we heard Tiny cry out. The front door slammed and he ran towards us. The earth buckled under the pounding of his feet, throwing Isla and me to the ground.

I had a moment to hope that the hill wouldn't collapse and then he was reaching out to grab us where we lay.

'Dollies,' he howled, tears tracking down his cheeks. 'Why you leave?' He held me up in front of him and I watched in horror as his mouth descended to me.

He was going to eat us now? Raw?

I struggled in his fist as his mouth got bigger and bigger. Isla screamed but all I could do was stare. And then his lips pressed up against the side of my body and he kissed me. My body went limp with shock.

'You beast,' Isla shrieked, pounding him with her fists.

Tiny jerked back from me and turned towards Isla. 'Owwwww,' he howled.

'Isla stop,' I yelled. 'You're hurting him.'

She stared at me, her eyes wide with shock. 'But, he *ate* you.'

'He kissed me.'

'He *what?*'

Before I could answer, Tiny lifted Isla towards his mouth. 'Oh. Euwwww,' she said, as he pressed a juicy kiss onto her face.

He turned and strode back towards his house and Scruffy charged from behind a rock and latched onto the bottom of his pants. Tiny didn't even notice as his steps swung Scruffy to-and-fro. He did, however, notice Aethan as he stepped into Tiny's path with an arrow notched in his bow. The swelling had gone from Aethan's face leaving him, instead, with a bad-boy black eye. He looked so fierce and brave that if I really had been in mortal danger I might have swooned at the sight of him.

'Another dolly.' Tiny clearly couldn't believe his luck.

'Don't shoot,' Isla and I yelled together. 'He's friendly,' I added.

Aethan didn't look convinced but he lowered his bow and let Tiny scoop him up. Scruffy growled and let go of Tiny's pants, chasing after us as we were taken back to the house. Tiny placed us all on the table and sat back into his chair.

I touched my chest and said, 'I'm Izzy.'

Isla copied me and then elbowed Aethan in the ribs. He immediately touched his own chest and introduced himself.

The look on Tiny's face was almost comical as he struggled with the puzzle. 'Not dollies,' he finally said.

I shook my head. 'No.'

His face crumpled and basketball-sized tears streamed down his cheeks.

'Oh,' Isla said, walking to the edge of the table, 'please don't cry.'

If anything, the tears increased in volume. He put his hands over his face and howled.

I jumped off the edge of the table onto his lap and scrambled up his shirt. One of his tears broke over my head like a bucket of water, but I kept on climbing. Finally I reached his face. 'Please don't cry,' I pulled on his fingers. 'You're a very nice giant.'

He lowered his hands. 'None of the other giants will play with me.'

I felt a tugging on his shirt and then Isla was beside me. '*We* would play with you,' she said.

'Isla,' Aethan whispered from the table, 'we have to go.'

She shot him a look and made a shut up gesture. 'But some of our friends are lost. We have to find them.'

Tiny stared at her and then smiled. 'Peek-a-boo?' he said.

'More like hide-and-seek.' She returned his smile. 'Will you help us look?'

'Hide-and-seek.' Tiny picked us up and put us back on the table and then he clapped his hands. 'We play hide-and-seek.'

'What's your name?' I asked him.

He stared at me for a second and then his head hung and I thought he was going to start crying again. He shook his head. 'The other giants won't give me a name.'

My confusion must have been written on my face because Aethan leaned in close and whispered, 'Giants aren't named at birth. They wait for their personality to emerge and then the community chooses a name. To not be named is to be declared an outcast.'

I felt as if someone had put their hand in my chest and squeezed my heart. 'Tiny,' I said, looking at the gentle giant. 'Your name is Tiny.'

I watched as his head came up. He stared at me with his huge, bugged eyes and his squashed nose and said, 'Tiny?'

'I also name you Tiny,' Isla said, placing her right hand on her heart.

'I name you Tiny.' Aethan touched his hand to his heart and then his head.

Tiny's mouth split into an enormous grin. 'Tiny,' he said, thumping his hand to his chest. 'My name is Tiny.' He jumped up from his chair and rummaged around in the kitchen, throwing things into a leather satchel. He tossed the satchel over his shoulder and a hat the size of a swimming pool on his head and lifted us off the table to place us gently on the floor. Scruffy rushed to my side and jumped up on me, licking my hands as I rubbed his head.

We followed Tiny out the door and back over the hills towards our deserted camp.

'Which way Tiny seek?' He looked over his shoulder and then spun in a circle.

'We are going to search that way.' Isla pointed back the way he had brought us.

'Tiny will seek that way.' He pointed further north than our intended path.

We watched as he strode off, the ground shaking in his wake.

Aethan shook his head as we watched him go. 'I wouldn't have believed that if I hadn't seen it.'

'What, a gentle giant?' Isla asked.

'No.' Aethan laughed and punched her on the shoulder. 'You being pashed by one.'

***

Aethan had left Lily and the packhorse at our camp and ridden on Adare to save us. I gave the black stallion a scratch behind his ears. He couldn't have recovered from the night before yet, and then had ridden for hours more. He had a big heart.

The walk back to our camp was much faster than the night before, partly because we could see where we were going, but mostly because we weren't so exhausted. But even with that it was late afternoon before we arrived.

We let Adare rest while we ate and then I repacked my bags. I took my small mirror out to wrap it in my blanket. Mum's face was floating on the surface.

Whizbang. I had raced out of the house without leaving a note and after my failed attempt to contact her had totally forgotten. Grams would have filled her in but that didn't mean she wasn't going to be royally pissed with me.

I pasted what I hoped was a nothing-to-see-here smile on, hoping I hadn't accidentally left on my got-chased-by-goblins-fell-in-a-river-and-kidnapped-by-a-giant one. Then I took a deep breath, waved my hand at the mirror and said, 'Speakius clearius.' Mum's face activated. Her eyes and nose were red.

'Izzy, thank the Dark Sky.' She took a deep, shuddering breath. 'I came home and you were gone.'

That had been days ago.

'But… didn't Grams tell you where I was?'

Mum's face scrunched up. 'No.' Her hand shook as she pushed her fringe back off her face. 'She's gone, Izzy. Your Grandma is missing.'

'What do you mean she's missing?'

'Nobody knows where she is.'

'She's not off looking at wedding stuff?'

'Lionel hasn't heard from her. He's frantic.'

Looking at her face I didn't think he was the only one who was frantic. I pushed my panic down. I had to believe she was safe. I mean this was my fun-loving, scatty Grams we were talking about.

'Mum, I'm sure she's fine. Remember that time she decided to see if the French Fries were better in France?'

Mum nodded, a small smile twitching her lips. Grams had gone only to discover that *their* French fries were no better than England's. She'd been quite put out (her words) and created a bit of a kerfuffle accusing the French of false advertising. The local police had called us to come and get her.

'She's probably in Venice racing gondolas.' If I hung onto that belief perhaps I would be able to concentrate on the trouble at hand.

Mum smiled, but the lost look remained in her eyes. I heard somebody call her name from another room.

'Who's that?' I asked.

'Hmmm?' Mum said. 'Who was what?'

'That voice.'

It called her name again. A man's voice, coming closer.

Now Mum looked flustered. 'There's no one here. You must be imagining things.' She glanced over her shoulder and shot me a guilty look. 'Got to go. Love you.' She blew me a kiss and ended the spell.

Huh. I sat back on my heels.

'You ready yet?' Aethan asked.

I jumped at the sound of his voice, ending up on my bottom on the dirt. 'It's rude to sneak up on people.' I batted away his outstretched hand and stood up.

'Who's sneaking? I've been here the whole time.' For the first time since Galanta's spell had kicked in, he smiled at me fully. His lips pulled up into that crooked smile I loved so much. My hand strayed of its own accord towards his face, but I managed to stop it before he noticed.

'Whatever,' I said, staring into my saddle bag to hide my red cheeks. I had to stop letting him make me blush. It was getting embarrassing.

'We can get a few miles under our belt before dark,' he said.

Before dark. Before we had to sleep.

I spun to face him as an idea hit me. 'Aethan,' I lowered my voice. 'We can meet Wilfred. Tonight.'

He tilted his head to the side and shook his head. 'Didn't catch that.'

I looked over to where Isla was loading her things onto the packhorse, and hoping I wasn't about to activate the Border Guard Secrecy Spell, whispered, 'Wilfred. Tonight.' I patted my arm where the armband would go.

Aethan's eyes widened. He also glanced toward Isla and then he nodded his head.

The next few hours of walking seemed to take forever. I watched the sun move towards the horizon, torn between wanting to get as much distance behind us, and wanting to go to sleep to see if Wilfred would be waiting for us.

Finally we set up camp, fed the horses and drew straws to see who would get the middle watch. Aethan drew the short straw. Isla was up first and I had the last one.

I curled up in my blanket with Scruffy and turned to watch Aethan. He brought his blanket over far closer than I expected and lay down next to me. Then he looked around to see if Isla was within hearing distance.

'If we don't find him you are not to go back in alone.'

I clenched my teeth and took a deep breath. Aethan and I had always had a spirited relationship, but I wasn't used to him treating me like I was an amateur. 'I will be perfectly safe.'

'Yes you will, because you won't be going in.'

Another deep breath. 'I will too.'

'No you won't.' With his chiselled jawline and his magic, dark eyes he had always been especially gorgeous when he was mad. It made me want to jump on top of him and chew on his neck.

'Will you two keep your lover's tiff down?' Isla stepped from the trees with her hands on her hips. 'May as well put a 'Here We Are' neon light out for the giants.'

'Sorry,' Aethan said. He turned back to me and hissed. 'It's still no.'

I moved closer so he could hear me whisper. 'What if Wilfred gets there later than us? What if we miss him?' I could see the hard look in Aethan's eyes softening. *Ah ha.* I had him now. 'What if he's hurt?'

Aethan's defiance crumpled. He ran a hand through his hair and said, 'Fine. But be careful. And it's only Wilfred we're looking for.'

I nodded my head. Even though I wanted to kill Galanta so badly just thinking about it made my toes curl up, I didn't want to compromise this operation any more than it already had been. While we were alive, we still had a mission.

'I want to report to Rako.' Aethan's face was only inches from mine.

'Are you crazy?'

'He needs to know.'

'So you want to go to Trillania, which he forbade us to do, to report that we are split up and in enemy territory?'

Aethan looked less sure of himself but he nodded his head.

'Plus,' I continued in a hushed whisper, 'we have Isla with us, and your thought bubble would have reached them by now. I'm guessing Rako is packing some serious heat from further up the faery food chain. Need I mention mummy dearest?'

Aethan winced and looked away from my gaze. 'He needs to know,' he mumbled again.

'Not my idea of fun. But hey, whatever rocks your socks. Come on, we need to get to sleep.'

He nodded, and to my delight, stayed right where he was, closing his eyes and evening out his breathing. I studied him, soaking up the moment. Like this, I could almost forget that he didn't know me, almost forget he didn't care. A deep ache set up in my chest and I sighed and closed my eyes.

***

Aethan was waiting with his back to me as he flipped his sword up into the air and caught it by the hilt.

'You don't want to mistime that,' I said, being careful to speak between tosses. Last thing I needed was him waking up with missing fingers.

He flipped it up one last time and it disappeared, reappearing in the sheath on his back.

'Show off.' I smiled at him.

'Are you planning on wearing that to hunt for Wilfred?'

I looked down at my clothing and let out a squeak. I was wearing a black negligee which did little to cover my skin and everything to show it off. That's what I get for falling asleep lying so close to him. I changed it to my Border Guard uniform of leather and fur.

'I kind of liked the other one better,' Wilfred said.

'Willy.' I spun around and threw myself into his arms. 'You're alive.'

Aethan clasped Wilfred's arm and, when I had disengaged myself, pulled him into a bear hug. 'It's good to see you man.'

'Likewise. Is Isla with you?'

Aethan nodded. 'So I'm guessing Wolfgang, Brent and Luke are with you.'

'Wolfgang's hurt real bad.' Wilfred started to pace up-and-down in front of us. 'Got banged up getting out of the river. Think his leg is broken.' He pulled a face. 'Well, I *know* it's broken. The bone's sticking out through the skin.'

'Buzznuckle,' Aethan said. 'Had to be the one of us that could heal that got injured.' He pinched the bridge of his nose with one hand and stared at the ground. 'So can you travel?'

Wilfred stopped pacing and pulled a face. 'Well therein lies our other problem. We were ambushed by a pod of giants.'

If the situation weren't so dire I would have burst out laughing. How do you get ambushed by one giant let alone a pod of them? You could hear them coming a mile away.

Aethan had obviously had the same thought. 'Ambushed?'

Wilfred grimaced. 'We didn't post a watch after our little swim. Not like we could have moved fast anyway, what with Wolfgang unconscious from the pain and us down a horse.'

'We've got one packhorse. You didn't get the others?'

'Got a couple of packhorses but Wolfgang's horse got more beat up than he did. They went down a waterfall. He managed to crawl out but his horse drowned. Found him about a mile down the river from where I got out. Brent was with him.'

'So where are you now?' I asked.

'They took us to a town. We're in a dungeon.' He shook his head. 'Not sure what part of the city. They put sacks over us.'

'Over your heads?' I asked.

'Have you seen the size of a giant's sack?'

Whizbang. Over half our team were locked up in a dungeon and we didn't know where it was.

'It was early morning when they took us and I could feel the sun on my right side.'

'So north,' Aethan said.

'They carried us and I reckon it took us about an hour to get there.'

I thought about how long it had taken us to walk the distance Tiny had covered in half of that. Looking over at Aethan I said, 'So about a day's walk.'

He nodded. 'We can do it in a few hours on the horses. Maybe longer.'

Wilfred pulled a face. 'I'm hoping it's shorter than longer. They're planning on eating us tomorrow night. Festival of Ookiyata, or something like that.'

'Ukita,' Aethan said. 'It's their God. You never did listen in class.'

'Nup,' Wilfred scratched his beard. 'That's what I've got you for. You're the brains and *I'm* the looks.'

Aethan put a hand to his own shoulder. 'I think Isla's trying to wake me. Must be my watch.' He faded from view leaving me there with Wilfred.

'What else can you remember from the town?' Anything he remembered might help us find them.

'I could tell when we entered the city. We must have passed through a gate. Their voices sounded different. Less hollow.' He paused and scratched his beard. 'Then I could smell manure and hear animals.'

'Maybe a market?'

He nodded. 'Possibly. That or a stable.'

'What then?'

'Well that went on for a while. So yeah,' he scratched some more, 'probably a market place. Then it became quieter, even the giants stopped yabbering on about which part of us they were going to eat. And I could hear their footsteps.'

'So a paved area? Or maybe cobblestones.'

'Possibly.' He scratched his beard again. 'I think I've got lice. I'm so itchy I can feel it in my sleep.'

'Stop it.' I batted his hands away from his face. 'You'll only make it worse when you wake.'

'They walked for a while on those cobblestones, or whatever they were. Then they opened a squeaky door and went into a building. We're in a dungeon in that building.'

I nodded and said, 'Simple.'

He grinned at me. 'Simple.' His face took on a more serious look. 'Hey what happened to you?'

'What do you mean?'

'Your magic. I thought you would have blasted those goblins off the face of the earth.'

Tears welled up in my eyes. Dark Sky, he thought we were in this mess because of me, and he was right. 'I tried,' I said. 'I really tried.'

'Hey.' He put a hand out and pulled me to him. 'I'm not blaming you, just wondering if everything's okay.'

I dashed an arm across my eyes and leant into the brotherly comfort of his embrace. 'Wolfgang said my magic is instinctual.'

Wilfred nodded his head. 'Makes sense.'

'Yes, well now I'm so busy thinking about *that*, that my magic doesn't get a chance to be instinctual.'

'You're over analysing it.'

I nodded. 'Before, I was so intent on the battle that things just happened. Now I'm so busy thinking about the things that should be happening that they don't.'

'It's a conundrum.' He scratched his beard again. 'Hey, what came first - the chicken or the egg?'

I stared at him. 'The egg?'

'You're sure?'

'Is it the chicken?'

'I don't know. I've just always wondered.'

I burst out laughing. That was one of the things I loved about Will, his ability to always keep his sense of humour. He was a good man to have in a bad situation.

'They're trying to wake me,' he said.

I hugged the big man. 'We'll come and get you,' I promised. 'Nobody gets to eat my Willy.'

He chuckled. 'You do know how bad that sounds, right?'

'Yep. Trying not to think about it.'

Still chuckling, he faded from view.

I thought about going back to my body and using the dream-catcher, but then I thought of Emerald. I closed my eyes and appeared in her cave. The signs of Aethan and my scuffle were still evident in the sand. She hadn't been back since then. Her bulk would have erased the marks.

I flickered from site-to-site, searching for her, but she wasn't there. Finally I went to the beach where I had last called her. The moonlight danced on the breaking waves. Sitting on a rock I stared into the distance, willing her to join me.

Isadora. A breath on the wind.

I looked over my shoulder, studying the tumbled boulders. Something moved in the depths of the shadows.

'Emerald?' I stood and walked towards it. Halfway there a prickle ran down my spine. Two bright lights shone from the shadow.

I took a step back, and then another as the lights brightened.

Isadora. A breeze blew towards me and curled around my body.

I took another step back and the shadow oozed from boulder-to-boulder, the lights glowing eerily. The wind increased its speed, whirling around me.

Isadora. My name was a hiss.

The shadow emerged from the last boulder, and flowed towards me, growing taller and taller. The glowing eyes pierced mine and the wind plucked at my clothes.

And then it was flying, speeding towards me. The wind slapped my face.

Isadora.

I screamed and threw my arms up as I willed myself back to my body.

Chapter Five

On The Shoulders Of Giants

I woke with a start as Aethan shook my shoulder.

'You okay?' He peered into my eyes.

I concentrated on wiping the look of terror off my face. 'Sure.' I coughed and sat up.

What had that thing been?

Isla looked like a kitten curled up in a ball. I stood up and pulled her blanket back across her and then beckoned for him to follow me.

'Did you get anything else?' he asked.

I nodded and filled him in on what Wilfred had told me.

'So the city's walled,' he said when I'd finished.

'Sounds like it.'

He shook his head in frustration. 'How on earth are we going to get in?'

'Hey.' I put a hand on his arm. 'We'll find a way.'

He stared into my eyes for a few moments, his frustration etched onto his face. 'You're right,' he said. 'We'll find a way.'

I smiled. 'Get some sleep.'

'Is he still there?'

'He's gone.'

Aethan started to walk towards his blanket but then he stopped and turned back to me. 'Isadora,' he said, 'they tell me that I knew you, that I've lost my memories of you.'

I tried to nod casually. I wasn't sure if I pulled it off or not. 'Nasty spell, that one,' I said.

'Were we...?' He moved his hand between us. 'Were we more than this?'

Well just rip my heart out and jump up and down on it.

I longed to tell him the truth. I ached to take him in my arms and kiss him till he felt it. But I couldn't do that. Apart from the fact it could destroy his real memories of me, to put that sort of pressure on him wouldn't be fair at all. He had to discover me again by himself, or not at all. And I had to let him. So I shook my head, pasted a smile on my face and said, 'We were good friends.'

'Just friends?'

'Yup.' If I nodded any harder it was possible my head might fall off.

'Oh. So if I were to....' He broke eye contact and stopped. 'Never mind.' Shrugging, he turned away from me.

I reached out a hand and touched his shoulder. 'If you were to what?'

'Nah.' He waved a hand at me. 'I'm just tired.' He turned and walked away. 'Night Isadora,' he said over his shoulder.

I clenched my teeth together to stop myself from yelling, 'Izzy. You used to call me Izzy.' Instead I found an area I could watch the camp from. We had enough to worry about without my emotionally confounding him.

The rest of the night passed uneventfully. I woke the others when the sun started to rise and after a quick meal, saddled Lily ready to go.

The one thing Aethan and I hadn't worked out was how we were going to tell Isla that we knew where the others were. We couldn't mention Trillania. Would it be enough just to tell her that we knew and to leave it at that?

I bit back a laugh. This was Isla we were talking about. There was no *way* she would let us get away with that.

The ground started to tremble as we moved out of the campsite.

'Here we go again,' Isla said, climbing down from her saddle.

We led the horses back into the shelter of the trees.

'Izzy. Isla.' Tiny shouted. 'Where are you?'

Did he think he was playing hide-and-seek with us?

Aethan stepped from the trees and held onto a trunk to steady himself as the tremors increased. 'Tiny,' he hollered. 'Over here.'

Worried about falling trees, we moved back into the open and concentrated on staying upright. I could see the silhouette of the huge giant coming towards us.

At the sight of us, his mouth broke into a huge grin, displaying his crooked teeth in all their glory. 'I find,' he said.

Isla sighed. 'You win.'

He shook his head. 'No, no. Tiny found friends.'

Did he mean what I thought he meant? '*Our* friends?' I clarified.

His grin intensified. 'Over there.' He pointed north. 'Nasty men have caught them.'

Isla looked over at Aethan and me. 'Does he mean goblins?'

If we hadn't spoken to Wilfred last night I would have assumed that as well. We were so used to thinking of giants as just that, that we hadn't realised they saw themselves as men and women.

'Men like you, but nasty,' I said.

He nodded, one of his eyes on me and the other pointing towards the sky. 'Must come quick. Tonight nasty men eat friends.'

Isla let out a yelp and leapt back into her saddle. 'What are we waiting for?' she said, turning her horse toward the town.

'A plan,' Aethan said. 'Tiny, can you get us to them?'

Tiny cocked his head to the side and stared into the distance. He reached a finger up and scratched the side of his nose. Just when I thought he hadn't understood the question he said, 'Can get you into town, but nasty men get suspicious if they see Tiny creeping around. You rescue friends and Tiny get you out.'

'Good enough.' Aethan flashed him a smile.

We mounted again but it was impossible to ride the horses with Tiny walking. We risked one of them breaking a leg if we tried.

'Tiny find more.' He pointed at Adare. 'Where nasty men caught friends.'

All we'd done that day was walk a few extra miles. Tiny had located the others *and* found their horses. He had us beat hands down at hide-and-seek.

'Is it on the way? I asked.

He nodded his head.

'Can you lead us there?' Aethan said.

If the shit hit the fan during the escape we were going to need all the horses we could get.

In answer, Tiny turned and started walking. We let him get far enough ahead that we could safely ride and then followed.

The others hadn't camped that far away from us and it only took us fifteen minutes to get to the horses. A little stream ran nearby and we took the time to water and feed them, before staking all of them so that they could get to the stream if they needed. Long, soft grass grew plentiful in the area. They could spend the day resting and grazing.

I could feel the day ticking away and we still weren't much closer to the others. Tiny took his satchel off his back and placed it on the ground.

'Tiny take you in bag,' he said.

I looked at the others. If we were wrong, if Tiny weren't to be trusted, it would be seven faeries and one small dog the giants would be eating tonight. But we didn't have any other options; we were running out of time.

'Come on,' I said, climbing into the bag with Scruffy.

Isla and Aethan followed me, none of us talking, but I'm sure we were all thinking the same thing.

Even with the top left undone, it was dark in the bag. Tiny lifted us carefully into the air and swung the bag over his shoulder. I let out a little squeal as the momentum forced us into the side of the satchel.

'Sorry,' Tiny said. But it sounded like he was amused.

A partially eaten loaf of bread was standing on one side of the bag. We wrestled it to the bottom to use as a bench seat, and the ride got more comfortable.

'Hungry?' Isla ripped a chunk off the side of the loaf and handed it to me.

After days of hard biscuits and beef jerky the bread tasted like heaven.

'Got any cheese?' Aethan asked, propping his feet up on a jar.

Isla snorted but ignored him. I looked at her in the dim light. It wasn't like her to not rise to a bait from Aethan.

'We'll get there in time,' I said, squeezing her hand.

'Oh, I know we will.' Her body language belied her words. 'I hope Wolfgang is okay.'

I stopped myself from mentioning his broken leg. There was no way I could have known about that. And besides, I didn't think it was really Wolfgang that had that line etched between her perfect brows.

The satchel swayed gently in time with Tiny's steps and I could feel my eyelids getting heavy. Scruffy nestled onto my lap and I closed my eyes and let my head fall back against the fabric of the bag.

'Halt, who goes there?' The giant's voice woke me from my nap with a start.

I gasped and sat upright. Aethan touched my arm and put a finger to his lips. For a glorious slice of time I had been suspended between reality and dreams. I felt like I had slept for hours.

'My name is Tiny.'

The other giant snorted. 'And what brings you to town... Tiny?' He said the name with enough scorn to make me want to pop out the top of the bag and teach him some manners. From the way Isla's hand twitched towards her sword I was guessing she was thinking the same thing.

'The festival,' Tiny said.

'Why don't you look me in the eye when you talk to me boy?'

A few other giants sniggered at the reference to Tiny's wandering eyes.

It felt like Tiny shifted from foot-to-foot and I silently willed him to stand his ground. 'I come to the festival,' he said, a stubborn tone to his voice.

'What's going on up there?' Another voice called from behind.

Oh great. We were causing a queue at the front gate to the town. We had giants in front and behind us. The knowledge caused sweat to gather on my brow.

'I go to the festival.' From the vibrations coming through the bag, I assumed Tiny was jiggling up-and-down on the spot.

'Oh for goodness sake Derek, let him in,' the voice behind us insisted.

'Yeah,' another voice, even further back called.

'Fine, Tiny.' More sniggers followed this, making me wish we had spent more time working on his name. 'Go through.'

The bag settled back into a gentle sway as Tiny recommenced his journey. As soon as he cleared the gate we were baffled with noise. Giants shouting their wares, others haggling over prices, and still more chatting in the streets.

Giants everywhere.

When we had come up with this ride-into-town-and-save-our-friends plan my mind had shied away from the reality of the situation. Well, reality had just shown up dressed in a psychedelic clown suit and carrying a placard that said, 'Here I am.'

How on earth were we to save them?

Tiny walked for a few minutes till we could hear animals bleating and mooing. Then he swung the satchel off his shoulder and slung it onto the ground. I let out an 'ooophff' as we were tossed off our edible seat and thrown across the bag. I landed in a heap, meshed into Aethan's body, my legs and arms entangled with his. His musky scent enveloped me as my face pressed into his chest.

'How much for the cow?' Tiny asked.

'What do you want with a cow?'

'I like milk.'

Seriously? He was buying a cow? Had he forgotten about our mission?

The store holder burst out laughing. 'This here is a bull,' he said. 'You'll not be getting any milk from him. But I have a fine dairy cow over here in this other pen.' His voice faded as he led Tiny away.

Isla poked her head out the top of the bag. 'Quick,' she said. 'Before they come back.'

She scampered out the top of the bag with Scruffy on her heels and Aethan and I disentangled ourselves with an awkward 'excuse me' and 'so sorry' and followed her. I tried not to think about the feel of his body wrapped around mine. That was not going to help at all.

Tiny had slung his bag behind the back wall of a pen, giving us full cover as we emerged.

I stared open-mouthed at the enormous animals. For some reason I had been expecting human-sized ones.

'Which way?' Isla asked.

The animal market stretched off into the distance in front of us. 'That way,' I said, praying I was right.

We crept along the back of the pen and stopped at the far end for a group of giants to pass. A quick glance backwards showed the stall keeper demonstrating how to milk the cow. We dashed across the path between that stall and the next, and then crept along behind it.

I'm more of a fighter than a creeper and the suspense wound me into a tight ball of nerves. The sweat that had formed before was now trickling down my face. All we needed was some giant to look in our direction at the wrong time, when we were exposed dashing from hiding spot to hiding spot, and it would be game over for all of us.

Not only would two thirds of the royal heirs be destroyed in a giant's cook pot, but the probability of the goblins winning the night faeries to their side would dramatically increase. The safety of the world depended on this mission and that added a whole heap more pressure to an already stressful situation.

We were about to make another dash across a street when Scruffy let out a low growl. I put a hand on Aethan's arm to stop him and a few seconds later a child appeared right where we would have been. 'They'll never find us here,' he called back over his shoulder.

We just had enough time to dive behind some hay bales before the speaker and another child appeared behind the stall. I peered between two bales as the boys made themselves comfortable on the other side. A lollipop stick protruded from between the leader's lips.

'I heard Mum telling Mrs Layton that the guard had caught faeries outside the city,' Lollipop said.

'No way.' The other youth pulled his own lolly out of his pocket and pulled off the wrapper. He tossed it over his shoulder and it floated down to land on my head. Lolly residue stuck the paper to my hair.

'Ahuh,' Lollipop continued. 'Said there were fifty of them.'

'That's way cool.'

I managed to get the wrapper off, but lolly goop stretched between the paper and my head. It finally released its grip on the wrapper, preferring instead to stick to my hair.

Lollipop took his sweet out of his mouth and examined it. 'You've never seen a faery, have you?'

'You haven't neither.'

'Yes I have.'

'No you haven't.'

'Have too.'

'You're a dirty stinking liar.'

'Am not.' Lollipop shoved his companion and for one awful second I thought he was going to roll into our hiding place.

He regained his balance and shoved back. 'Are too. My Mum said lying runs in your family.'

'You take that back.' Lollipop balled up his fist.

'If you boys are going to fight back there you can piss off to another stall.' Heavy footsteps bounced us, as the store owner rounded the end of the building.

'Sorry Master Hammon,' both boys said in meek voices.

For a few moments all that could be heard was the sucking noises. Then lollipop boy said, 'Do you want to see one?'

His companion pulled his sweet out of his mouth. 'What, now?'

'Ahuh.' The look on Lollipop's face embodied the spirit of naughty children everywhere. 'Mum said they put them in the church crypts.'

I looked over at Aethan and Isla, unable to believe our luck.

'The crypts are dark.'

Go on, I willed them. *Lead us to the church.*

'Scaredy-cat.'

'Am not.'

'Are too.'

'Boys!' Master Hammon's voice blasted from the other side of the stall.

'Prove it.' Lollipop stood up and started walking up the street in the direction we had been going.

We dived back out to behind the stall and scuttled along our hidden alley as we tried to keep up with glimpses of the boys. The problem was not only that their legs were three times as high as us, but that we had to maintain a look out as we ran. We ducked and dived, hiding behind animals and stalls and hay bales as we made our way after them, but they got further and further ahead.

'They're getting away,' Isla muttered.

Just before we lost total sight of them, they darted to the right, down an alley. When we got to the start of the alley we saw them turning right at the end. There was no shelter down the alley. We were going to have to run it with nowhere to hide.

'No guts no glory,' Aethan said.

We sprinted down the alley, the mouldy walls of the buildings towering ominously on either side of us. The gloom and dampness amplified the feeling of doom. My nerves wound tighter and tighter, my breathing coming heavier than it should have from the exertion of the run. Nowhere to turn, nowhere to hide.

Finally, when I thought I might start screaming, we reached the corner the boys had taken. Another cobblestoned alley stretched in front of us. There was no sign of the children.

We ran down the alley until it reached a T-intersection.

'Shit.' Aethan ran his hands through his hair as he looked left and right.

We were so exposed.

'That way,' I pointed to the left. A tall spire stretched towards the sky. I was betting it was the church.

Using the doorway shadows for cover, we moved towards the spire.

Where was everyone? If today was a religious festival why weren't they all coming to the church?

A low hum started up as we got closer to the building with the spire. Singing.

Of course, the reason there weren't any giants in the alleys coming to church was because they were already *at* church.

The end of the alley opened into a large, paved courtyard in front of the church. A wide set of stone stairs curved from the ground to a soaring arch filled with two ironclad, wooden doors. A smaller entry was serviced by a path that wound through a garden and ended at a stone arch on the edge of the courtyard.

We darted across the courtyard to the stone arch and hid in its shadow. As we listened, the singing got louder and then there was a squawking creak as the main doors were pushed open. A giant, dressed in robes stood in the entry.

I scooped Scruffy beneath me as we cowered into balls, face down and pressed into the base of the arch as the priest started down the stairs. Counting on the colour of our clothing to camouflage us in the shadows, we stayed absolutely still as the congregation trailed after him in a long column.

It felt like forever as their footsteps thundered past us, their singing echoing around the courtyard and down the alley. Sweat drenched my body as I controlled the urge to flee.

And then they were gone.

I let out the breath I had been holding and sat back on my knees. Aethan grabbed me before I could stand.

Lollipop boy pushed open the small entry door. 'They'll be gone for at least an hour.' Instead of heading down the path to where we hid, he led his companion across the garden towards the staircase. He broke a branch off a tree and whipped it from side-to-side before tossing it back to the ground.

'Little vandal,' Isla hissed.

They jumped up onto the stairs and made their way to the still-open doors of the church.

As soon as they had disappeared inside, we followed. Of course it wasn't quite so easy for us. The stairs were shoulder height and took us longer to navigate.

We had an hour to find our friends and get the hell back out of there. I was hoping the crypts weren't too far down.

We heard Lollipop as soon as we crept into the church. Hiding behind a pew we could see him struggling with a door. 'I'm sure it's down here.' He turned the handle and rattled the door backwards and forwards and suddenly it popped open.

His companion stuck his head into the opening. 'Coooooolll,' he said. 'The stairs go down.'

'Where did you think they'd go?' Lollipop pushed past him and disappeared down the stairs. His friend followed and the door began to close.

We broke from our cover and raced towards the door. If it shut we were never going to get down there.

'Quick.' Aethan grabbed one end of a door stopper and I got the other. We wedged it in between the door and the frame with inches to spare.

'That was close.' Isla looked down the stairs. 'It's dark.'

'Maybe you should stay up here and stand guard,' Aethan said to her.

She looked at him with one eyebrow arched. 'Trying to keep me safe, brother dearest?' She patted him on the cheek and stepped past him, jumping down the first stair.

Aethan turned to me.

'Nahaaha,' I said. 'I'm coming. You may need my superior fighting skills.'

The corner of his mouth quirked up. 'We need someone to stand watch.'

I looked at Scruffy. 'You stay. Bark if someone comes.'

He whined and pawed at my leg.

'Love you too buddy. Now hide.'

He darted underneath the nearest pew and pressed his body up against the leg. No-one would see him unless they got down on their hands and knees and looked.

About halfway down, the staircase began to lighten. We progressed more quickly once we could see, and it only took us a few minutes to make it to the bottom. The light came from a tunnel off to our left. We slunk down it, freezing when we heard the boy's voices.

'Coooollll.'

'I told you there were faeries down here.'

Aethan gestured for us to follow and we crept into the room and hid behind the legs of a chair.

The boys had their backs to us as they peered into the cell that held our friends. Fine mesh covered the cell bars from ceiling to floor. We could see Brent, Luke and Wilfred standing behind the mesh.

'Faeries are arrogant.' Lollipop jabbed the wire mesh with his finger. 'My Mum says so.'

'Mind who you're calling arrogant.' Wilfred puffed his chest out and stepped closer to the mesh.

'Arrogant, arrogant, arrogant.' Lollipop stabbed the wire with each word.

On his third stab, Wilfred leapt forwards, pulling his sword out of his sheath and stabbing it into the end of Lollipop's finger.

'Oowwww,' Lolly shrieked, leaping back from the wire. He stuck his finger in his mouth and sucked on it.

Aethan stepped out from behind his chair leg and waved. Wilfred's eyes widened as he saw him, but then he turned back to Lollipop as if nothing had happened.

'Think you're pretty tough coming all the way down here by yourself,' Wilfred said.

'I am tough.' Lollipop took his finger out of his mouth and put his hands on his hips. 'I could take you on any day.'

Wilfred, Brent and Luke burst out laughing.

'Yeah right,' Brent said. 'My Grandmother's tougher than you. And she can't walk.'

Luke and Wilfred laughed again, slapping their legs as if it were the funniest thing they had ever heard. What were they doing? Were they trying to get killed?

'I am so tough,' Lolly said.

'Why don't you come in here and show us how tough you are?'

And then of course I understood what they were up to. There was no way we would be able to get them out of there. The lock was too high for us to undo. The boys though? Well they were another matter entirely.

Lolly looked around and spied a set of keys hanging from the wall. He stalked over, grabbed them and took them back to the cell.

'I don't know if this is such a good idea?' his mate said.

'No one will know.' He fumbled for the correct key. 'We'll just squash a couple of them. I get the orange, hairy one.'

Brent, Luke and Wilfred backed away from the door to the other side of the room as Lolly opened it.

'Not so tough now are you?' Lolly's laugh reminded me of the bullies from my schooldays. Did they take lessons on how to make that sound?

'Nope.' Wilfred shook his head. 'But my friends are.'

He pointed in our direction and when the two young giants turned around we were blocking their exit from the cell. Aethan and I had drawn our swords and Isla had my bow with an arrow notched.

'Hello boys,' Isla said, pulling back on her bow string.

When Lolly went to rush us, she let the arrow fly. It thudded into the flesh of his thigh and he let out a squeal and fell to the ground. 'Plenty more where that came from,' she said.

Wolfgang lay on a mattress near the far wall. Brent and Luke picked it up and carried him out of the cell. His face was pale but his eyes were open and he managed to give me a small smile.

'How are we going to keep them in there?' Wilfred said, as he stood in the doorway with Aethan and me. Lolly's mate stepped towards us and we waved our swords to warn him off.

'I think I can manage.' Wolfgang's voice was weak.

We stepped back as Brent and Luke closed the door. Lolly's mate rushed at the door, but before he could force it open there was a clicking sound and the key turned in the lock. The mesh prevented them from being able to undo it.

'Well done,' I said, turning towards Wolfgang. His eyes were closed and his breathing came in small rasps. I exchanged a worried look with Isla.

'You'll never get away with this,' Lolly said. A small trickle of blood seeped from the arrow wound.

'Oh,' Isla said, 'I think we just did.'

We could hear their yells fading behind us as we climbed back up, but we had more important things to worry about. It took all of us to get Wolfgang up the stairs. Three each side, we lifted the mattress onto the next step and then clambered up after it. By the time we neared the top I was panting and covered in sweat.

With one step to go, Scruffy let out a little ruffing bark.

Whizbang. Someone was coming.

We lifted Wolfgang the last time and dragged the mattress towards the door. I stuck my head out through the opening. I could see a priest up the front moving around and lighting candles. Singing could be heard coming into the church from outside.

'Quick,' I hissed. The parade was almost there.

The first of the congregation marched up the stairs, their song echoing around the church. We carried Wolfgang's mattress and slipped it under the nearest pew, sliding in next to him.

'The door,' Aethan whispered, darting back towards it.

We had left the doorstop propping it open. The last thing we wanted was someone investigating the crypt while we were still in the church.

I followed him. Grabbing either side of the wooden stop, we wiggled it from side-to-side. The pressure of the door on it stopped it from coming easily. Any second a giant was going to come up the side aisle and see us there wrestling with the damned thing.

It inched outward, until Wilfred joined us, putting his back to the door and pushing it open. We yanked the stop out and placed it back against the wall, diving back under the pew as the first shadow darkened the aisle. Scruffy pushed up against me, and I scratched him on the head.

Still singing, the giants entered the church. They filed back into the pews and we pressed ourselves against the side leg, trying to remain upright as the ground shook. They took their seats and silence fell over the room. The light dimmed as the entry doors started to shut.

'Excuse me,' a familiar voice said. 'Want to talk to God.'

The doors creaked back open and murmurs and mutters of disapproval could be heard.

'Let him in,' the priest said from the front. 'Anyone who wants to talk to Ukita can enter his home.'

There was more muttering and then the sound of feet shuffling and Tiny walked down the side aisle. If we were to escape he had to sit near us. But if we were seen trying to attract his attention we would all be caught, and he would no doubt be punished. In the end I reasoned most of the giants would be looking at him, so I stepped to the other side of the leg and waved an arm in the air.

Aethan yanked me back beneath the pew. 'What are you doing?' he whispered.

'Getting his attention.'

We felt Tiny stop walking as he got to our pew. 'Tiny sit here,' he said.

'This is my seat young man,' a giantess said. 'Go find your own.'

'Tiny's seat.' He shuffled sideways into the pew and we saw the legs of the lady sliding sideways.

'Why, I never,' she muttered.

Tiny let out a satisfied grunt as he sat down. He chucked his bag onto the floor and kicked it under the seat. I resisted the urge to clasp his hairy leg and kiss it.

Isla, Aethan and I rushed to the top of the bag and pulled back the lid.

'What are you doing?' Wilfred whispered in my ear.

'This is our ride out of here,' I said.

He stared at me with his eyes wide and his bushy eyebrows raised but at the sight of Isla and Aethan preparing the bag he shrugged.

The priest's voice droned as we wrestled Wolfgang's mattress into the bottom of the bag next to the bread. Then we climbed in and, just before I flicked the lid back down, I reached out and patted Tiny's leg.

A few seconds later we heard him stand up. More mutters of disapproval followed. 'Finished,' he said, swinging us up into the air.

I think we all held our breath as the giant doors creaked back open, and then Tiny was walking down the stairs and away from the church. I couldn't believe we had gotten away with it.

He strode through the alleyways and back through the marketplace. We huddled around Wolfgang's mattress and waited. Nearly there. We were nearly free.

'Oiy Tiny.' It was Derek from the front gate. 'Where are you going?'

'Tiny go home now.'

'Thought you wanted to see the festival.' I squeezed my eyes shut as Derek's voice got closer.

'Spoke to God. He told me to go home.'

Derek burst out laughing. 'I bet he did. Why would he want a lumpkin like you at his birthday party?'

By the movement of the bag I thought Tiny was shuffling his feet again. 'Tiny not a lumpkin.'

'Let it go man,' Aethan murmured under his breath.

'What'd you say?' Derek's voice was quieter but it held a menacing undertone.

'Tiny not a lumpkin,' Tiny shouted.

Oh boy. Here we go.

In the dim light of the bag I could just see Brent and Luke start to draw their swords. Aethan shook his head and motioned for them to re-sheath them. If the bag got tossed around it was us that would feel the sharp length of steel.

'Well looky here. The mutant grew some balls.' There was a soft smacking sound and I pictured Derek punching a fist into the palm of his other hand.

'Not mutant,' Tiny roared and then we were dropping down and moving forwards. The bag jumped around wildly, swinging from Tiny's back to his side like a pendulum. Derek let out a cry and a shockwave from the contact of Tiny tackling him flowed through the bag.

Then we could hear flesh pounding flesh. I prayed it was Tiny's flesh pounding Derek's and not the other way round.

Derek let out another roar and the bag was flung out to the side. Tiny grunted and like an elevator out of control we crashed to the ground.

It was crowded with the eight of us in the bag. I cradled Scruffy in my arms as we tumbled over each other, a gigantic ball of body parts. Wolfgang let out a low moan as we came to rest.

I was guessing the score was one all.

'What ya got in here?'

We were hefted back into the air so suddenly that, for a split second, when we reached the top of the arc, I was weightless.

'No,' Tiny yelled. '*My* bag.'

The bag jerked and the fabric stretched horizontally as they wrestled for control.

Oh Dark Sky, don't let it rip down the middle. A picture of us tumbling from the ruined bag flashed into my mind.

One big tug in Derek's direction and the bag was free, but in Derek's possession.

'You been stealing boy?'

Oh, had he ever.

'Tiny not steal.'

'Well let's have a look, hey.'

I shared a look of horror with the others. We had been so close. So close. And now because of this bully we were going to be captured. And eaten.

I hated bullies. Despised them with my whole heart. I felt a pressure building inside me. I'd had enough of them trying to ruin my life. I'd be damned if I were going to let this Derek end it for me.

'Wolfgang.' Aethan's low tone held a note of urgency.

Wolfgang opened his eyes, but pain glazed them like a frosted window. 'Isadora,' he croaked.

'I can't... I don't.' If it were up to me, we would die for sure.

'Instinct,' Wolfgang gasped. 'Don't think. Do.'

Isla grasped my arm as the flap of the satchel lifted, flooding light down through the opening. 'I believe in you,' she whispered.

I couldn't let Derek see us. Not like this, with Wolfgang wounded and us all trapped. I threw my arms up in the air above us.

Don't see us. Oh please don't see us.

The light shifted and bent around us, touching the sides of the bag. Not one ray of sunlight landed on any of us.

Derek's face appeared in the opening and peered down at where we lay in a tumble of disarray.

'Huh,' it said. 'There's nothing here, except....' A hand descended towards us and Brent and Wilfred shoved the half-eaten loaf of bread into the outstretched fingers. 'This bread.'

Derek shoved the bread into his mouth and took a bite. 'Thanks, I was hungry.'

He let the bag fall from his fingers and I tensed with my hands still up, waiting for another hard landing, but before we hit, the bag was swung back up and around and I guessed we were back on Tiny's shoulder.

The gentle swaying motion of Tiny's walking recommenced. The noise of the town fell behind us and we were free.

I dropped my hands and slumped back against the side of the bag.

Isla crouched down beside Wolfgang and put her hand on his brow. His chest hardly moved as he took short, sharp breaths. My eyes dropped to his leg. It lay at an awkward angle to the rest of his body. He had to be in such pain.

Aethan put his hand on my arm. 'What did you do?'

'I don't know.' I *never* knew.

'She wove an illusion.' Wolfgang opened his eyes. His lips pulled up in an attempt at a smile. It looked more like a grimace. 'In a fashion. She manipulated the light rays so that he couldn't see us.' He winced and closed his eyes, shifting his body as if trying to stop the pain.

'Shhh.' Isla took his hand in hers.

'I wove an illusion.' I shrugged my shoulders. 'I'm pretty useless really.'

'I wouldn't call that useless.' Aethan gave me his cutest, dimpled smile. 'You saved us.'

He had the same look on his face that he used to get when he told me that he loved me. Searching, intense, admiring. Like he was drinking in the sight of me and storing the memory for later.

I met his stare. Trapped by the depths of his midnight-blue eyes, I could feel him stripping my soul. But then he blinked and turned away. Without telling me that he loved me. Not that I had expected him to, but the absence of it was a painful reminder of what I had lost.

I took a deep, shuddering breath and looked back at Wolfgang. Isla still held his hand but now she watched me. Her head was cocked to the side like she was trying to understand something.

'Can you heal him?' She nodded her head down at Wolfgang.

'Oh, no… I've never healed before.' Heaven forbid I try and blow him up instead. I could imagine trying to explain *that* one to Rako.

Wolfgang opened his eyes again. 'I could lead you,' he said in a weak voice. 'Show you.'

I shook my head. 'I could hurt you.'

He barked out a dry laugh and then closed his eyes again, tensing at the pain from his leg. When the moment had passed he looked at me again. 'You will at least try? For me?'

Did he know what he was asking? What he was risking? I was like a loaded gun in the hands of a group of blind children. Anything could happen.

'I'll think about it,' I whispered. It was the most I could give him.

Chapter Six

The Rat Is In The Trap

I closed my eyes and pretended to sleep for the rest of the ride back to the camp. But instead of sleeping, I worried. I worried about Grams, I worried about Emerald and I worried about killing Wolfgang. And when I had finished worrying about them I moved on to Galanta and Santanas.

Where was the Goblin Queen? What was she planning? I ached to be off after her, but I knew our mission was a vital piece in the big picture. If, Dark Sky forbid, we didn't stop her in time, we would need the night faeries as allies.

That of course brought me back to Wolfgang. Without him our chance of success dramatically decreased.

Tiny stopped walking and lowered us to the ground. 'We're here,' he said, lifting up the flap.

Isla let go of Wolfgang's hand and bounded out the top. 'You were wonderful,' she said, looking up at Tiny.

I followed her and threw my arms around his ankle. 'You're our hero.'

The gentle giant's face erupted into a blush. He clasped his hands behind his back and hung his head while dragging the tip of one shoe through the grass.

Aethan and Luke emerged, stepping backwards as they pulled the end of Wolfgang's mattress. Wolfgang seemed to have passed out again. His colour looked even worse than when we had first found them. And it was up to me to heal him.

Eeeekkk.

Luke put down his end of the mattress and turned to Tiny. 'I am forever in your debt.'

Brent bowed low and said, 'We will tell stories of Tiny the Brave.'

If possible, Tiny's face went even redder.

'You're the man.' Wilfred punched the side of Tiny's leg.

'You are certainly as brave as your mother.' Wolfgang tried to sit up. Isla rushed back to him and helped him into an upright position.

'Mother?' One of Tiny's eyes pivoted to Wolfgang. 'You knew mother?'

'If I am not mistaken you are Berdina Flatfoot's son.'

Tiny nodded, then his face crumpled. 'Mother left cause Tiny ugly.'

'Is that what they told you? Dear boy. Your mother loved you very much.'

The sudden hope on Tiny's face was painful to witness.

'She came to us in the Dark Years with crucial information. Then she stayed to help us fight.'

'Mother help?'

Wolfgang nodded. 'More than you could ever know.'

'She never came home.' A huge tear trickled down Tiny's cheek.

'She died in battle.' Wolfgang shook his head. 'She died a hero.'

'I'm sorry Tiny.' I wrapped my arms around his ankle again.

Tiny sniffled and a tear narrowly missed my head. 'A hero. Mother was a hero.' He sniffled again and, as if trying the words on for size, said, 'She loved me.'

'Will you be all right?' I asked. 'I mean with the other giants?'

He nodded his head and let out a snort. 'Tiny too dumb to save you.' He laughed again.

I could see Lily watching us from the trees where she stood with the other horses. I was about to head over to her when Wolfgang said, 'Isadora. It is time.'

I felt like running away. I felt like hiding. But mostly, I felt like vomiting. What if I got it wrong? What if I…

'Hey.' Aethan shook my shoulder gently. 'You can do this.'

'I don't know if I can.' The words came out in a rush. 'I've never been able to control my magic.'

'Well if you fail you fail. But at least you'll know you tried.'

If only it were that easy. I shook my head. 'I blow things up. Accidentally.'

'Ahhhh.' He stared into my eyes. 'I don't know you well, but what I know is that you are good and kind, and that you always do your best. Wolfgang obviously thinks you can do it.'

As I met his stare, the urge to blither hysterically seeped away. Instead, calm settled over me. 'Okay,' I said. I turned and walked to where Wolfgang lay. 'What do you want me to do?' I sat cross-legged beside him and took his hand.

'Empty your mind.'

I closed my eyes and concentrated on the sound of my breathing.

'Now reach out to me.'

I pushed my mind outwards and felt Wolfgang there waiting for me. He led me back to his body. His life energy flowed over him like a gentle wave. It tingled beneath my awareness.

'That's right,' he murmured. 'Let yourself go.'

I flowed into his energy, becoming one with it as it travelled around his body. Over his head, down his chest, past his hips and... I felt it... like a sickness. A dark patch in his energy.

Shards of bone pressed through his flesh, jagged edges digging deep. Tendons twisted, ligaments torn. Muscles ripped and flesh destroyed.

I didn't know how Wolfgang was still conscious let alone talking. Only his training could have kept the agony at bay.

Without even thinking I flowed into the wound, pulling the bits of bone together and knitting them into a strong piece. I kneaded muscles and re-attached ligaments and tendons.

I could feel him shuddering under my hands, but I ignored it.

I ordered his tissue back to its rightful position and stroked it into place with my power. When it was all as it should be I sat back and opened my eyes.

Wilfred and Aethan had a shoulder each and Brent and Luke had the legs. Wolfgang panted as he stared at me with wide eyes.

'I'm sorry it took me so long.' I knew from first-hand experience how painful healing could be.

'But child,' Wolfgang squeezed my hand. 'It hardly took any time at all.'

'Really?' I felt like I had been at it for ages.

'A few seconds,' Wilfred said. 'Fastest healing of a wound like that I've ever seen.'

'And it didn't hurt.' Wolfgang sat up. 'At all.' He flexed his leg experimentally and then rose and put his weight on it. 'Remarkable,' he said. 'Not even any after pain.' He walked around the clearing a few times. 'I'm curious as to how you knew where to put everything.'

I stared at him. 'I didn't. I let it go where it wanted to.'

He grinned. 'Ingenious.'

I could feel the hairs on the back of my neck standing up. 'What did you think would happen?'

'Not sure. I figured anything was better than the pain.'

I could feel my eyes starting to bulge as I glared at him. He had thought I was going to mutilate him and he had let me do it. He had let me risk failure; or worse still, the possibility I would hurt him further.

I turned and stormed off into the trees as I tried to regain control of my temper. Picking up a fallen branch, I slashed the leaves at the tree trunks as I passed.

Stupid faery.

Thwack, crack.

Had been so surprised when I'd healed him.

Swish, thump.

Wouldn't have been so pleased if his leg had exploded.

A hand grasped my shoulder and I let out a squeal and spun, bringing the branch around like a baton. Before I could hit him, Aethan caught my wrist, locking my arm out straight. My heart raced like a playing colt as I stared into his eyes. What was it with men setting themselves up for me to hurt them?

Consciously, I slowed my breathing and let my arm relax. It dropped to my side but he didn't let go of my hand.

'I came to make sure you were okay,' he said.

I *had* been okay. I had been happy with my anger. Now though, my heart beat fast for a different reason. Now my knees felt weak and my breath caught in my throat. All I had to do was stretch my neck and tilt my head and our lips would touch.

Our gaze seemed locked together as he shifted closer. I stretched towards him, flexing the balls of my feet to lift me up. His free hand rested lightly on my hip and I shuddered at the contact. I wanted those arms wrapped tight around me. I wanted them holding me in place as his mouth ravished mine. And all the time he stared at me, his dark eyes setting me on fire.

A branch cracked further back in the woods. His eyes widened in surprise as he looked over my shoulder. Lifting one finger to his lips he moved backwards around the trunk of an elm. He pulled me with him and pushed my back up against the trunk. If he weren't loosening his sword in its sheath I would have thought all my fantasies were about to come true.

He leant against me and peered around the trunk. 'Goblins,' he whispered in my ear.

Goblins?

Buzznuckle. Here I'd been thinking all we had to worry about were giants.

'Do you think they saw us?' I was *far* too aware of the feel of his cheek brushing against mine as I whispered in his ear.

An arrow thudded into the side of the trunk an inch from Aethan's face.

'Think so,' he said as he turned, dragging me back the way we had come.

We zigzagged through the trees as we ran, the sound of pursuit obvious behind us.

'Incoming,' Aethan yelled as we approached the others.

We burst into the clearing to find them with their weapons already drawn. Isla loosed an arrow past my shoulder. I heard a grunt and turned to see a goblin collapse not a dozen paces behind me.

Wolfgang threw out his arms and I felt two shields form. One was a half-bubble floating over the horses, the other a semi-circular shield in front of us. A half-dozen arrows thudded into it and bounced harmlessly to the ground.

Eight warriors broke from the trees, dropping bows and drawing cruel daggers. If I hadn't fought them before I would have been quaking in my boots. Easily seven-feet tall, their teeth were filed to points and their faces filled with rage. Human bones decorated the leather supporting their loin cloths, and oil coated their dark brown skin. They roared as they charged.

The two fastest reached Wolfgang's shield first, bouncing off it and collapsing to the ground like birds smacking into a window. If the situation hadn't been so dire I would have laughed at the sight.

'Go,' Wolfgang yelled as he dropped the shield in front of us.

Isla bounded into the air, releasing two arrows into the downed goblins before she landed again. Tiny yelled as he stomped his feet, reminding me of someone trying to squash ants. The goblins dodged and weaved, but not all of them made it through.

'Hoi,' Wilfred yelled. 'Leave some for the rest of us.'

Isla flashed him a smile. 'Don't worry, I have a feeling there will be plenty for all of us.'

As if on cue another dozen goblins emerged from the trees. These approached more warily. Of the six that were left from the original charge, four were caught up in battle and the other two had become giant road kill.

I smiled as two of the late-comers ran at me. I'd always found killing goblins a wonderful way to work off a bad mood. Not that my mood was that bad any more. Not with the feel of Aethan's body imprinted into my mind.

I leapt into the air, turning a somersault as I swept my sword down to cut through the side of one of their necks. Blood arced out in a rhythmical spray and he was on the ground with glazed eyes before I landed. The other licked his lips and backed up.

They'd obviously targeted me for a specific purpose, and I was guessing it was because they'd thought I was an easy kill.

Really, Galanta should train her warriors better before she sent them into battle. What a pity this one wouldn't get a chance to improve.

I ran at him and he lifted his dagger straight out like I had been sure he would. I wound my weapon around his and spun, ripping it from his grasp. Then I thrust my sword back under my right arm with both hands, feeling the sudden resistance as it speared into his chest.

My next victim was already approaching as I kicked backwards, forcing the dying goblin off my blade. This one grinned as he stalked me, tossing his dagger from hand-to-hand. He pulled a second one and wheeled the blades through his fingers, spinning them faster and faster. *A blades master. Great.*

I wasn't sure if he expected me to feel fear. All I know was that I was as surprised as he when one of Tiny's feet crushed him to the ground.

'Not hurt my Izzy,' Tiny yelled, grinding him into the dirt.

Isla was backing up towards a tree as she fended off an attacker. She flicked her blade through a flurry of motion, but was unable to break through the goblin's attack. She was in trouble once she got to the tree. There would be nowhere for her to go.

I ran towards her, but before I could get there another goblin charged me from the side. He lifted a spear and hurled it at me. Without even thinking I flicked a hand. He and the spear flew backwards through the air. I heard a nasty crack as he slammed into a branch, his body flexing backward so that his head and feet touched. I doubted very much he would be coming back from that.

I leapt into the air and landed on the back of the goblin attacking Isla. Grasping his head, I ripped it to the side. There was another crack and his arms fell limply. I jumped clear as he collapsed.

'Thanks,' Isla panted. She picked up her bow and loosed a couple of arrows at a goblin attacking Wilfred. 'How many more do you think there are?'

I looked around the clearing. Tiny was in the process of picking up some goblins that had popped out of the trees at his feet. One-by-one he threw them as far as he could back over the top of the woods.

Wolfgang was shooting fireballs into the tree line where dark shapes dodged and weaved trying to escape a fiery death. Aethan, Brent, Luke and Wilfred were fighting two goblins each, their blades flicking through complex patterns.

But like a rodent plague, as fast as we killed them, more crept out to replace them. It was only a matter of time before one of us got tired and made a mistake.

'Cover me.' I closed my eyes and reached out with my mind, pushing out into the woods. Darkness and evil swarmed around us, black hearts beating in anticipation of our deaths. Like homing pigeons they came.

I heard the bell-like chimes of metal striking metal; Brent crying out in pain; Wilfred laughing like a mad man as he fought; and ever closer our deaths crept. Wolfgang's spells killed most of them before they got to us, but even that was not enough against what was coming. Galanta had prepared a surprise for us. A hundred more warriors crept through the trees. A hundred more warriors for us to kill.

It was too many. Too many by far.

I opened my eyes and stared at Isla, the horror must have shown on my face.

'That bad?' she whispered.

I nodded and closed my eyes again.

There had to be *something* I could do. There *had* to be.

I felt for their hearts.

Thundering hearts pushing thick, black blood. Coming closer, ever closer.

I sent out tendrils of power; one for each heart, they wound through the woods. Growing like saplings, a fine net of power, woven around each heart. Then I cracked the tendrils, and a hundred whips ripped hearts from goblin chests.

I felt them fall. Like a field of wheat being harvested, they collapsed where they stood, their souls hurled into the ether. And then my vision faded, my legs betrayed me, and I sank to the ground as my mind fled to an oblivion of its own.

***

The familiar twilight of Trillania surrounded me as I lay on my back and stared at the sky. I put my hands to my ears and shook my head. The echo of a hundred screams was tattooed on the inside of my mind.

Best not to think about it.

I pushed myself up to my knees and climbed unsteadily to my feet. The others needed me, I had to go back. But try as I might, I was unable to return to my body.

Hmmmph. The only other time that had happened was when I'd been trapped by Galanta's blood bond. I was pretty sure that wasn't the reason this time, so I had to assume I was unconscious, *not* asleep.

I may as well make use of my time here.

Did I dare track Galanta?

If she were here, she would assuredly have a large force of warriors with her. It wouldn't have bothered me so much if I knew I could leave whenever I wanted, but I couldn't.

I sent my mind out to Emerald. Still nothing. I tried to return to my body to no effect.

A piece of hair stuck to my forehead, dangling into my eyes. I brushed it to the side while I thought my way through my problem.

If I snuck up on Galanta I might be able to see what she was up to. I didn't *need* to reveal my presence. I wasn't kidding myself enough to not admit I would kill her if I could. But the chance was slim to nothing. She would be wary. I know *I* would be.

Mind made up, I closed my eyes, and projected myself to near where she was. I didn't want to appear right in front of her – although it opened up the possibility for a quick kill, I was more likely to end up with a dagger between my shoulder blades. And while *she* could leave for healing, *I* couldn't.

I found myself surrounded by trees. Why did it always have to be in a forest? There were plenty of things to worry about in a Trillanian forest even *without* stumbling onto a goblin. I added a crossbow to my arsenal. If a buffo charged me it would come in handy.

Galanta was off to my left. I could feel her. I turned that way and scuttled from trunk-to-trunk, pausing to check there were no unwelcome visitors in between.

Whatever she was doing here, she was doing it quietly. No drums, no chanting, not even any of the guttural goblin language.

It took me a few minutes, but eventually I reached the place I could feel her. I peeped around the edge of a tree trunk to where I knew she should be, but she wasn't there.

I pulled back behind my trunk. Where was she? I could feel her. Was she hiding behind another tree? But no, the sensation of her was coming from the small clearing I had peeped into.

Ever so carefully, I stepped into the clearing. My head swivelled from side-to-side as I checked for movement. Night birds called and a light wind rustled the leaves, but there was no sign of anyone else there.

I tip-toed to where she should have been and stared at the ground. A small black splotch of blood darkened the earth.

Was she injured?

I could feel a feral smile curl my lips. It was time to hunt.

Closing my eyes I reached for her. North. She was further north.

I willed myself there, crouching low in a dense stand of bushes. Arrow nocked, I stared over the top to where I could feel her. She wasn't there.

Rising, I stalked to where I could feel her life force. More blood. A larger patch this time. Was she running from someone? Excitement hummed through my veins.

Now I could feel her off to the west. I transported myself there, releasing an arrow as soon as I appeared. It flew through the spot where she should have been, but she was already gone.

I hopped further south and found a sizeable amount of blood.

Back north to find a clump of hair caught on a bramble bush.

I was closing in on her, I could feel it. Could almost taste her desperation as she flicked again and again. Losing more blood each time, getting ever weaker.

East to where she had lost her dagger.

North to where she had left her spear.

She was mine. I could taste the victory as I chased her.

One last jump. This time the feel of her was overwhelming. She was here. I knew it.

I spun in a circle, my sword loose in its sheath and an arrow ready to fly. Dark brown flickered through the trees as she staggered away from me. I took off after her, ready to end this once and for all. I had let her get away once, that wouldn't be happening today.

Isadora.

I ignored the sound as I raced after Galanta. The distance between us was closing.

Isadora.

A black shape, off to my left, flickered through the trees. Galanta darted to her right and I followed, cutting the corner and gaining time.

Isadora.

Blackness grew on the edge of my vision. But Galanta was so close. I sighted her down my arrow and released it. It thudded into a tree, inches from her head. She threw a desperate glance over her shoulder, her eyes wide, her mouth open as she panted. She pressed her hands to a wound in her side and she staggered.

Looking back on it all, there were so many things that didn't make sense. Where were her warriors? Why didn't she leave Trillania?

But there, at the time, with the feel of her in front of me and the taste of her death on my lips, I wasn't capable of rational thought. I let out a snarl and hurled myself after her.

The blackness swelled as it raced towards me, twin lights blazing from within its inky depths. I let out a screech and loosed my arrow into it. The arrow flew wildly as if I had not aimed at all.

I threw out a hand, loosening a lightning bolt towards the shadow. It glanced off a sheet of light and a tree to the right burst into flames.

Now it was my turn to flee.

Isadora.

The hair on the back of my neck stood on end as fingers of dark reached out towards me. I could see Galanta off to the side, her head thrown back as she laughed.

A trap. It was all a trap.

And I had fallen for it.

The shadow wrapped itself around me, cold and damp it slithered over my skin. I closed my eyes and willed myself away.

My daughter.

Why couldn't I leave? I tried again and again, but the shadow pinned my arms to my side and held me in place.

Look at me, daughter.

I opened my eyes and stared at the glowing lights. Dread walked down my spine. 'I am not your daughter,' I whispered.

A shadow hand reached up and brushed back my hair. 'Of course you are.'

I shook my head trying to deny who trapped me. Part of me wanted to start screaming hysterically, the other part wanted to curl into a ball and hide. But as the shadow formed a man, Galanta came to stand at his side. I could no longer deny who held me.

'Your brother, Alexis, is my father.'

He threw back his head and laughed. 'If *I* am not your father, why does my blood trap you?'

That's *what was going on?*

'No,' I shook my head again. 'My mother would not lie to me.' Well, not about this I hoped.

How was I to break this blood bond? I couldn't do what I had with Galanta, because he had no blood to drink.

'Come.' He lifted me bodily and drifted through the trees.

Galanta followed off to the side, a triumphant sneer on her face. 'Did you think I couldn't feel you?' She let out a laugh. 'We are blood bonded. I always know when you are near.'

I was *so* going to have that talk about blood bonds with Wolfgang when I got back.

If I got back.

I banished that thought from my head. Defeatism would only cripple me.

Galanta had said she always knew when I was near. Prickles ran over my skin. If *that* were true, she had known I was there the night she had raised Santanas's spirit.

'That's right.' Her lips pulled back to reveal her pointed teeth. 'I knew you were watching. I wanted you to know what you had done.'

'Gloating's not very nice.' I was proud my voice didn't show the panic the rest of my body experienced. What *were* they planning to do to me?

'Nice isn't in my vocabulary.'

'There's a lot of things not in *your* vocabulary.'

She turned to Santanas. 'Let me cut out her heart.'

Sweat formed on my brow as bile pooled in my gut. I fought back the urge to vomit. I would *not* show weakness in front of her.

Santanas let out a sigh. 'You are not going to gut her Galanta. We need her.'

I resisted the urge to giggle in relief. They weren't going to cut out my heart.

Galanta stuck her bottom lip out and eyed me. 'Surely a little cut wouldn't hurt.'

'I'll think about it,' he said as we flowed on through the forest.

'Where are we going?' Normally I liked surprises. Christmas, birthdays – I was all for it. Today I wasn't feeling so adventurous.

'Your new home.'

I stayed quiet for the rest of the trip. The answers I was getting weren't helping with my attempts to remain calm. Would Aethan and Wilfred realise I was here? Would they come for me?

We drifted through the forest and across a large plain. Then up into a mountain range that stretched as far as the eye could see. Was it the Black Mountains?

Near the top of one of the peaks a stone castle stood. Part of the turrets had plummeted to the ground where they lay in discarded piles of stone, but the rest of the castle was intact.

Galanta pulled open double wooden doors, leading the way into the castle and down a flight of stairs.

'Remove her weapons,' Santanas said.

Galanta shoved and pushed at me as she took my sword, daggers and bow and arrows. I let her. There were plenty more where they came from.

'Home, sugar, home.' She pulled open a door to a cell.

'It's home, *sweet*, home,' I said as Santanas deposited me in the room.

She pulled back a hand to slap me, but Santanas loomed in between, a barrier of shadow.

'You will not harm her,' he said.

I stuck my tongue out at her and waved as she slammed the door shut.

In the small amount of twilight peeping through the window high in the wall I could see a mattress lying on a pallet on the straw-covered floor. A bucket filled with water sat in the opposite corner. I paced the room, measuring it as I walked. One wall was five paces, the other four.

I rattled the door and looked for cracks in the walls, but there was no easy way out. I stood pressed up against the wall furthest from the window and tried repeatedly to release a lightning bolt. The only thing I got for my efforts was a stress headache.

Okay, so if I couldn't escape I could at least protect myself. I summoned a sword, but nothing happened. I had the same result with every weapon I could think of.

Despondent, I slumped onto the bed, wriggling around to get comfortable. A lump persisted, digging into my spine.

I pulled the mattress up and felt along the wooden pallet. Half a nail stuck out of one of the planks. The wood was split and warped along its length. I pushed the mattress off the pallet and grabbed the end of the plank, straining upwards till, with a mighty crack, a chunk pulled free.

I smacked it into my hands a few times. It wasn't a baseball bat, but it would do. It would have to.

By the time I had finished, my head was pounding so I lay back down with my weapon hidden under the edge of the mattress. How was I going to get out of this mess?

I wasn't sure how long I'd been lying there before the door rattled. I grabbed my plank and stood by the door, wiggling my feet till the stance felt right as I raised the wood to the side of my head.

Batter up.

A few seconds later a plate was pushed through a hatch near the bottom of the door.

Hmmmph.

I'd been looking forward to smacking Galanta in the head.

I stared at the food. Without enough light I couldn't be sure what it was, but its putrid smell was enough to tell me not to eat it.

I drank the water and sat on my mattress and waited for the door to open. I paced the room, running my hands over the walls and yelled till my throat was raw. Another couple of trays turned up, each as foul-smelling as the first.

How long had it been since I'd been captured? Trillania didn't have days, and time here didn't correlate to Isilvitania. All I knew was that my stomach grumbled so fiercely that the clumps of meat were starting to smell edible.

The door rattled again, but this time, instead of the noise of the bottom latch working free, I heard a key in the lock. I grabbed the plank and stood by the side of the door.

If I hit her hard enough it would be game over. Without her, Santanas's spirit would be lost.

The door pushed open and a shape too short to be a goblin stepped into the doorway. I swung the bat back, waiting for them to step into the room.

'Ithadora?' the small shape lisped as it peered into the darkness.

Friend or foe? I couldn't be sure. The plank felt heavy in my hands as I stared at the small head.

'Ithadora? We muth go now if you are to ethcape.' The voice was low enough to belong to a male.

Escape? I lowered the plank and stepped into the opening of the door.

'Come,' the figure beckoned when he saw me. 'We go.'

He stepped out of the doorway into the light. I tried to follow but an invisible barrier held me in the room. I ran my hands over it and then beat at it, but it would not yield.

'Come, come,' he said.

'I can't.' I peered at him. Was he a mudman? Why would a mudman be helping me?

'Yeth,' he said. 'Blood bond cannot hold you. You share blood.'

I stared at him while my frantic mind contemplated his words. And then I got it. It was the fact that I was of his blood that was giving Santanas his current control. But that meant that I already *had* his blood running in my veins, I didn't need to taste his at all. His tenuous hold over me had come from my lack of knowledge on the subject. I had thought he had control over me and therefore he did.

Santanas's blood bond was only effective because I believed it was.

As soon as I realised the truth, I was able to pass through the doorway. I resisted the urge to shout in triumph. Stealth was still better than confrontation.

'Thank you,' I said to the mudman. 'I need to go now.' The block preventing my return was gone.

'Wait,' he said. 'You muth thee.'

'See what?'

He didn't answer but beckoned for me to follow. Was it another trap? I couldn't be sure. But the little man had rescued me - why I wasn't sure.

I armed myself and then crept down the passage after him and up a flight of stairs. We wound our way through the castle, eventually exiting a door on the opposite side of the castle from where I had entered.

A large wooden building stood off to the side. A stable or a store house.

I could hear Santanas's voice booming from within. 'You served me before. You will again.'

An animal roared its displeasure and light flared from gaps between the wooden logs.

Santanas laughed. 'You think to harm me? You cannot touch me, dragon.'

I froze in horror. Dragon?

Emerald? I sent my mind out towards the barn and encountered emptiness. She wasn't there.

'You muth thave her.' The mudman tugged on my arm. 'Your friend.'

I shook my head. 'No. That's not my friend.'

'Yeth,' he said. 'Your dragon.'

I sent my mind out to her again, this time flowing through the entire barn. Galanta stood near the side wall and Santanas's spirit hovered in the doorway. I couldn't feel Emerald, but I also couldn't feel any other dragon. Inch-by-inch I scoured the air until I realised what I had been missing. There was a void in the middle of the barn. My mind skated over and around it, but I couldn't penetrate it.

She'd been here the whole time, trapped in a shield. I beat at it, trying to reach her, but it held firm. I was going to have to free her the old-fashioned way.

The mudman beckoned and led me around the back of the building. He bent down and pointed to where a chunk of wood was missing. I clambered to my knees and pressed my eye against the gap.

Emerald crouched in the middle of the barn. Her lips pulled back from her massive teeth as she spewed fire at Santanas. The shield lit up like a light globe as the fire curled inside it.

'Yield,' he yelled, cracking a whip at her.

The tip of the whip lashed the side of her face and she shook her head, her eyes wild with pain. He slashed again and this time the whip gouged a chunk of flesh from her flank.

She roared and poured fire towards him but she didn't so much as flick a wing.

'We can do this the easy way, or the hard way,' he said, cracking the whip in front of her face.

The bond between us yanked tight, squeezing the air from my lungs. I had to help her. I had to save her.

Santanas's whip had showed me that the shield was one way. If I could get to her, perhaps I could free her, but I was only going to get one go at it.

I nocked an arrow and ran around the side of the building. Bursting through the doors I loosed the arrow at Galanta. She let out a shriek and disappeared from view. It would take her a few seconds to re-orientate herself and get back.

'Stop.' Santanas's voice was laced with power but it no longer had the ability to control me.

All I could see was Emerald, her beautiful body streaked with blood, her majestic head held proudly. The anger in her eyes changed to hope as I sprinted towards her.

I knew as soon as I was through the shield. Our minds collided in a whirl of conversation.

You must leave.

Not without you.

He has bound me with ties you cannot break.

I let my mind roam over her. Invisible bonds bound her wings and her legs.

If I can free you where will you go?

Isilvitania. He cannot reach me there. Not yet.

I reached her side and lay a hand on her flank. She was right. I wasn't going to be able to break the bonds. Not in time for her to escape.

He comes.

The terror behind her thoughts made my mind up for me. I couldn't leave her here. *I wouldn't* leave her here. I slashed with my mind, ripping the shield into two pieces and tossing them to the side. Then I yanked the bonds off her body and let them flow over mine.

No!

You must go. If he caught her again all would be for naught.

She bent her head and touched her snout against my forehead. A large tear wet the side of my face. Then she stretched her wings and let out a roar and promptly disappeared from view.

I fell to the ground as the bonds tightened fully. They bound my feet together and pinned my arms to my side. Galanta flickered back into view and I smiled at them both as I shut my eyes and willed myself back to my body.

Chapter Seven

When Day Meets Night

I was trapped. I couldn't move, or open my eyes, or yell for help. I beat at the inside of my body like a person buried alive. But it made no difference.

'She's going to be fine. Her energy is strong.'

'Why is she still unconscious?'

My friend's voices filtered through my panic.

'She's not technically unconscious any more.' That was Wolfgang.

'Well, what *is* the technical name for this?' Aethan sounded worried. If I could have, I would have smiled.

'More like a deep sleep.'

Somebody whistled an off-key melody, stopping the eerie tune to ask, 'What did she do?'

There was silence and I could imagine them all looking toward Wolfgang, waiting for the answer.

What had I done? There'd been a battle. I remembered that.

'I'm not exactly sure.' Wolfgang sounded like he was holding something back. 'I need to talk to her.'

Had I done something bad?

'I've never seen anything like it.' Brent sounded shocked.

'Me neither.' I could picture Wilfred shaking his head. 'All those goblins with their chests ripped open.'

'Stop it.' Isla's voice cracked like a whip. 'She saved our lives.'

Chests ripped open?

'Are you sure she's okay?' A feather-light hand pressed against my forehead.

'Her familiar would be upset if there were something wrong.'

I could feel Scruffy; a soft, warm weight on the centre of my chest.

'But it's been five days.'

Five days?

I felt Scruffy move. It sounded like he yawned and then scratched at his ear with his hind paw. He sniffed a couple of times and then a wet nose pressed to my cheek. He let out a little ruff and jumped off my chest.

Five days? Mum would be in a right state.

'What's he doing?' It sounded like Wilfred was trying not to laugh.

'I'm not sure,' Wolfgang said. 'What's up boy?'

'It looks like he wants you to go somewhere,' Isla said.

'Either that or he really likes your shirt.' Wilfred barked out a laugh.

I could picture Scruffy tugging on Wolfgang's shirt sleeve with his little teeth.

'What is it boy?' Wolfgang's voice came from right above me.

Scruffy's weight reappeared on my chest and he ruffed and licked me on the forehead.

Cool hands cradled my face and I felt the light tingle I associated with Wolfgang messing around in my head.

'She's back,' he exclaimed.

The tingle intensified.

Help, I screeched at him.

Isadora?

Oh thank the Great Dark Sky, he could hear me.

Yes.

What happened?

Galanta trapped me. I escaped but I've got bonds on me.

I wasn't sure why I didn't mention Santanas. I knew without a doubt that if Aethan found out the truth he would forbid my returning to Trillania. To be quite truthful I wasn't really in a hurry to, now that I knew Emerald was safe, but I also wasn't going to tolerate him dictating what I could do.

More tingling along my arms and legs.

Ahh. I see. Quite a neat trick.

'Wolfgang,' Isla said. 'Is she going to be all right?'

'Quite all right my dear.'

Join with me. This will be easier with the two of us.

I imagined myself reaching out to take his hands in mine. Immediately I felt him there with me, inside my body.

Nicely done. See here.

He directed me to my legs where black smoke ghosted around my ankles.

We're going to blow it away.

That simple?

If you can imagine it, it will be.

Together we blew towards the smoke ring. I imagined it pulling apart and it shifted and swirled and finally tore apart and floated away. I sighed inwardly as I stretched my toes.

'She moved her legs.'

I heard footsteps as the others moved closer.

Now your arms.

I flexed my arms against the smoke but it held me firm.

Not like that. Wolfgang sounded amused. *Blow it away.*

A picture of the three little pigs popped into my head as I huffed and I puffed. As with my legs, the smoke fragmented into tiny black whiffs and floated away.

'That was all you,' Wolfgang said as I stretched my arms above my head.

I opened my eyes and sat up, reaching out to rub Scruffy's head.

'You're alive.' Wilfred scooped me up in a bear hug. 'What happened?'

I pulled a face as he put me down. 'I'm not sure.' Even if I wanted to tell them the truth I couldn't have, not with Isla there. The Border Guard Secrecy Spell would have prevented that.

I met Aethan's probing stare and shrugged my shoulders. 'I'm not,' I lied. 'Where's Tiny? Is he safe?'

'He's fine,' Isla said. 'He wanted to come, but we convinced him to go back to his home. If he'd gone missing at the same time as we did, they may have worked out that he helped us.'

I was sad I hadn't gotten to thank him but relieved he was alive and well.

'Very brave giant, that one,' Wolfgang said.

I clambered up off the pile of blankets I had been lying on and bent forwards, stretching out my lower back. 'That feels good.' It felt like I hadn't moved for a month. 'Where are we?'

'All going well we will reach the night faery border tomorrow.' Aethan sat back down and picked up his sword, inspecting its edges in the dim light of a fire. A sharpening stone lay at his feet.

'Have you had any more trouble?'

Wilfred snorted and shook his head. 'After what you did? I doubt there were any goblins left on this side of the river.'

What had I done? Goblins had been attacking us. There were too many for us to defeat. I had reached out towards them and then I had...

A hundred screams echoed in my head. Screams of raw pain and terror.

'Great Dark Sky.' I stumbled backwards, tripping over the pile of blankets.

Wolfgang reached down a hand and pulled me to my feet. 'Perhaps we should talk,' he said.

I followed him away from the fire and into the trees. We walked for a few minutes before he said, 'Ahh, this will do nicely.'

We stepped out from the tree line to the bank of the river. A group of low, smooth stones lay scattered in a half circle. Wolfgang took a seat on one and I perched on the one next to him. Scruffy sniffed around the remaining ones before returning to lie at my feet.

'How's your leg?' I was stalling. I wasn't sure if I wanted to have this conversation.

'I think I may understand a little more about how your power works.'

I let out a small sigh of relief. Not the direction I thought the conversation was going to take. 'How?'

'You visualise what you need done and your magic makes it happen. Sometimes the results aren't what you expected. But the end point will ultimately be what you wished for.'

I could just make out his face in the shadows of the night. 'I don't get it.'

'Your magic responds to your need, not your command.'

Hmmmm. Well that sucked bigtime. What was the use of having powers if you couldn't get them to do what you wanted?

'But I used to try to elevate things and they would blow up.' I had lost count of the times I had had to clean vegetable parts off my bedroom walls.

'What were you thinking when you did it?'

I cast my mind back to the last time I had tried before I had given it up as a bad idea. The watermelon had refused to lift no matter how hard I had tried. Finally I had imagined it disappearing from where it sat. The resulting explosion had been spectacular. 'I wanted it gone.'

'Your skill lies in the field of battle. In violence.'

I shivered. I wasn't sure how I felt about that. 'But I used to be able to make some spells work with my wand.'

'Witch magic. I'm guessing that is no longer available to you since you successfully joined your witch and faery sides?'

I nodded. The only thing my wand was useful for now was communication. And if I were totally truthful, I didn't need it for that. All my life I had thought I would use a wand, and now, even though it was virtually useless, I couldn't bring myself to get rid of it.

'There is another matter we need to talk of.'

I winced. I knew where this was heading and I *so* didn't want it going there.

'Do you remember?' he asked.

I thought about pretending to be ignorant of what he referred to, but the screams still lingered, and I wasn't sure I was going to get rid of that unless I talked about it.

'A little,' I said. 'I remember we were grossly outnumbered, and I knew we would all die unless I did something.'

'What did you do?'

I took a deep, shuddering breath. 'I killed them.' My voice came out in a harsh whisper. 'I killed them all.' Tears I didn't know had been forming slipped down my cheeks.

'You know that was wrong child.'

I shook my head. 'Why? How?' We were killing them anyway.' The tears came faster. It seemed even though my mind wasn't there yet, some deep part of me knew what I had done was wrong.

'You used black magic.'

His words sucked the breath right out of me. Bright dots danced in front of my vision as ice crawled over my skin.

Black magic?

'No,' I shook my head. 'No, no, no.' I gulped as tears poured down my face. I couldn't have, I wouldn't have. That would make me as bad as... 'But I saved us.' My words were weak.

'You did. But at what cost?'

I rubbed my hands over my face and stared at the river. 'How was what I did any different to what you did?'

'I used my power as a weapon, like you would use your sword or your bow.'

'You threw fire at them.'

'I left the enemy choices. They did not *have* to die by my hand. They could put up a shield, or hide behind a tree. They could have run away.' He paused for a moment while the words sunk in. 'You didn't. They had no chance to save themselves. You murdered them in cold blood.'

I sank to my knees in the soft grass and crawled to the side. I hadn't eaten for five days but my body still tried to throw up. I heaved until acid burnt a path up my throat.

Black Magic. Oh Great Dark Sky. Was I evil?

'There, there.' Wolfgang's hand rubbed my back. 'All is not lost.'

I looked up at him through my tears. 'I thought we would all die.'

'Better that, than your performing black magic again. Once, you will get away with if you are truly contrite. But do it two or three times and your soul will be scarred. You will be unable to see the difference between good and evil.'

'I will become evil,' I said.

He nodded his head. 'Just remember, there is always another way.'

I was silent for a second before asking, 'Do the others know?'

'I'm sure they suspect.'

I sagged in relief.

'But only Aethan knows for sure.'

'You told him?' I gasped.

'He guessed.'

I could feel myself curling up inside. I had done something despicable and dark, something evil, and Aethan knew about it. There was no way he would ever want me now.

I sniffed and wiped my face on the back of my arm.

'Come on,' he held a hand out to me. 'Let's head back to the others.'

I clasped his hand and let him pull me to my feet. We turned back towards the trees and Scruffy let out a low growl.

A line of men, totally clothed in black, stepped out from the tree line. Their faces were covered with black masks and they each held a bow and arrow, some aimed at Wolfgang and some at me.

'You will come quietly,' one of the men hissed, gesturing his bow back into the tree line.

'Do as he says,' Wolfgang whispered.

I bent and scooped up Scruffy, holding him partly to protect him, and partly for comfort. Then I grasped Wolfgang with my spare hand and headed back into the trees.

It didn't take us long to reach the campsite. Wilfred, Brent, Aethan, Luke and Isla sat in a row. Their hands were tied behind their backs. They didn't say anything as Wolfgang and I joined them.

I placed Scruffy at my feet as one of the black-garbed men approached us. He secured Wolfgang's hands and then pulled my hands roughly behind my back and tied them with a rope. I was suddenly, ridiculously hungry. My stomach grumbled loudly as if in protest at my inability to feed myself.

That wasn't the worst of it though. Faery magicians used their hands as witches and warlocks used wands. With our hands tied behind our backs Wolfgang and I were powerless.

'Nobody talk,' the leader hissed, 'or I will cut out your tongue.' He pulled a dagger out of a leg holster and waved it at us. 'Anybody want to go first?' When none of us answered he re-sheathed the weapon. 'Good. It seems you learn fast. Now we walk.'

They forced us to our feet and tied a rope between us. Then they poked and prodded us like a group of cattle till we walked through the trees in single file. They did the same with the horses, linking them together so that one man could lead them all. Scruffy was tied to the last horse in the line.

We walked for hours till they let us rest, pushing us down cross-legged in a row. One of the men walked along our line, holding a water skin to our mouths. I got more water on me than in me, but I wasn't about to complain. Not when the leader held his knife, staring at us as if wondering who he was going to gut first.

Far too soon they prodded us back to our feet. My stomach screamed for food and my legs felt weak. My head spun as I stood up and I stumbled forwards, falling to my knees.

The leader growled and reached down. Grasping my hair at the base of my neck he yanked me to my feet and then slapped me across my face. 'You will walk,' he hissed.

I wanted to walk, I really did. But my body had other ideas. I stumbled as I tried to remain standing. The leader raised his arm to strike me again but before he did Aethan intervened.

'She needs food.'

The leader turned towards Aethan. His face was unreadable under the black mask, but I was guessing he was smiling as he stalked towards him. 'You dare to speak?' His voice was low and ominous.

'She needs food.' Aethan had a stubborn look on his face that I knew all too well.

Two of the other men grabbed him from behind, securing an arm each, as the leader stopped in front. 'It speaks,' he said, his voice caressing the sibilant sounds of the words.

He reached out and grasped Aethan's face with a hand. His other hand held the dagger. The two men behind struggled to control Aethan as the leader squeezed his face till his tongue protruded from his mouth.

The rest of the group seized us as we fought. Two to each of us, except Wilfred, whose wild struggles required three men to control.

'I warned you what would happen if you spoke,' he hissed. 'Now it seems I must cut out your tongue.'

Aethan thrashed from side-to-side as the knife got closer to his face.

'If you treasure your eyes stay still.'

Rage took over as the knife descended towards Aethan's face. 'No,' I screamed. I felt the power leave me, linked to that word by my anger and my love. It expanded like a smoke ring, bigger and bigger until it smacked into the first of the men. One-by-one they froze where they stood. The knife stopped mere millimetres from Aethan's mouth.

For a second I thought I had frozen my friends as well, but then I realised they were all staring at me in shock.

I shouldn't have been able to do that, not without the use of my hands.

'Come on,' I said, pulling away from my captors.

With some inventive manoeuvring we managed to get our daggers and cut each other's ropes. I rubbed my wrists, working the circulation back into my hands as I trotted back to untie Scruffy.

'Here.' Isla handed me one of the hard, dry biscuits.

I took a bite and pulled a face. 'I see they don't improve with age.'

She tipped her head to the side and watched me as I ate. I was relieved when she didn't voice what she was so obviously wondering.

'Let's get out of here,' I said. 'I have no idea how long that will hold.'

'Wait.' Aethan walked to the man that had been going to cut off his tongue. He ripped the soft mask off his face and blew out a soft whistle. 'Thought so,' he said.

Wilfred went to stand beside Aethan, peering through the soft dawn light at the man's face. 'Night faeries,' he said. 'How do you want to play it?'

Dark Sky. These were the people we were meant to negotiate with on Orion's behalf. We were going to be taking one of these savages home with us. No wonder Isla had been upset by the idea.

'I say we go home and leave them here to rot.' Isla ripped the mask off one of the men that had held her. She stared at him for a second and then slapped his cheek. The noise of her hand connecting with his flesh scared a flock of birds from a nearby stand of trees. *That* was going to hurt later.

Aethan let out a big sigh. 'We've been through this a thousand times. We need them.'

She threw the mask onto the ground and stalked away. 'Fine. But when this goes pear-shaped don't say I didn't warn you.'

With a half-smile Aethan said, 'Is there any chance you'd let me forget that you warned me?'

Isla threw her head back and looked down her nose at him. 'Certainly not.'

'So we take them,' Brent said, starting to pull the masks off the rest of them.

'This one's a woman,' Luke said.

'Well heeelllooo good looking.' Wilfred sidled up in front of her. She had raven-black hair and almond-shaped eyes.

Isla snorted. 'Dream on.'

'You know just how to cut a man to the quick.' Wilfred put his hands over his heart.

'Yes, but that's *all* I cut. She'd cut your heart out before she'd even look at you.'

We removed their masks and their weapons, tying those to the horses. Then we secured their hands behind their backs and roped them together. It was a bit like playing with life-sized dolls.

'Right.' Aethan rubbed his hands together. 'Wake them up.'

Everyone stared at me. I stared right back. I didn't know how to wake them up. I hadn't meant to freeze them in the first place.

'Urmmm, wake-up.' I flicked my hands at the line of night faeries. Not surprisingly, it didn't work.

Wilfred chuckled. 'You always were a brilliant child.'

'Shut up Will.' Isla punched him on the arm.

'You don't know how to, do you?' Aethan's voice was half frustration and half mirth.

'Of course I don't.' I waved my arms in the air as my voice rose. 'I *never* know.'

Wolfgang sidled up next to me. 'Would you like me to take it from here?'

'Please.' I stuck my tongue out at Will and turned to Wolfgang. 'How?'

'Just relax. I'll do all the work.'

I felt a tickling at the edges of my mind. Then Wolfgang was there with me, inside my mind. I'm not sure exactly what he did but it felt as if one minute I held the reins to a team of out-of-control carriage horses and the next he was sliding those reins from my hands. A struggling turmoil was lifted from my shoulders and I was free.

I sagged against him and said, 'Thanks.'

'It was a lot of minds to thrall in one hit.' He smiled. 'Don't think I could have done it.'

'But you hold them now.'

'The holding is the easy part.'

He turned towards the night faeries and wiggled his fingers at the leader. 'Obey.'

'What the…?' The leader struggled to free his hands.

'Obey,' he said again before nodding at Aethan.

'We go in peace to your land,' Aethan said. 'You will follow us.' He set off at a fast pace but the night faeries stayed exactly where they had been.

'Urrrr Aethan,' Wilfred said.

Aethan stopped and looked back over his shoulder at the still stationary faeries. 'Wolfgang?'

'Guess I should have been a bit more specific.'

He wiggled his fingers again and said, 'Obey him.'

This time the night faeries followed Aethan when he left.

The sun was high in the sky when the night faery leader said, 'We are home.'

'This is Emstillia?' I asked.

'Emstillia. Home of the night faeries, the greatest jewel in the land.'

Isla let out a snort. 'We'll see about that.'

We travelled for another hour before we encountered a night faery patrol. They took one look at us, with our prisoners, and they flipped black masks onto their faces and unsheathed their swords.

'Stop them.' Wolfgang's voice was calm.

'Halt,' the leader called out. 'In the name of King Arracon. They come in peace.'

'If they come in peace,' one of the other night faeries hissed, 'why are you tied?'

'We ambushed them and took them captive. They overcame us but did us no harm. They have brought us safely home.'

'Is it just me,' I whispered to Isla, 'or do they all sound like snakes?'

'Sound like snakes, act like snakes....'

The other group of night faeries stayed as they were, masks lowered and weapons drawn. They studied us until their leader held up a hand. 'We will honour your truce,' he said.

The masks flipped back off their faces as they rode towards us, but I didn't relax until their swords were all re-sheathed.

'Why have you come to Emstillia,' the new leader asked.

'The matter is between us and your king,' Aethan said.

They eyed each other as if in a staring contest. Finally the night faery said, 'Come, we will take you to him.'

'Do you swear on the shade of your mother and your mother's mother that no harm will become us?'

The other man watched Aethan for a minute. 'I see you have had dealings with us before.'

'In other words he sees that we know they are a bunch of treacherous cowards,' Isla whispered in my ear. She *really* had it in for them.

Aethan inclined his head.

The other man sighed. 'I swear on the shade of my mother and my mother's mother, that no harm will come to you while you are under my protection.'

'Good enough,' Aethan said. He fell in beside the other man.

And just like that, we entered the capital of Emstillia.

Chapter Eight

Caught Between A Rock And A Hard Place

'You have to admit,' I tried not to smirk as I looked at Isla, 'that *is* impressive.'

'I'll admit no such thing.' She lifted her chin and flicked her braid back over her shoulder. 'Not in public, anyway. I have an image to uphold.'

We were staring up at Emstillia castle. The whole thing, turrets and walls and even the bridge over the large moat, glistened like a black jewel in the sun.

We had been stopped by yet more guards and now we waited for King Arracon to be notified of our presence. I was taking advantage of the break to scoff another couple of rock-hard biscuits. I had given my share of the dried meat to Scruffy. He was starting to look lean from all the walking, and while *I* thought it suited him, you could tell by the way he begged for food that *he* wasn't happy about it.

'What's it made of?' I wondered out loud.

Wolfgang took a seat beside me. 'Ice.'

I stared at him while I chewed my latest bite of biscuit till I'd generated enough saliva to swallow. 'You're kidding, right?'

'Made by magic, from magic, within magic.'

'That doesn't make any sense.'

He stared at the castle for a few moments longer. 'I don't suppose it does,' he said. 'I read that. Can't remember where.'

A few minutes later a guard strode back across the bridge. 'The King welcomes you Prince Aethan, brother of Prince Orion, son of King Arwyn, and all your friends. We will take you to your rooms and your horses to stables.'

Aethan eyed him for a moment. 'Our mounts are not to be stabled in the same stalls as your hagons.'

The man shrugged one shoulder. 'Of course not, Prince. We would not think of it.' But a twitch of his mouth made it obvious he might have thought of it if Aethan had not mentioned it. 'We will take the dog as well.'

'My familiar stays with me,' I said, sweeping Scruffy up in my arms.

'A witch?' He fairly spat the words.

'Part witch, part faery.' I stared at him, just daring him to take offence. I was trying to be open minded, but Isla was rubbing off on me.

He met my eyes, and I was reminded of how similar and yet different the night faeries were from the land faeries.

Being the same height and build, from behind it might be possible to mistake us for each other. But while land faeries' skin was snowy white, night faeries' was an olive brown. Also our eyes were rounder than their almond ones, and whilst our hair varied from blonde to dark, all of the night faeries I had seen, had jet-black hair.

'Very well,' he finally said, 'the familiar stays with you.' His tongue flashed out of his mouth and licked his upper lip and then he turned and strode back towards the bridge.

I stared after him. 'Was his tongue...?'

'Forked?' Isla said. 'It's why they sound like they do.'

'They're born like that?'

She looked at me and squared her shoulders. 'They do it to their new-born babes. Something for Orion and his new bride to fight about.'

With that bouncing around in my head we were half-way across the bridge before I thought of my other question. 'What's a hagon?' I said to Wilfred.

'Cross between a dragon and a horse.'

'Well the original hagons were,' Wolfgang added. 'They trapped the souls of baby dragons and forced them into horses.'

I could feel my eyes bulging as I imagined Emerald's soul being forced into a horse. It made me want to hit something. 'They must be hard to train.'

'The originals were impossible to train, so they bred them. The resulting animals are not as intelligent as the originals, but they can still breathe fire.'

As we crossed the threshold, the cold of the castle hit me like a wall of snow. We turned left into a hallway which curved with the shape of the castle. Walls of ice towered above us, dominating us with their cold presence. I reached out a finger to touch one but Isla stayed my hand.

'Ever touched dry ice?'

I shook my head.

'Well don't,' she said.

I stared instead at the icy, black walls. Soft lights glowed from within and illuminated our path. The hall seemed to go on forever, spiralling gently upwards, room-after-room opening off it.

When my legs were starting to complain about a night and day of walking, our guide stopped and opened one of the doors. 'This will be your suite.' He gestured for us all to enter.

The door opened into a cavernous room made of black ice. Thick, white, fur rugs littered the cold, hard floor and chandeliers of black crystals hung from the ceiling. Black cushions were scattered around the edges of the rugs and more doors opened off the room. It was bitterly cold and oppressive and I wanted to run all the way back down that hall till I burst into the warmth of the sun.

But instead I opened one of the doors to reveal a smaller room. This one housed a bed piled high with blankets and fur. A small ensuite opened off it.

'Rest,' the guide said. 'We will bring you your evening meal.'

'I bags this one.' I entered the room and deposited Scruffy on the bed with my saddlebags. I hoped those blankets were going to be enough to keep us warm.

While the thought of a warm shower was inviting, I doubted I would be warm for long once I turned the hot water off. So instead, I pulled as many layers of clothing on as I could and crawled under the blankets pulling Scruffy in with me.

I stayed like that for a few minutes before guilt got the better of me. Mum would be frantic by now. The small mirror was close enough that I didn't have to leave the blanket nest to get it. I held it up in front of me and concentrated on thoughts of Mum.

She appeared suddenly, her face a mask of surprise as she stared at me. I gathered by the damp tendrils of hair that clung to her face and the steam that whirled around her, that she had just hopped out of the shower.

'Isadora,' she yelped, pulling her robe closed around her.

'What's that love?' A man's voice asked.

The look on her face turned from surprise to horror. 'Nothing,' she yelled, holding a hand up in front of the mirror.

'I can still see.' I peered around her hand. Who was there with her?

Mum whipped her wand out of her hair and flicked it. A towel rose from the floor and hovered in front of the mirror.

'Mum?' I said.

'How did you do that?'

'Do what?'

'Activate the spell from your end. How did you even know where I'd be?'

'Lucky guess,' I lied. 'I can call back later if this is inconvenient for you.' That voice had sounded familiar.

'Hang on a minute.'

I heard the bathroom door close and then a few minutes later the towel dropped from in front of the mirror. Mum had replaced the robe with a pale-green dress. Her cheeks were flushed and her eyes sparkled.

'Is there somebody there?'

'Hmmm? Why would you think that?'

'That man's voice.'

She laughed a little too loudly. 'I had the television on in my room. Some terrible movie. I turned it off.'

I didn't call her on her obvious lie. 'So, you haven't been worried about me?'

'Of course I have. I've been worried sick. What with you and your Grams both off Dark Sky knows where.

'Grams is still missing?'

'She contacted me.' Mum sniffed. 'Wouldn't tell me where she was though. Was acting all secretive, checking over her shoulder every thirty seconds as if someone might be following her.' She let out a laugh. 'Sometimes she's such a drama queen.'

'Ahhh Mum.' I paused unsure of how to phrase my question. There wasn't any easy way to ask her if she'd had relations with Santanas. 'Are you sure who my father was?'

Her eyes narrowed and her lips pinched tight. Okay so perhaps that *hadn't* been the best way to phrase it.

'I don't mean it like that,' I said. Goodness knows I wasn't accusing her of being a slut. 'I mean it was definitely Alexis wasn't it? It couldn't have been somebody pretending to be him.'

The I'm-going-to-make-you-wish-you'd-never-been-born look relaxed off her face and I let out a sigh of relief.

'Well I was assigned as his personal assistant so I was with him the whole conference,' she said. 'All the other dignitaries thought it was him. So did all the other faeries. What's this all about?'

'Oh nothing,' I said. 'I was just wondering why he hasn't come to see me. You know, now that my presence is common knowledge.'

'Last I heard he was an ambassador in Australia. Perhaps he doesn't know about you yet?'

'Maybe,' I said. That hadn't been my true line of investigation but now, for the first time, I was curious about my father.

'I've got to go,' she said. 'I'm going to be late for book club.'

I resisted the urge to say, 'Yeah right.' It looked like Grams had been right about the whole book club thing. Mum was doing something naughty and I was dying to know with whom.

I packed my mirror back in my saddlebags and then dug around until I found my dream-catcher. I hung it on the bed head and lay back, pulling the pile of blankets right up over Scruffy and me, tucking the edges in underneath us.

The cold seeped in if you left any gaps. And then I thought about Grams.

Was someone following her or was it all just another one of her games? That thought would normally have been enough to give me a sleepless night. But as soon as I closed my eyes, it drifted from my mind and, before I knew it, I was sound asleep.

***

'What are they waiting for?' Aethan paced up-and-down the manicured lawn of the Royal Gardens.

'I say we leave.' Isla had been pushing for that the entire three days we had waited to be summoned before the king.

Aethan didn't even bother responding. He just threw a glare at her as he continued his pacing. The waiting was making him cranky.

I sat up and crossed my legs. 'Anyone want to walk to the fountain?' We spent our days in the garden soaking up the warmth of the sun. I dreaded returning to the cold of the castle.

'I'll come.' Wolfgang unfolded himself out of the painful looking yoga position he had been holding and jumped to his feet. 'I need to stretch my legs.'

'You looked like you were stretching them pretty well already.'

He chuckled as we walked away from the others. 'That was a static stretch.'

We followed Scruffy as he sniffed and peed his way down the garden. There was a question I wanted to ask Wolfgang, but I was scared of the possible answer. I grasped my courage in my hands and said, 'Did you want to continue my training?'

He scratched at his cheeks with both hands. 'Not having to shave every day only just makes up for the itching.' When he'd finished scratching he said, 'Frankly I don't think there's much point in continuing your training.'

My heart sank. He didn't think it was worth training me. I was a total loss.

'Oh,' I said. 'I see.' I tried not to let my disappointment show in my voice but I mustn't have been successful.

He glanced over at me, his bushy eyebrows wiggling up-and-down as he examined my face. 'Not like that.' He shook his head. 'I mean I don't think training can help you. Hmmmm. That didn't come out right either.' He paused and stared up at some birds circling overhead. 'You can already do everything you need to; you just need to have faith in yourself.'

'But what about my limitations? How will I know what I can and can't do?'

'That's the beautiful thing about the way you wield the power. Most of us have to think about cause and effect. You need only imagine the effect.'

'But it's so unpredictable.'

'Yes,' he nodded his head, 'it is. But unpredictable can be advantageous when you are engaging the enemy.'

I could see the fountain in the distance. I spent a large portion of each day there letting the enormous spouts of water gushing into the air soothe my fractious boredom.

'Izzy, Wolfgang.'

We spun to see Luke running towards us.

'We have been summoned.'

'Finally,' Wolfgang said, smoothing down his robes.

We trotted back to the others and formed two lines with Wolfgang at our head. Aethan and Isla stood behind him, and then Wilfred and I. Luke and Brent took up the rear. Like that, we followed the messenger into the icy castle.

Instead of heading up the path we normally took to our rooms, the messenger wound around to the right, circling down into the bowels of the castle. The icy walls threw out enough light to see where we put our feet, but the cold grew in intensity, icy fingers wrapping around my bones till my teeth chattered as we walked. I hugged Scruffy to my chest and hoped we didn't have to go much further.

Down, down, down we wound till I couldn't feel my fingers or the tip of my nose. The lights in the walls dimmed until shadow clothed our features. I yearned for warmth and light. I ached to feel the sun kissing my skin.

Just before I lost control and starting sprinting back up the way we had come, the messenger stopped and rapped on a door.

A voice boomed from the other side of the door. 'Who dares to enter the Royal Throne Room?'

'Prince Aethan and Princess Isla Gabrielle of Isilvitania,' Wolfgang said. 'We come with a retinue to discuss a proposal with King Arracon.'

There was silence for a few moments before the same voice said, 'Come in peace.'

A gust of warmth hit us as the door creaked open to reveal a room very different from any other I had seen in the castle. Stone ringed the circular space and paved the floors. A huge fire roared in an ornately carved fireplace. Animals, frozen in time by a master craftsman, continued up the wall and around the tops of the arches and pillars, as if they were leading a merry chase around the room.

A row of high-backed chairs stood on either side of an enormous throne. Men, dressed entirely in black, sat in the chairs, but the throne was empty.

As if nothing were wrong, Wolfgang strode to stand in front of the throne. 'We come with bad tidings and an offer of a new beginning.'

The man to the left of the throne stood. 'Peace cousin. We have had no emissaries from Isilvitania for years. We would share a meal and talk of pleasantries before we hear of these bad tidings.'

I could see the muscles in Aethan's cheeks bulging and practically hear his teeth grinding. We get ignored for three days and now this? No king, *and* they want to eat first.

I placed Scruffy on the floor as we followed the men to an adjoining room. A large fire roared in this one as well and I wondered why the rest of the castle was so cold. To keep visitors off centre? None of us had had a good night's sleep since we'd gotten there. We were definitely not at our best.

A long table had been set ready for a meal. We sat down one side with the dignitaries on the other. I managed to get close enough to the fire that I could feel the warmth through my clothes.

We sat in silence as a line of serving women bustled into the room carrying baskets of flat bread, jugs of icy water and platters of meat and vegetables. The silence continued as we filled our plates and ate. So much for the talking pleasantries bit.

When all our plates were empty, the serving women cleared the table, reappearing with pots of steaming tea. We waited while they poured the tea into eggshell-thin porcelain cups. When they had finished, Wolfgang cleared his throat.

'King Arwyn and Queen Eloise send their respects and ask after the health of King Arracon and Queen Titania.'

The man at the head of the table bowed his head. 'I am Tyfon, I speak for the King. Unfortunately Queen Titania is not at her best. King Arracon is with her even as we speak.'

Aethan's shoulders relaxed and he sunk back into his seat. 'Please convey our wishes that she may recover soon.'

'Oh the Queen is not sick.' Tyfon took a sip of his tea. 'She is with child. It has not been an easy pregnancy.'

Aethan nodded. 'Well, please convey our best wishes and congratulations.'

'You spoke of ill news,' Tyfon said. 'Is all well in Isilvitania?'

'All is well,' Wolfgang said, 'for now.'

I watched the looks on the night faery men's faces as Wolfgang told them of Santanas's release.

'This is ill news indeed,' Tyfon said when Wolfgang had finished, 'but why have the Prince and Princess's lives been risked to bring us this news?'

Aethan hopped up and paced around the table to stand in front of him. He dropped to one knee and bowed his head. 'I come on behalf of Prince Orion, Crown Prince of Isilvitania. He seeks a truce to help us combat the dark years to come. In good faith, he offers himself into marriage with a night faery maiden of marriageable age and Royal Blood.'

There were a few seconds of silence when Aethan had finished talking. Tyfon rubbed his chin while he considered Aethan's words. 'I see,' he finally said. 'I will convey your best wishes and your message to their Royal Highnesses. Please enjoy the comfort of our home while they contemplate your words.'

Nobody spoke until we were back in our rooms. 'Contemplate our words?' Aethan kicked one of the cushions across to the other side of the room.

'I mean really, I don't know why you expected anything different.' Isla dropped delicately into a cross-legged position, looking very Zen in comparison to Aethan's anger.

Wolfgang sat beside her. 'It could have been worse.'

'How?' Aethan waved his arms around. 'We're stuck here while we are needed elsewhere.'

'Perhaps you should have considered that *before* you set out.' Isla's icy composure only made Aethan madder.

'If I had my choice, we would be hunting Galanta.' He glanced at me in a way that would have made me cringe if I'd thought he knew about my failed hunting expedition in Trillania.

'Well, go hunt her.' Isla threw a hand in the direction of the door.

'I can't.' Another pillow followed the first. 'I promised Orion. And he's right. This is too important.' He slumped to the ground and lay staring at the ceiling.

I hated seeing him like this – so frustrated and... alone.

'I'm going out.' I picked up Scruffy and walked to the door. It was unbearable being near him and not being able to soothe him.

Even though I jogged down the ramp, it was still too long till I was back outside. The castle suited the people who lived in it. Cold as ice. I couldn't wait to be gone from this place.

Taking our time, Scruffy and I wandered back down towards the fountain. I found my favourite spot on the far side of it and sunk into the long grass. The warmth beat down on me and I closed my eyes. I wouldn't go to sleep. I would just lie there enjoying the warmth. I felt Scruffy turn around and around in the grass next to me before settling down against me.

The sound of the water cascading back into the pond increased the danger of my falling asleep. I opened my eyes and stared at the sky. It would be foolish to fall asleep here.

I sat back up and perched on the edge of the fountain. The water felt so silky and smooth as I dragged my fingers through it. I pulled my hair up on top of my head and tied it in a loose knot. The water felt delicious on my face and neck. I unzipped my vest just a little and wet my upper chest through my tank top. For one wild minute I contemplated the thought of stripping off to my underwear and swimming in the fountain, but the thought of having to explain what I was doing to the row of tight-lipped men we'd lunched with stopped me.

I spun around so that the water was behind me. Scruffy was sound asleep with his legs in the air. I cocked my head and concentrated. Off to the left, it sounded like somebody was … what *were* they doing?

I crept to the manicured shrubs and threaded my way through them till I came to a grassy lawn. Aethan stood with his back to me. He held a sword extended to his side as he peered down the shaft. He was stripped bare to his waist and his back muscles bunched in anticipation of his next move.

I licked my lips and moved closer.

He leapt into the air, spinning so fast he was a blur. Landing on one knee, he thrust the sword upwards to the front. Then he tucked and rolled in the other direction, coming up onto his feet and kicking his left leg to the side.

His sword swept through a flurry of motion as he moved forwards against his imaginary opponent.

He was magnificent as he flowed from one fighting stance to the next. His long, hard body made the movements seem easy. Then he flicked backwards through two one-armed backflips, spinning on the last one so that he was facing my direction. He landed with the tip of his sword pressed against my throat.

Breathing hard, he stared into my startled eyes. Then he lowered his blade and stepped back, running his free hand through his hair. 'Want to train?' he asked.

I took a deep breath to steady my wildly-beating heart. 'Is it helping with your bad mood?'

His mouth quirked up at one corner. 'Something like that.'

'I didn't bring my sword.'

He slid the sword back into its sheath and unbuckled the waist band. 'Free hand?'

'Sure.' I pushed my way out of the shrubbery and unzipped my vest, dropping it on the ground near his sword. Scruffy emerged from the shrubs a few seconds later and climbed on top of it, massaging it with his paws till it was deemed comfortable enough to lie on.

'Do you want me to tie one hand behind my back?' The look on his face said he was serious.

I snorted. 'Oh please.' And then I dived through the air, sweeping an arm out behind me as I rolled past. I timed it perfectly, connecting with the back of his knees with enough force to collapse his legs.

He went down to a crouch and I leapt on his back, forcing him onto his face. I grabbed one arm and twisted it up behind his back till he grunted in pain.

'If I want one of your arms tied,' I whispered in his ear, 'I'll do it myself.' Then I jumped backwards, putting enough distance between us that I would have some warning of his attack. He was going to make me pay for that move and I was going to enjoy every second of it.

He sprang to his feet like a cat and spun to face me. 'Point taken,' he said, spitting a piece of grass out of his mouth.

He advanced on me slowly and I resisted the urge to squeal and run off into the trees like I had sometimes done in the past. But that had always been so he could catch me and kiss me, and there wasn't going to be any of that going on today. Which was a pity, because I had always found that an enjoyable way to cure a bad mood.

He jabbed twice with his left fist and I patted it away, knowing what he would do next. Sure enough, he followed it up with a right uppercut and a left hook, but I knew they were all camouflage for the kick that was about to come.

I bobbed and weaved around his strikes and then ducked under his trademark roundhouse kick, darting in close enough to palm strike him in the face. His head whipped back and I leapt up, ball-kicking him in the chest as I turned a backward somersault.

He staggered back as he shook his head, blood dribbling out of his nose. His eyes narrowed as he stared at me and then he charged.

I leapt to the side, but he swept an arm out wide, collecting me around my waist. He tossed me onto the ground but before he could pin me, I rolled, spinning over onto my knees and then leaping back to my feet.

The huge smile I could feel stretched across my face mirrored the one he wore. It was just like old times, the only difference being that I had the advantage. I knew his fighting style; knew his favourite moves and his dirty tricks. I knew his weaknesses and his strengths. And he had *no idea* about mine.

Out of all the things that had come from Galanta's spell, this was the only one that didn't suck.

'Right,' he said. 'I was going to go easy on you. Don't say you didn't ask for this.'

'Bring it on big boy.' I danced from foot-to-foot.

He attacked with lightning speed, jabbing and hooking, forcing me backwards across the lawn as I dodged and blocked. I flicked his fists and darted left, jumping into the air to superman punch him. His head rocked to the side, but he spun, swinging his leg around in a low arc. It collected with mine, sweeping them out from beneath me.

My breath exploded from me as my back hit the ground, but before he could take advantage of my vulnerable position, I rocked back onto my shoulders and flicked my legs up into the air. I wrapped them around his waist, hooking my ankles behind his back, and then I twisted, dragging him to the ground.

I unlocked my legs and leapt on top of him, punching my fist down towards his cheek. He moved his head at the last second and my fist drove into a rock that was hidden in the grass.

I was good, but I wasn't made of steel, and my fist came off second best against that rock. The unmistakeable sound of bones breaking preceded the pain by mere milliseconds. I screeched and nursed my fist to my chest, wiggling backwards out of range. I was going to have to fight one-handed.

Pain radiated up my arm and tears threatened at the corners of my eyes as I readied myself for his next attack.

'Hey,' he said, sitting up. 'You're hurt.' He pulled me down onto his lap and gently took hold of my hand. It was already starting to swell. 'Well you certainly taught that rock a lesson.' He reached up and wiped away the unshed tears lingering in the corners of my eyes, and for one glorious second, things were as they had been. Uncomplicated and honest. Just a man loving a woman.

'You'd better not have hurt her too much you brute,' Isla said as she stepped from the trees. Aethan let out a low oath, tipping me from his lap as he sprung to his feet. And just like that the moment was over.

'Sorry, sorry,' he said, grabbing my good arm to help me up. 'We'd better go find Wolfgang.'

'The healing is going to have to wait.' She pulled an apologetic face. 'That's what I came to tell you. King Arracon has requested an audience with you and Wolfgang. Wolfgang has gone on ahead to avoid insult by making him wait.'

'What about you?' I asked. 'Why aren't you invited?' She was an heir to the throne as well.

'It's complicated.' She spun away from me but not before I saw a line of tension between her eyes.

Aethan set off at a run towards the castle. Isla and I followed at a much more sedate pace. I felt a layer of depression settle over me as we entered the castle. The sloping hall that wound around the inside of the external wall meant that none of the rooms had windows. And even though light emanated from the walls, the black ice threw a shadow over everything. How did they stand living here?

Shivering, I wrapped my good arm around my chest.

'I know how you feel.' Isla's eyes took on a haunted look.

I stared at her for a moment, wondering if she would tell me what she was thinking. But she never had before, so I wasn't surprised when she didn't this time.

Wilfred, Brent and Luke were playing cards when we got back to our chamber. 'You found him?' Wilfred asked.

Isla nodded her head and plonked down on a cushion next to him. The pain from my hand had dulled to a throb. I kicked a few cushions together and lay down, resting my broken knuckles against the icy floor. It turned out there was one thing a castle made of ice was good for.

'What happened?' Luke lowered his cards and nodded in my direction.

'Izzy tried to beat a rock into submission.'

'Huh,' Brent said. 'How'd that work out for you?'

'Hunky dory.' It was going to be a while before they let me forget about this one.

'Were you caught between a rock and a hard place?'

I poked my tongue out at Wilfred. 'That wasn't even funny.'

'I know. It's this place. It's drained the funny out of me.'

'Well hopefully we'll have an answer today,' Isla said.

I closed my eyes and tried to ignore my hand. I wasn't looking forward to the healing, but the pain was getting old fast. It felt like forever before the door banged open and Wolfgang and Aethan returned.

'What did he say?'

'What happened?'

'Can we get out of here now?'

Our questions jumbled over each other.

Aethan ran his hands through his hair and said, 'Yes and no.'

Wilfred picked up a cushion and threw it at him.

He laughed and grabbed the cushion out of the air and tossed it onto the ground. Taking a seat he said, 'Arracon agrees that a union between our nations is desirable. And since the initial union didn't work out,' he threw a guilty glance in Isla's direction, 'that a marriage between a Royal maiden and Orion would be suitable.'

Isla snorted. 'Suitable? Just suitable? We're offering him our crown prince.'

'Down girl,' Wilfred murmured, placing a hand on her arm.

For a second I thought she might punch him, but instead she shook her arm till his hand fell off and turned her back on him.

'There will be a banquet tonight, at which the chosen lady will be presented to us.'

'And then we can go home?' Brent's face broke out into a broad smile.

Aethan shook his head. 'No,' he said, 'and then I get to court her on Orion's behalf.'

That made me sit up. Court her, like he'd courted *me*?

I gritted my teeth as pressure grew inside me.

I would have to sit and listen to their pretty conversation, while he charmed her on Orion's behalf?

It felt like every single hair on my body was standing on end.

I would have to witness her fluttering her eyelashes and giggling at his jokes? I would have to watch her leaning into him till they were close enough to kiss?

The power pulsed through me and my vision turned red. If she lay one pretty little nail on him, I was going to do things to her that had never been done to a living person before. If she even thought of gracing his lips with her own I would...

'Isadora.' I snapped open my eyes to find Aethan staring into my face. 'Is it the pain?'

'Yes,' I growled. Oh, it was pain all right, just not the kind he was thinking.

'Wolfgang,' Aethan said. 'I think Isadora broke her hand.'

The look on everybody else's faces told me they knew *exactly* what was going through my mind; sympathy from the men and malicious glee from Isla, as if she were hoping that I would tear the chosen night faery limb-from-limb.

Aethan, however, was totally clueless. 'I'm hoping you'll spend some time with her as well,' he said to me. 'So that she has at least one friend when we get home.'

I'd be her friend once she was married to Orion, but while she was treating Aethan as her future husband, I would be her mortal enemy.

'Sure,' I spat out, struggling to contain the fury that wanted to punch holes through the castle walls. 'Maybe we can paint each other's nails.'

Wilfred let out a chuckle. 'Perhaps you should let her heal,' he said.

Wolfgang was watching my face with a concerned expression. 'Come along Isadora,' he said.

I followed him to my bedroom and sat on the edge of my bed.

'You need to control yourself before I can heal you,' he said. 'If I were to join my power with you like this, it is possible you would take control of it as well. I don't fancy having to explain to the night faeries why their castle blew up.'

I took a deep breath, and then another until I could feel the tension melting out of me.

'That's better,' Wolfgang said when I finally opened my eyes. 'Now give me your hand.'

I placed my damaged limb into his. Now that the rage was gone, the throbbing had returned. He closed his eyes and I felt a tingle run down my arm and through my hand.

'It's broken all right.' He stood and walked back to the doorway. 'I'll need some assistance please.'

The others filed into the room while I lay back on the bed. Brent and Luke took my legs and Wilfred pinned down my uninjured arm. Isla laid a cool hand either side of my head, and Aethan held down the shoulder of the arm that was to be healed.

I closed my eyes as Wolfgang's power surged into me. White, hot lances spiked into my fist again and again. Flesh bubbled and boiled inside me, steam tearing apart my cells. I arched my back and struggled to pull away from him as a scream ripped from my throat.

Then the heat was gone and a wall of ice rammed into my head. Inch-by-inch it crept over my body. I could hear crackling as my flesh solidified.

Scruffy let out a howl and started scrabbling at the side of my body.

'What's happening?' Isla's hands jerked away from my face as my skin froze beneath her touch.

'I don't know.'

'Do something.' Aethan's face distorted as my eyeballs solidified.

I tried to scream but my mouth froze open in a macabre grimace as the ice continued its path through my cells.

'What's going on here?' I recognised the sibilant sounds of a night faery man. 'Why are you using magic within our walls?'

'She broke her hand. I was healing her.'

For a moment I could make out a shadow man peering down towards me, but then, as my eyes finished freezing, even that was gone.

'Interesting,' he said. 'Normally it is the spell maker that is affected by the punishment curse.'

'What's happening to her?'

'She is dying.' He didn't sound at all concerned.

If I had thought the healing was painful it had *nothing* on being turned into a snowman.

'Do something,' Aethan growled. There was the sound of cloth tearing.

'Release me,' the night faery snapped. 'The price must be paid.'

'We were not warned,' Isla said.

'We do not need to warn *you* oath breaker. It is our home.'

Scruffy let out a bark and I heard the night faery swearing. 'Get him off me. Stupid dog.'

There was more tearing and then a smacking sound and Scruffy let out a low whine.

He had hurt him. That stupid night faery had hurt my dog. I didn't care that he was willing to watch me die. That was the sort of behaviour I would have expected from them. But *nobody*, and I mean **nobody**, hurt my familiar and got away with it.

I ignored the pain from the ice and concentrated on the white heat of my fury, filling myself with it till I thought my legs and chest must be glowing white. Then I forced it upwards to where the ice met healthy flesh.

'Help her or die,' Wilfred growled.

'Do not threaten me bear. You brought this on yourselves.'

I ignored their fighting as slowly, ever so slowly, I forced the glacier back up towards the tip of my head. I wanted to cry out with the pain of the steam bubbling in my cells, but instead I concentrated on my anger. I would make him pay if it were the last thing I did.

'What's happening?' I felt a soft hand on my chest. 'She's warm again.'

'That's not possible.' The night faery sounded torn between disappointment and confusion.

The thought of wrapping my hands around his throat gave me the strength to keep going. Up past my neck, into my face. I wondered if steam was oozing off me. I blinked my eyes as my lids unfroze, and then, as my eyeballs liquefied I did let out a scream. Burning, stabbing, white hot pokers in my eye sockets, but when the pain finally ebbed I could see.

Pushing, pushing, the ice fought me every inch. I knew if I let go, even for a second, I would lose the battle. Up my forehead, to the tip of my head. One last push and with a roar I forced the spell out of me. But that wasn't enough. I wanted to make sure that it never did that to any other person.

I felt the spell fleeing back to where it had come from and I followed it. Down through the walls of the castle we raced. Round and round as we circled deeper and deeper. Tendrils of the spell embedded in the castle ripped out like a weeded creeper. And then we were diving through the floor, to a huge, black gem buried deep within the earth.

Anger and hate pulsed from the stone. I almost gave up as the toxic emotions washed up against my psyche. But then I remembered the feel of it stealing my life away and I poured myself into it.

Jealousy raged inside me, clawing me apart from the inside out. Aethan was mine, **mine!** The pulsing of the stone grew stronger as it fed off me. It was the cause of the discontent within the land. A parasite. The gem encouraged pain and then fed off it.

No wonder the night faeries were the way they were. No wonder they had changed so much from what they had been. The magic from this stone infused the castle. It was evil. It had to die.

I pushed away my jealousy and concentrated on happy thoughts. I thought about Mum, Grams and Sabby and how much they meant to me. I thought about all my friends within the Border Guards. And then I thought about Aethan. Love filled me till I could feel it bursting out of me. I took that love and I channelled it into the stone.

It fought me, plucking negative thoughts and feelings out of my head and throwing them back at me. But I ignored them, infusing it with love until the black pulsing energy dimmed and slowed and finally stopped. A small crack started in the heart of the stone, spreading out towards the edges like a cobweb. Dark light pulsed one more time and then died, the previously translucent gem now a lump of dead rock.

When I was done, I flowed back into my body. The whole fight had taken no more than a few seconds. Ignoring the residual pain, I sat up on the bed and turned to face the night faery.

'What did you do?' The look of shock on his face was priceless. 'You should be dead.'

I stood up and stalked towards him, grasping his neck with my hands.

'I'm sorry,' he said, eyes bulging wide, 'I couldn't save you. Once the spell is activated it is unstoppable.'

'You hurt my dog,' I hissed, shaking him with each word till his head rattled from side-to-side.

'Your *dog*?'

'My dog.' I gave him one last shake and tossed him aside. 'Don't do it again.' I pivoted to the side and scooped Scruffy into my arms, placing him on the bed. He looked up at me with his amber eyes and gave my hand a lick.

The night faery man scrambled from the room and pulled the door shut behind him.

I clenched my hand into a fist and relaxed it again. 'Well that feels better,' I said, looking at the rest of them for the first time.

Nobody had moved and they were all staring at me.

'How?' Wolfgang licked his lips. 'How did you do that?'

'Turns out I've got a lot of repressed anger.' I laughed and then punched Wilfred on the arm. 'What? No wise-arse response?'

'Still getting over the vision of you turning from icicle to flame.'

'When you're hot you're hot.' A wave of exhaustion hit me and I sat down on the bed.

'You need to rest,' Wolfgang said. 'It will take you days to get over that.'

'Perhaps you should stay here tonight,' Aethan said.

'And miss all the fun?' And not see the woman he was to court? 'Not likely.' I gave him my broadest smile. 'Isla will you wake me with enough time to get ready?' For some reason, I knew in *this* instance, I could depend on her. The rest of them would probably let me sleep 'for my own good'.

She nodded. 'We can get ready together.'

They filed out of my room as I crawled under my blankets with Scruffy. The nice thing was, with the warmth still flickering through my system, the cold from the castle didn't touch me. I closed my eyes, and had the best sleep I'd had since we'd arrived at the cursed place.

Chapter Nine

Mirror Mirror On The Wall...

When Isla shook me awake I felt like I had slept for days. 'The banquet starts in an hour. I thought you might want to shower first.'

She was right. I did. I had been sweaty after my fight with Aethan but that was nothing compared with how much I had sweated while I'd slept. The blankets touching my skin felt wet.

When I emerged from the bathroom I found she had laid a dress out on my bed. 'Thought we should look the part,' she said.

'Isilvitania Royal women versus Emstillia Royal women?'

She nodded her head. 'Round one. Ding ding.'

I laughed and picked up the dress. Sky-blue silk fell to the floor in elegant waves.

'I thought it would bring out your eyes,' she said.

'What are you wearing?'

She pointed to a ruby red dress of the same cut and pulled a face. 'Sorry I only brought two dresses.'

'That's two more than me.'

We were quiet for a while as she brushed out my hair. I closed my eyes and let myself pretend I was a child again. It had been too long since someone else had brushed my hair.

Feeling emboldened by the contact between us I said, 'Isla, why did that man call you oath breaker?'

The brushing stopped and I opened my eyes and turned towards her.

'You heard that?' Her eyes were huge in her beautiful face.

I took the brush from her and started working the bristles through her hair. She stared straight ahead for a few moments and then she let out a sigh and slumped down onto the bed.

'It was a long time ago. Well before you were born.'

My hand hovered above her head. Before I was born?

She let out a tinkle of a laugh. 'You didn't realise how old I was. I guess being brought up amongst such short-lived people, ninety years would seem a lifetime.'

'It *is* a life-time.'

'And yet amongst the fae I am still considered a young woman.'

I commenced my brushing. Something to think about later.

'This is not the first attempt to bind our people with the night faeries. When I was still a child, my hand was promised in marriage to a night faery.' She let out a rough laugh. 'I was so young and naïve. So excited about marrying Arra. He was handsome and charming; everything I thought

I wanted in a husband.' She paused again and for a moment I feared she would not continue. 'The week before our wedding he came to my rooms and forced himself upon me. He was not so charming then. Every night he came and every time the beatings got worse. He took pleasure in my pain.' Her voice trembled as she continued. 'I could not marry him. To commit myself to a lifetime of that? I would rather have died.'

I stopped the brushing and sat on the bed next to her, taking one of her hands in mine.

'He was so clever. He knew by taking my virginity he had sealed my lips. I was too ashamed to tell anyone. So I ran away.' She straightened her shoulders and pushed her hair back from her face. 'It was a total disaster of course. Relationships with the night faeries deteriorated almost to the point of war. I sometimes wonder if that was what he was really after.' She stared into the distance for a long moment and then shook herself. 'Anyway that is why they didn't support us during the Dark Years.'

'What happened to him?' Would he be there tonight?

'Oh,' she said, 'he made a better marriage for himself. I have been officially pardoned, if not forgiven. If he had married me, he never would have become king.'

'King?' My voice shot up an octave.

She laughed lightly. 'Silly me. Did I leave that part out? Yes, Arra married the daughter of King Lanon. Strangely enough, all his other heirs died before Lanon did.'

I shivered. This was the man Aethan had to deal with?

'Come,' she said. 'We must hurry or we will be late.'

She expertly twisted my hair up on top of my head, braiding some pieces and leaving others to fall loosely around my face. The braided bits she looped and twirled till my hair was an artwork. 'Here,' she handed me a pair of moonstone earrings and pointed to her make-up box before starting work on herself.

Once she had finished her hair she took over my make-up, muttering to herself about how young women these days weren't taught practical arts. In all honesty though, with how my life seemed to be progressing I was pretty happy I had mastered the sword and not the eyeliner pen. Hopefully by the time I was ninety I would be proficient at both.

There was a knock on the door and then it opened a fraction and Wilfred stuck in his head. He let out a low wolf-whistle as he glanced at us both, but I noted how his gaze lingered on Isla.

'It's time,' he said.

'Will you do me the honour?' Isla held her hand out to him.

He swept it up and placed it daintily onto his arm. 'It would be my great pleasure milady,' he said in his best pirate-impersonation voice.

I desperately wanted to ask Aethan to escort me, but seeing as how his job that night was to court our future queen, I didn't think it was appropriate. And of course *that* thought had me gritting my teeth again. If I could get through dinner without shedding blood I would be doing very nicely.

Wolfgang was waiting for me in the chamber. 'The others have headed down,' he said. 'They wanted to get the lie of the land, or something like that.' He held his arm out to me and I copied Isla, placing my hand upon it.

Isla and Wilfred swept out of the room and Wolfgang and I followed. Down, down, down we circled until we reached the front entrance. A night faery waiting there directed us outside to the garden.

I could feel some of my tension leave me as we entered the garden. Lamps, hanging from branches, lit our path to a large pavilion. Little lights glowed in the air as if moving gently on the breeze.

'Garden faeries.' I was pleased to see something familiar. Holding my finger out, I watched as one of the lights drifted closer.

'Izzy, I wouldn't...,' Wilfred began.

Before he had finished the sentence the light rocketed towards me and latched onto my finger. I let out a shriek as something sharp pierced my skin. Wolfgang grabbed my hand and flicked off the tiny animal.

I stuck my finger into my mouth and sucked off the blood. 'What was that?'

'A sprite.' Wilfred let out a laugh. 'I did try to warn you.'

'I'm not going to turn into something now am I?'

'What?' Wilfred laughed harder. 'Like a were-sprite?'

'Something like that.' It was all right for him to laugh. His mother was an orc. He'd been a part of this magical world his whole life. There was still so much I didn't know.

'Leave her alone Will.' Isla slapped him playfully on the arm and then in a sing-song voice said, 'It's show time.'

She was right. We were almost at the marquee where a welcoming committee waited for us. A group of night faeries, all dressed in black, blended into the fabric of the marquee.

'They really take the whole night thing seriously don't they,' I whispered to Wolfgang.

A smile flashed across his face as he reached out his hand to greet the first one.

I could see Isla's back getting stiffer and stiffer as we made our way through the throng and into the marquee. We were led to one of the long, low tables where Brent and Luke already sat. Aethan was nowhere to be seen.

'Well I never,' Isla sputtered when we sat down.

'What's wrong?' I leant over Wilfred and whispered.

'Our greeting party was made up of the least important members of the royal court. I fear things will not go well tonight.' She chewed on her bottom lip, a motion that made her, for the first time since I'd met her, seem uncertain of herself. 'Perhaps I should not have come.'

'Why not?' Aethan slid onto a cushion on the other side of her.

His shirt was of the deepest blue and matched the colour of his eyes perfectly. His dark hair was rumpled up just the way I liked it - as if it were begging me to run my hands through it. The dark stubble on his face highlighted his cheekbones.

He turned his head toward me and my breath caught as he met my gaze. For a few seconds we sat like that, our eyes trapped by each other's. But then Isla leant into him and started whispering in his ear and he turned his attention to her.

I took a sip from the goblet sitting in front of me while I tried to regain my composure. What had he seen while he'd gazed at me? A young pest of a girl? A friend? Could it be possible that he had seen something else? That desire had been kindling in his eyes?

I took a deep breath and another sip from my goblet. Thoughts like that were not going to help. Especially not tonight. Tonight was about King and country, about the big picture. And where the big picture was concerned, the feelings of one half-witch half-faery didn't count.

Aethan stood and returned to the milling men, chatting as he circulated the room. I turned to Wolfgang but he was busy staring off into the far corner of the marquee. I followed his gaze but could see nothing of interest there. Brent and Luke were also scoping the room and I decided to follow their example. I should be doing my job, *not* mooning over Aethan.

The first thing I noticed was that apart from our party, everybody was wearing black. I wasn't so surprised about the men, but even the women had on flowing black gowns. Isla and I stood out like peacocks amongst a flock of crows. I was guessing that *that* had been her intention.

The next thing I noticed was that while the men moved about the room, the women sat demurely on their cushions talking amongst themselves. A lot of the conversation seemed to involve Isla, if the looks they cast in her direction were anything to go by.

'Lady.'

I jumped in my seat and turned around. A serving woman held out a pitcher of wine. She nodded to my goblet which, apart from the couple of sips I had drunk, was still full.

'No thank you, I'm fine.' It would be a big mistake to drink too much amongst this lot.

'Please allow me to top you up.'

Before I could decline again she leant past me, forcing me to the side so she could reach my goblet. As she stood back up, she pressed a piece of paper into my hand.

'Thank you,' I said, trying to keep the shocked expression off my face.

I waited till she was long gone before I glanced down at what she had given me. A small piece of folded paper nestled in the palm of my hand. I looked around the room while I flicked it open with my thumb. I wasn't very good at subterfuge.

A quick glance down at the paper showed me one word scrawled in a bold hand.

BEWARE

I leant down as if to adjust my slipper. While I was down there I refolded and tucked the piece of paper into my bra.

The message created about a million questions and answered none. Who had sent it? Was it a personal message to me or to the group? Were we in danger or was it about our mission? I felt like screaming in frustration. Surely they could have given me more information than that.

Perhaps I should go after her. I searched the room for her but she was gone.

'Wolfgang,' I said, nudging him with my elbow.

'Hmmm? Yes?' He looked away from the corner of the room.

'The serving women. Are they night faeries?' The ones I could see all appeared shorter than the average night faery.

'You mean the slaves?'

'They're slaves?'

He nodded his head. 'Once upon a time the Ubanty Tribe roamed these lands. When the night faeries broke from our people...'

'Wait. We used to be one people?' That thought gave me the heebie-jeebies.

'Yes. There was an argument over a succession and the faeries that followed our King Rowan stayed. A small band of followers loyal to his twin brother, Randa, left. They came here and set up Emstillia. The Ubanty people weren't so keen on the idea and a battle followed. They lost and their descendants have been slaves to the Royal Court ever since.'

Before I could comment, a bell tolled twice.

'And now it begins,' Isla said.

Everybody who was still standing made their way back to their seats. At the front of the room I recognised the men we had lunched with. A single cushion in the middle of their row remained empty.

'All rise for the King.'

We stood, and a statuesque figure wearing a black fur cape over the obligatory black clothing, strode to the front of the room. Isla had been right. Arracon was handsome, in a devil-may-care way. His full lips were framed by a strong nose and high cheekbones. Long lashes curled thick around eyes that studied the room. His gaze fell on Isla and a small smirk appeared.

I didn't think I could have sat there so calmly if a man who had ripped away my innocence had been smiling at me like that. I was guessing by Aethan's lack of reaction that he didn't know the full story.

'Welcome,' Arracon said in a deeply-resonating voice. 'It has been too long since we have had guests from Isilvitania.' He smirked at Isla again and I had an urge to smack him in the mouth. 'We are here to celebrate a possible union between our two peoples. We have given great thought to which female would be a suitable candidate to join with Crown Prince Orion.' He stopped and looked around the room. 'We have decided that there is only one female fit enough to be worthy of such a salubrious marriage.'

He paused again, this time to look back in the direction from whence he came. 'Prince Aethan, on behalf of your brother, may I present to you Princess Ebony, Jewel of Emstillia and heir to the throne.'

Isla let out a gasp, but I wasn't looking at her. Ebony flowed into the marquee and moved to stand beside her father. Like all night faeries, her hair was of the deepest black and her skin a softly burnished mocha. But where their eyes were all dark, hers were the softest sea green. They glowed in a face that was perfect in proportion and form. Full lips pursed sensuously as she gazed at Aethan. Lustrous black hair tumbled down her shoulders to her waist, and her black dress clung to her breasts and hips.

I felt despair roil over me. Ebony, in all her glory, made Isla look plain. And until that second, Isla was the most beautiful woman I knew. I hated to think what I looked like in comparison. Aethan had to court Ebony, had to make her want to come to Isilvitania and marry his brother. I felt sick at the thought of them spending time together.

'Easy,' Wilfred whispered, placing his hand on my arm.

I looked down to find I was holding a knife. I hadn't even realised I'd picked it up off the table.

'Jealous much?' he murmured plucking it from my fingers.

Aethan stood and made his way up to the front. Arracon formally introduced them and then Aethan brought Ebony back to the table and waited while she seated herself. I could see far too much bosom when she leant towards Aethan.

Picking up my goblet, I took a swig of wine. I tried not to listen to their conversation, honestly I did, but her bell-like voice was easily heard over Isla and Wilfred's low murmurs.

'So your brother Orion,' she said, 'is he as handsome as you?'

Aethan laughed softly. 'Lady, you compliment me. I can assure you that Orion is far more handsome than I am.'

'I'm not sure if that is possible,' she said. 'Before I saw you, my father was the handsomest man I had ever seen. Now I am not so sure.'

I was glad the goblets were made of metal and not glass or I would have needed Wolfgang to heal me again.

'Orion is handsome and strong and wise. He will make a good king and an enviable husband.'

'Strong is good,' she said. 'Men should be strong enough to look after their wives. I know some women like to play at fighting, but I think it is unseemly. Wives are the softness that complements the husband's strength.'

Great Dark Sky if that were true, I was in deep trouble.

'That's a nice way of looking at it,' Aethan said. 'It is pleasant spending time with a woman of grace.'

What? Since when?

I leaned to the side as a serving woman – no, *slave* – placed a meal in front of me. It smelled of spices and roasted meat, but suddenly, I wasn't hungry. What if this Aethan really did like his women soft? What if the other Aethan, *my* Aethan, never came back? Years of unrequited love suddenly stretched in front of me. I picked up my fork and used it to move my food around my plate.

'Not hungry?' Wilfred asked.

'Who can eat?' I rolled my eyes and nodded towards Ebony and Aethan.

'Everything will work out,' he said around a mouthful of food.

I sighed. 'You said that once before. How do you know?'

He swallowed and put his fork down. 'Things always do. Sometimes not how we imagine they will, but they do.'

'Not helping.' I stabbed at a piece of meat and handed it down to Scruffy.

'You two are meant to be together. This is just the blacksmith's fire.'

I shook my head. 'I don't follow.'

'When a blacksmith makes a sword, he heats it and beats it and heats it again. If he doesn't do that, the sword won't be as strong. It will shatter on its first use.'

I worked my way through his analogy. 'So you're saying we'll be stronger *because* of this, not in spite of it?'

'Exactly.'

Isla leaned past Wilfred and said, 'Not bad for a big, red bear.'

'You're imagining me naked, aren't you,' he said to her.

'Why yes.' She looked straight into his eyes and gave him a small smile. 'I most certainly am.'

Wilfred's face blushed as red as his hair as he turned his attention back to his meal.

I chuckled as I speared a piece of meat. That was Wilfred's standard pick-up line, but I'd never heard it turned on him before.

It didn't take long for Wilfred to get over his embarrassment. He spent the rest of the meal whispering to Isla, who laughed wickedly at whatever he was saying. Wolfgang seemed totally pre-occupied with the corner of the marquee, so I ate my meal in silence. When we had finished the main course, the table was cleared and I found myself hoping that was it for the evening. I itched to get Aethan away from Ebony.

'Would you care to go for a stroll?' Aethan stood up and offered Ebony his hand.

'That would be lovely.' She giggled as she 'accidentally' tripped into him, forcing him to wrap her in his arms to steady her.

A low growl came out of my throat before I could stop it.

She turned her radiant face towards me, looking at me as if I were an unsolved puzzle.

'Excuse me,' I said, putting my hand in front of my mouth. 'It's the spice.' I wasn't keen on her thinking I had burped, but there was *no way* I was admitting I had growled at her.

'I burped once,' she said, smiling at me like I was a wayward child, 'when I was a baby. I don't remember it myself.'

Aethan looked like he was holding back a laugh as he escorted her away.

'I burped once,' I mimicked her soft voice.

Wilfred laughed and said, 'Bet she's never growled.'

I poked my tongue out at him and stood up. 'Excuse me, I need to use the ladies'.'

I breathed a sigh of relief when Isla and Wilfred continued their whispered conversation. I had feared she would offer to go with me and I really had no intention of finding the toilet. I needed a walk too, and well, if that walk just *happened* to take me near where Aethan and Ebony were strolling, well that would be a *huge* coincidence.

By the time I made it outside the tent, Aethan and Ebony were nowhere to be seen.

Bugger. Which way would they have gone?

'Any ideas boy?' I said, looking down at Scruffy. He was staring back into the tent where dessert was being wheeled in.

'Do you want to stay with Wilfred?' I said.

He looked up at me and wagged his tail and scampered back to Wilfred. I saw him pawing at the big man's arm as a platter piled high with delicacies was placed on the table.

Trying to pretend I was just going for a stroll, I turned left and headed into the garden. A sprite bobbed innocently towards me. 'Don't even think about it,' I said, flapping my hands at it. Its light flickered from white to red before it headed off in another direction. I was guessing that that was the sprite equivalent of giving me the finger.

A quick pass through the closest parts of the garden didn't reveal Aethan. After another five minutes of unsuccessful searching I decided to head to the fountain. Lights lit the cascading water and smoothed away the shadows from the surrounding trees. The snowy, white marble structure was the only friendly thing I'd encountered since we had arrived. I sat on its edge and trailed my fingers in the water.

'They brought it with them when they came.'

I jumped up and backed away from the dark figure standing in the tree line.

'They pulled it apart and piece-by-piece they carried it here from Isilvitania.' The man stepped away from the trees and moved towards the fountain. 'Now it is the only reminder of what they once were before they let Randa's anger and jealousy warp them.' He mimicked my previous position and sat on the edge, trailing his fingers through the water. 'That was all a long, long time ago.'

Wary of his body language, I stepped back to the fountain, and re-took my seat. 'You are Ubanty.' It was a statement, not a question. If his shorter stature were not enough of a giveaway, black tattoos twirled up his arms and danced along the top of his collar bones. Half-crescent moons were inked beside each eye.

He nodded his head. 'I am Samuel.'

'Isadora.' I held my hand out to him and he took it in a clasp. Engraved metal bands encircled his wrists.

'The one they speak of.'

'Pardon?'

'The witch that brought down the castle defences. We have waited a long time for you.'

I stared at him with my mouth opening and closing, but I couldn't find the right words to say.

He froze and peered to his right, as if he could hear something I couldn't. 'They come.' He stood and backed towards the trees. 'Never fear, I will follow and we will come for you. Hold strong.'

I stared after him as he disappeared into the shadows. He was certainly an interesting fellow. Perhaps he was the local crazy. Every town had one.

A stick cracked to my left and I jumped and then laughed nervously. He really had freaked me out. It was probably for the best if I headed back to the marquee.

I took a step towards the muted glow of the party and another crack echoed to my right. 'Aethan? Ebony?' Perhaps I had found them after all.

Dark shadows sprinted from tree-to-tree. I grabbed my knife from my ankle and spun in a circle. There were three, no four, no *six* people circling me, weaving in and out of the trees in an elaborate dance. I held my ground and waited for them to attack.

Two of them raced towards me and threw their arms out. A large net sailed through the air and hooked over my head. I would have flicked it off easily if two more nets had not followed in rapid succession. My struggles to remove one, only increased the hold the other two had on me.

I stopped fighting the nets and turned to see the six standing in a circle with me at their centre. Each of them held a rope attached to one of the nets. As I watched they started the elaborate dance again, running under and over each other's ropes. By the time I realised they were making a net big enough to encase me, it was too late. They ran in a circle looping the ropes around my ankles as I hopped from foot to foot. When they had finished I was encased in their net and controlled by a rope. One of them jerked on the rope and my feet were whipped out from under me.

'Right,' I said. 'I think that's enough.'

I thought about what I wanted – to be free – and gestured with my hands. Nothing happened. There was no need to panic though; it wasn't the first time my powers had failed the first time. I reached inside me for the glowing patches that contained my power. I could feel them, but I couldn't reach them.

'That's enough witch,' one of the shadow men said. 'You can't access your powers with this net upon you.'

I ceased my struggles and stared in bewilderment. Who were these people and what did they want?

'They will know she is missing soon,' another one of the masked figures said.

'Yes, we must hurry.'

'Help.' I felt like such a big girl having to yell that word. 'Heeeellpp.'

I pulled my knife from its sheath on my ankle as I continued to shriek. They picked me up and hurried away from the castle, away from the party. Away from my friends. I dragged my dagger over the rope but the sharp edge didn't even fray it.

As I hacked at the net the piece of paper scratched at my breast.

BEWARE.

I was an idiot. The Ubanty had warned me and I had immediately disregarded it. I'd been more worried about a night faery trollop than my own safety. I'd grown arrogant and stupid and… there weren't enough words that meant idiot to describe what I had become.

All my attempts with the knife failed. There was nothing I could do while I was in the damned net. I would have to wait for them to free me before I could escape. That knowledge rankled.

I tried to relax and save my strength, but the ropes dug into my flesh where it supported me. Trying to get comfortable only earned me a sharp prod. I resisted the urge to poke back with my knife. I didn't think that would help the situation.

A few minutes later we came to a low ridge line. Four of the six ran ahead while the other two carried me up the steep hill. Hidden amongst the peaks was a building. The open door emitted the glow of a fire. At least I would be warm.

I was bundled inside and thrown on the floor next to a fire pit, close enough to the dancing flames that the heat burnt the side of my face. I wiggled and rolled away from it. There was warm and then there was *warm*.

'Where is her familiar?' The voice rasped like nails on a chalkboard and the hair on the back of my neck stood on end.

The six masked figures bowed low as a shape entered the room. It shifted and twisted so that one second I was looking at a person, the next a large cat, then a crow. The eyes remained constant; glowing yellow, they burned from within the face of the creature. I stared into those eyes as the face twirled around them. A bear, a pig, a dragon - the never-ending change was mesmerising.

'He wasn't with her.'

'It will do, I suppose.'

The face changed to a wolf and the creature snarled, rearing up in front of me. An eagle's taloned claw reached out towards me, trapping me as I tried to wriggle out of reach. It clasped my head and squeezed, the tips of the nails drawing blood. Power roared into me, not gently the way Wolfgang did it, but hard and fast, ripping at the edges of my sanity.

The yellow eyes whirled faster and faster, transfixing me. Even though every cell in my body wanted to fight the creature, I couldn't twitch a muscle. It made everything Galanta had ever done to me look tame.

A brown, worm-like tongue protruded from the mouth and wiggled towards me. It licked the length of my face and then forced its way past my rigid lips and into my mouth. I wanted to retch at the taste of rot but I couldn't. Helpless, I lay there as the tongue made its way to the back of my mouth and started down my throat. The face drew closer as the whirling, yellow eyes hypnotised me.

Pain lanced through my chest as the worm pierced my oesophagus. It tore through flesh as it burrowed towards my heart. Horror gave me strength as I fought the invisible bonds. I twitched a finger, then another but that wasn't going to be enough.

What was it doing to me? I may not have known but I was pretty sure none of it was good. Fire burned in my lungs as I struggled to draw air. I wasn't sure which would kill me first, the tongue or suffocation.

My heart beat like a crazy animal and blood dripped from my lips. Roaring sounded in my ears as white lights blinked before my eyes. Pressure, agonising pressure, as the worm closed around my heart.

I tried to scream through the blood as the creature's lips touched mine. And then it was gone, the tongue retracting back the way it had come. It jumped off me and turned with a snarl. I swallowed blood and coughed helplessly as I fought for air.

Tattooed Ubanty fought like madmen. More jumped from the rafters and circled the creature. I saw Samuel, firelight glinting off his bare chest as he spun his sword. As I watched he beheaded two of the six night faeries.

I sucked in some air, and then some more, rolling onto my side to cough up blood.

The creature changed to a lion and swiped a huge paw, catching a Ubanty in the chest. Then it spun back towards me. 'Mine,' it hissed, reaching out to grab the net.

Samuel leapt over the fire, blade cutting through the lion's arm. The dismembered limb turned to smoke and flowed back to the creature.

'Be gone,' Samuel yelled.

'Mine.' A snake reared up, venom dripping off its fangs as its eyes whirled.

Samuel pirouetted with his blade held wide, but it was the two Ubanty attacking from behind that cut off the head of the snake.

A wail filled the air as black smoke raced around the room. I cowered in the net and put my hands over my ears. And then it was gone, racing out through the doorway and into the night.

I stared up at Samuel while my mouth worked soundlessly. 'What,' I stopped and coughed up more blood, 'was that?' My voice came out in a painful rasp.

'A 'retcher'.' He squatted beside me and started to unravel the net. 'We did try to warn you.'

I should have been thankful that they had saved me, and I was, but I was also a bit pissed about the warning. 'Beware? That's the warning? How about next time a little more information. Dear Izzy, Do not leave the party by yourself or a retcher will try to eat your heart.'

He chuckled as he continued his work. Three of the others came to help him and it didn't take them long to peel it over my head.

'Not that I'm not grateful,' I added, nodding my head at them. Mum would slap me if she heard me being so ungracious.

Samuel held out a hand and helped me to my feet. I put my hand to my chest and pressed. 'Why has it stopped hurting?'

'The Retcher's saliva has unique healing properties. It hides how the victim was killed by sealing up the wound.'

I could still feel the tongue forcing its way down my throat. That was going to give me nightmares for weeks. 'It was going to eat my heart wasn't it?'

He nodded and led me out the door and down the hill. 'By swallowing your heart it would have gained your powers and then it would have been unstoppable. Come, we must get you back to the party before they start searching for you.'

'But,' I stopped and stared at him. The other Ubanty were pulling the night faery corpses from the building. 'The night faeries tried to kill me.'

He shrugged. 'Only a small faction of them. The ones that worshipped the retcher. The others are oblivious to tonight's activities.'

There were so many other questions I wanted to ask as he led me back towards the castle. How did they know? Why had they saved me? But the only one I had time for was, 'Why me?'

He stopped near the fountain and turned to face me. I could see the other Ubanty fanning out around me. I was guessing I still wasn't safe from the retcher.

'There are things you do not know,' he said. 'Things I cannot tell you.' He stopped and unclipped one of the metal armbands from his wrists and then flipped it back into place. 'All I can tell you is that you have freed us, and that we will be there with you at the end. But it will not be because of us that you will triumph. It will be because of who you are.' He put a hand over his heart and then backed away from me and into the trees. The others did the same.

I stared after them for a second before I remembered the retcher. The whole incident could not have taken more than half an hour. I lifted up my skirts and raced back towards the marquee.

'Izzy?' Wilfred called my name from the darkness to my left.

'Over here.' I heard rustling and then he pushed out from between two bushes.

'Where have you been?' He peered at my face and then grabbed my arm, twisting me so that the light from the marquee shone onto my face. 'Why is there blood all over your face?'

Whizbang. I'd forgotten about the blood. 'I fell,' I said, 'and my nose started bleeding. I've been trying to make it stop.' I wasn't sure why I was lying to Wilfred.

He sighed and dragged me towards the party. 'I've been worried sick. Scruffy started to cry and well, I assumed the worst.'

The rest of them were waiting out the front for me. I was happy to see that Ebony wasn't with them.

I held up a hand to forestall them and said, 'Nose bleed. Nothing to worry about.'

Scruffy ran to my side and jumped up, scrabbling up my body and into my arms. He let out a long, loud fart as he jumped.

'Wilfred, what did you feed him?' I waved my spare arm in front of my face.

'Trifle and ice-cream.'

'Don't forget the meringue,' Aethan said.

Isla reached over and scratched behind Scruffy's ears. 'It could have been the honey buns.'

'Or perhaps the apple tart,' Brent added.

'It had to be the pecan pie,' Luke said. 'That stuff gets me every time.'

'But I saw *you* eat a huge piece of pecan pie,' Isla said.

Luke smiled an evil smile and everybody moved away from him.

I shook my head and smiled. From a near-death experience to this, all in a matter of minutes? It sure was good to be alive.

Chapter Ten

All Hail The King

'Isadora.' Wolfgang's voice accompanied a soft tap on the door.

'Come in.' I had showered and was sitting on the bed running a brush through Scruffy's fur. I wasn't ready to empty my head for sleep; too many bad memories from the evening were hovering in the back of my mind, waiting their chance to strike.

He closed the door behind him and crossed the room to sit on the edge of my bed. 'I came to see if you were all right.'

'My nose? Hunky dory.'

There was a pause before he said, 'I think we both know that's not what happened.'

I stopped brushing and stared at Scruffy's coat. Tears welled in my eyes and I struggled to contain them. 'Ridiculous,' I said, wiping at my face with the edge of a blanket. 'After everything that happened today *now* I start crying.'

He moved closer and wrapped his arms around me, rocking me gently. I buried my face in his robe. The horror of being helpless against that *thing* while it forced its way into me welled up, and before long my sniffles turned to sobs.

'There, there.' He continued to rock me while I cried myself out.

'What was it?' I sobbed.

'From the blood around your mouth and what I felt during dinner, my guess would be a retcher.'

'That's what Samuel said.' I hiccupped and pushed myself upright.

'Samuel?'

'The Ubanty saved me.' I didn't mention they had tried to warn me. I was guessing that would have earned me a sound lecture. And besides, it was now a moot point.

He sagged back against the headboard, staring at the ceiling.

'Is that why you were staring at the corner of the marquee all dinner?'

'I wasn't sure,' he said. 'I haven't felt one for so long.'

'It was there?' My voice came out more shrilly than I would have liked.

He sighed. 'It seems things are progressing more quickly than I would have liked.'

'What do you mean?'

'That Santanas is already affecting our world.'

I stared at him while I tried to make the connection. 'What does that *thing*,' I shuddered, 'have to do with Santanas?'

'During the Dark Years, Santanas brought the retchers through to our world and set them free. The fear and panic they incited suited his purpose.'

'Are they like dragons?'

'No, he found them bodies and used black magic to bring them. But it took many bodies to bring one of them through.'

'The animals,' I said. 'They kept changing.'

He nodded his head. 'Yes, he used animals. It added to their fear. When he was trapped they were, for a better way of explaining this, sucked back into Trillania.'

'Samuel said it was after my power.'

Wolfgang's eyes widened in surprise. 'That's new. They normally hunt indiscriminately.'

'But why would he send one after me? He said he needed me.' I realised what I had said as soon as the words left my mouth.

Wolfgang's eyes narrowed. 'And when did he tell you this?'

I cringed and whispered, 'Don't tell Aethan.'

'I can't make promises like that till you tell me.'

'Oh okay.' I stuck my bottom lip out in a sulk and stared at the blankets as I plucked at them with my hands. 'You know how I told you that Galanta trapped me in Trillania?'

His face didn't lose its intent expression as he nodded.

'Well she wasn't alone.' I turned to face him fully. 'You and I need to have a long talk about blood bonds.

Donna Joy Usher

Anyway a mudman helped me escape, but Santanas had trapped my dragon. So I freed her.'

'A mudman helped...? Never mind. I'm guessing you got those bonds freeing your dragon?'

I nodded. 'When they first caught me, Santanas wouldn't let Galanta hurt me. He said they needed me.'

Wolfgang rubbed his beard with his hands. 'And why can't I tell Aethan this?'

''Cause he won't let me go back in.'

He looked amused. 'And when has that ever stopped you from doing what you wanted?'

'Ha ha.' I poked my tongue out. 'It makes things difficult. I'd rather not have to fight him every time I turn up there.'

'I see. And what about the retcher? Why have you kept that information from him?'

'Night faeries tried to kill me. He is taking the heir to the night faery throne home to marry his brother. If you are correct in that Santanas is already active in this land, then we are going to need them on our side. I don't want him doing the chivalrous thing on my behalf and destroying this mission.'

I felt chivalrous as the words came out of my mouth. I could have used this to my advantage as a way to get him away from Ebony. The eighteen-year-old girl inside me was screaming for it, but the Border Guard-trained part had taken over.

Wolfgang stared at me as his eyebrows rose up and down. They did that when he was deep in thought. 'On one condition,' he finally said. 'I'll keep these secrets if you promise not to go back into Trillania by yourself.'

'No fear there,' I said. 'Galanta can tell when I am there.'

'Blood bond? Yes, we really do have to have that conversation soon.' He stood and walked towards the door. 'How are you feeling?'

'Better, thanks.' It was the truth. I did feel better for having talked about it.

'Well then, sleep well.'

'Thanks,' I said. And true to my word, I did.

***

'Where are you off to?' Isla had a sullen look on her face as she stood in the doorway to my room.

'The library.'

'Again?' She strode to my bed, curling her legs up under her like a cat as she perched on the edge.

'I thought there might be some stuff there that could help us.' In truth, I'd been looking for information on retchers.

'I'm bored,' she said, sucking on a piece of her hair.

'Who's chaperoning today?'

'Wilfred and Luke.'

I had been relieved from chaperoning Aethan and Ebony when I had accidentally/on purpose knocked her drink over her when she had leaned in too close to Aethan.

That had been a week ago and I was much happier for not having to see them together.

'How come you aren't racing off to the garden every second you can?' she asked.

I paused in the process of putting my writing pad and pen into a bag and turned to face her. 'I hadn't realised,' I said. 'But you're right. Being in the castle doesn't bother me any more.'

She yawned and stretched. 'Me neither. Weird. Hey, how come *you* get flowers in *your* room?'

The flowers had started showing up the day after the banquet. I was guessing the Ubanty women were placing them there when they cleaned, but I had no idea why. If anything *I* should have been taking *them* flowers.

'Not sure.' I shrugged. 'You can have them if you want.'

She hopped off the bed and danced over to them, bending over to smell them. 'Thanks, but I might go and gather some of my own. You want to come?'

It was tempting. I hadn't been out to see the garden since the party. But my gut told me I needed to find something on the retchers.

'Maybe tomorrow,' I said, picking up my bag.

Wolfgang was waiting for me in the main chamber. That was another advantage of going to the library; I got to pick Wolfgang's brain. We had finally had the blood bond conversation – turned out I had pretty much worked most of it out myself. But he was researching a way for me to hide myself from Galanta. The day before he had pulled a particularly large and dusty book from the top, back corner of the library that he thought might contain some useful information.

'I thought there would at least be librarians here,' I said, as we pushed open the creaky door to the library.

'There were the first couple of days I came,' he said. 'Now they all seem to be off scratching their heads over some problem. Ahhhh,' he pulled the book toward him and blew some more dust off the cover. 'Come to papa.'

I wandered off to scour the shelves for something that might be of use to me. I'd spent a lot of my school days hiding in the library and I felt quite at home in them. There was something peaceful about so much information just waiting to be found. As if a huge beast of knowledge slumbered within the walls.

I trailed a finger along the spines as I read them: History of the Seven Seas – interesting, but not likely to help me; A Hundred Ways to Light a Candle – I was sure *that* contained more than the title suggested, at least I hoped so; Hypnosis, How to Control People Without Them Knowing – that one should be burnt.

The 'H' area of the library wasn't turning up anything that seemed remotely like what I was after. I grabbed the ladder on wheels and dragged it to the far end of the shelf, then I climbed to the very top. Rows and rows of books stretched out in front of me. You could spend a lifetime here and not read one tenth of the information. That made me feel very small.

I propped a hand on the shelf to support myself and stood on tiptoes, peering across the top of the bookshelves. It was a whole different world up here. While down below was an organised chaos of information battering to be read, up here was peaceful. Like floating above the clouds.

I swept my eye across the vastness of the library and noticed a small book sitting on the top of the bookshelf two rows down. That was weird. Perhaps someone had left it there while they had been doing the very same thing I was.

I climbed back down the ladder and continued my search, but the little book plucked at my mind.

'Of fine,' I muttered. 'It's not like I've found anything else useful.'

I moved to the correct row and dragged the ladder to the place where I thought the book had been. Then I climbed back to the top of the library. The book was sitting just out of reach. Rather than move the ladder, I leant on top of the bookshelf and stretched my fingers towards it, clawing at it with the tip of my nail till it was within reach.

It was smaller than it had looked; a hand-written book, dirty with years of dust. Tucking it under my arm, I climbed back down the ladder. I pulled it back out and blew at the dust while I walked towards Wolfgang.

'Isadora.' He pushed his glasses back up his nose and turned towards me. His obvious excitement made me forget about the book I had saved from obscurity. 'It's so simple.'

Before I could ask him what was so simple, the front door of the library banged open. 'It's inconceivable,' a man said. 'Impossible.'

'And yet it has happened.'

'We must tell the King.'

A chorus of voices shouted down *that* suggestion.

'We need to find a cure.'

'It is *broken*. There *is* no cure.'

'That's the problem with you Lactar. You always assume the impossible.'

Someone, probably Lactar, snarled in response and there was the sound of flesh smacking flesh. It seemed the librarians were a feisty lot.

'Stop, stop. Fighting will not help. You are both right. We need to tell the King, but that news will go down better once we've found the cure. Spread out and start searching.'

In the time they had been arguing Wolfgang had closed the book he'd been reading and quietly returned it to the shelf. He beckoned to me and I picked up my notebook, hurriedly stuffing it into my bag. We crept towards the front of the library, pausing so Wolfgang could peer around the last bookshelf from where we had heard the voices. He nodded and we tiptoed towards the front door.

The librarians had their backs to us as they searched the shelves. Before anyone could notice, we slipped through the partly open door and out into the corridor.

'What was *that* about?' I waited till we were well clear of the area to ask.

'I don't know, and I'm guessing we're not meant to.'

It wasn't till I got back to my room that I realised I still had the little book. Buzznuckle. Now I'd have to take it back, and if the librarians were there, they weren't going to be happy.

I wiped my sleeve across the title and tilted it to catch the light from the wall. Creatures of the Dark One. My breath caught in excitement. Was it possible that I had accidentally taken the exact book I needed?

I flipped open to the first page and started to read the old, spidery script.

Many animals have been used by the Dark One in his bid to rule the world. While some of these were trapped and forced against their will, others served him willingly. This book will attempt to categorise these creatures.

I flicked through the pages. Someone had painstakingly drawn pictures of the animals they were describing. On the back page, the following was written:

Very Good Cedric. Sound information presented in an interesting way. I particularly liked the illustrations. 'A plus'.

I flopped back onto my bed. I had stolen somebody's school assignment. That was typical of how my week had been going. Still, perhaps there was something in here that would help. I mean he *had* gotten an A plus.

I turned back to the beginning and started leafing through the pages. None of the animals in the book were ones I'd ever heard of. I was guessing by the names of some of them that the whole thing was made up.

Cedric had had a vivid imagination, painting creatures such as the snugalofs and six-toed gurantha as blood-thirsty killers, happy to do dark and dirty work. In contrast, the poor narathymia were trapped into serving the Dark One when their pups were stolen and held hostage.

I was chuckling by the time I got to the end of the book, really enjoying the graphic illustrations. That is, until I turned to the second last page.

Retchers

These abominations steal the soul from their prey by consuming the still-beating heart. They remove this heart in an appalling method – using an appendage like a tongue to reach down the victim's throat and through their chest to their heart. The removal of the heart is an excruciating process and of course, leads to death. Interestingly enough, the retcher's saliva has remarkable healing properties.

I was happy that Cedric found that remarkable. I certainly didn't as I stared at the page in horror. Was it possible he had fluked this one? Maybe heard the story when he was a young boy and not realised retchers were real? Because if that were not the case, then it was possible that everything in this book was also real.

I shuddered and threw the book across the room away from me.

'Izzy.' My door burst open and Isla danced into the room. 'We're going home.' She jumped onto my bed and bounced up and down. 'Aethan's convinced Ebony to marry Orion.' She stopped bouncing and peered more closely at my face. 'What's wrong? You look like you've seen a ghost.'

I pasted a smile on my face. 'No ghosts here. Yes, that's wonderful.' I managed to refrain from asking what form the final convincing had taken. If kissing had been involved, blood *would* be shed.

She laughed. 'You should see the fierce look on your face. Don't worry, nothing like *that* happened. Did you really think it would?' She studied me for a second. 'She's going to marry Orion, Aethan would never lay a finger on her.' Her face took on a mischievous look. 'Not that she didn't try to make him.'

I took a deep breath, determined not to let her rile me for her own amusement. 'But she's so....' Beautiful didn't cut it.

'Naïve. Young. Spoilt.' She let out a snort. 'I wish you'd gotten over your jealousy. The last couple of days have been a riot. You should have *seen* the look on Aethan's face when she asked him what flower she most reminded him of.'

I attempted to keep a straight face – *nothing* about that situation was funny – but my traitorous lips pulled up at the corners.

'What did he say?'

'A rose, of course. I think it's the only flower he knows. I mean you know how bad he is at that sort of stuff. Remember that poem he wrote for you.' She burst out laughing again. '*Awful!*'

It *had* been awful. But some of the things he'd whispered to me when we'd been alone had stolen my breath away. He might have the body and mind of a warrior, but I knew that in there, somewhere, hid the soul of a shy poet.

'You must tell me how you guys met someday. From things Wilfred's said, you've known each other for quite a while.'

'Yep, one of these days.' When snugalofs flew backwards. 'So when do we leave.'

'First light. Give us time to re-stock and Ebony time to pack. She wasn't very happy about not being able to bring her retinue, but even Arracon could see the necessity for us travelling light and fast.' She pulled a face when she said his name.

'I don't know how you stay so composed with him around.'

'It was a long time ago.' She sat down cross-legged on my bed. 'It took a while for me to come to terms with the fact that I would be single forever, but once I got over my anger, I started enjoying life.'

'Single forever?'

'I was ruined by the scandal. No-one would marry me after what I did to him.'

'After what *you* did to *him?*' I stood up and shook my head.

'That's all anyone else saw. They didn't know about the rest.' She placed the tip of her first finger onto her lips as if to remind me it was a secret.

The few scratchy remnants of my perception of Isla as a scatty, spoilt princess melted away. 'So you're happy about Ebony marrying Orion?'

She let out a laugh, but her eyes were hard as she said, 'If I could, I would slit her throat and leave her to die. But I can't. So instead I will guard him.'

Aethan had been right, all those weeks ago when he'd said he hoped there was more to Isla then there seemed. 'Why,' I asked, slowly picking through my words, 'have you let me see the *real* you?'

She cocked her head to the side and studied me. 'I don't trust Ebony, not one little bit, and I need your help protecting my family.'

'No-one was there to protect *you.*'

'Exactly.' She dusted her hands together as if my helping was a done deal. 'I won't let that happen again.

Anyhoo, places to go, people to do.' She laughed wickedly and skipped back out of my room.

***

'I'm sorry,' Aethan said to Ebony, 'you can't bring that many packhorses.'

'But my clothes.' Tears trembled on the ends of her lashes.

I wondered if he were still enjoying spending time 'with a woman of grace'. When he got his memory back I was *so* going to make him pay for *that* comment.

'You can get more made in Isilvitania.'

I glanced over at Isla. A small smile hovering on the edges of her lips told me she was enjoying this as much as I was. She was right, If I could have gotten past my jealousy I would have seen the funny side of this long ago.

'One. That's all you can bring.'

'I thought they'd all be here to see her off,' I whispered to Isla.

'Night faery custom. They never say goodbye. Bad luck or something like that.'

'What about my slave? I suppose you want me to leave *him* at home as *well*.' Ebony stamped her slippered foot and put her hands on her hips.

'He can come.'

'Boy.' Her skirts frothed around her as she turned away from Aethan. 'Pack as many of the cases as possible onto one horse.'

'No,' Aethan said. 'I don't want your horse dropping dead on the first day.'

Ebony's slave stepped out from behind one of the packhorses. He may have worn the baggy, brown clothing of a slave, and those armbands may have proclaimed him one, but the proud, black eyes that burnt in his face told a different story.

Samuel.

He stood with his head slightly bowed, awaiting Ebony's next demand.

'Oh very well.' She flicked her long, silken plait back over her shoulder. 'Boy, bring my animal.'

Samuel bowed and disappeared around to the side of the castle where the stables were. He returned with two horses. One was a sturdy brown mare with a short, shaggy coat. I was guessing by the bow and quiver full of arrows hanging off the back of the saddle, that *that* one was his. The other, towering above the brown, was the same midnight-glossy black as Ebony's hair.

'Oh great,' I said to Isla, 'she's colour co-ordinated her horse with her hair.'

'That's not a horse,' Isla said.

Samuel led the animal over to a mounting stone and Ebony sprung lightly onto the side saddle. The animal danced to the side as Ebony adjusted her skirts, and flung its head in our direction. Cat eyes stared at us, the pupils twirling gently as it looked us up and down. Steam flowed out of its nostrils as it snorted softly. Small scales glistened on its haunches and each leg ended in five scaly, taloned toes.

'A hagon,' I said. Rage filled me at the sight of the animal and I hoped that wherever Emerald was, she was safe.

'Pick a horse,' Aethan said.

Ebony ignored him while she continued to play with her skirt, her lips pursed into an angry line. 'Are you sure?' She looked up at him through her lashes, her green eyes glowing with unshed tears. 'Could I bring two?'

'One,' Aethan snapped. 'And hurry.'

I couldn't help myself. I trotted Lily past her and said, 'Lucky you like your men strong.'

She lifted her nose into the air, sniffed and turned the other way. 'That one,' she said, pointing to one of the animals. More slaves appeared from the side of the castle and started leading the other animals back to the stable.

Samuel leapt onto his horse and tied the lucky packhorse's rope to the pommel of his saddle. Two swords were sheathed in harnesses that criss-crossed his back, and daggers shone against the black tattoos on his biceps.

Wilfred eyed him up-and-down, finally giving him a nod of approval. He may have been a slave, but when the shit hit the fan it was going to mean one more sword on our side.

The first day progressed smoothly, which only served to make me edgy. After all the trouble we'd had, I couldn't believe that a whole day would go by in which not one thing tried to kill us. It was, to be quite honest, a little boring. And listening to Ebony prattle on to Aethan was only amusing for a while before it became annoying. I mean seriously, who had that much to say?

By the time we set up camp for the night I had started to feel sorry for Aethan. After my convoluted emotions of the last week or so, that was a nice change.

Samuel set up Ebony's tent a little away from the rest of ours and then prepared her evening meal. He fed and watered and curried both their animals and polished her saddle, but the whole time there was a certain air about him. As if he were ready to drop whatever he was doing and pull out those swords. It was obvious by the way the rest of the men eyed him that they felt it too.

When she had finally retired to her blankets (her words) he pulled a piece of dried meat from one of the saddle bags and sat on a log by himself. I hadn't heard him utter a word the whole day.

I refilled my bowl with stew and grabbed a bread roll, carrying them both over to him. He looked at Ebony's tent as I approached and I nodded my head. I handed him the stew and bread and went back to the others. We would be back on the hard travel tack in another couple of days, but until then we had enough to share.

The next day continued as the first had, with Ebony chewing off Aethan's ear and the rest of us trying to stay out of earshot.

The shadows were long from the setting sun when Wilfred pulled his horse in next to mine and whispered, 'Aethan wants to go in tonight.'

I turned to him in surprise and he pulled a face and nodded his head towards Isla.

'He wants to try to find Rako and let him know we are on our way back.' With Ebony, was the unspoken part of *that* sentence.

'Okay,' I said, managing to keep my voice steady.

I waited till he had drifted off again before I nudged my horse towards where Wolfgang rode. What with the librarians, the book I had found and then the news that we were going home, I had totally forgotten about Wolfgang's research.

'Did you find the answer to my blood bond problem?'

'With all the excitement I had quite forgotten. The answer is quite simple.'

That surprised me. *Nothing* in my life was ever simple.

'We need to mark crosses over your pulse points and third eye.'

'That's it?' I couldn't believe it.

'Well there is one small problem.'

I rolled my eyes. '*Of course* there is.'

'It has to be done in someone else's blood.'

I blew out a big puff of air. 'How much blood would I need?'

'Enough for ten crosses.'

That wasn't so bad. 'You realise it has to be you, right? None of the others know about this.'

'I'm assuming you are going in tonight?'

I nodded my head. 'Aethan wants to contact Rako.'

The rest of the day dragged until we set up camp. We followed the same routine as the night before; Ebony retired early and we shared our dinner with Samuel. Aethan made sure that he, Wilfred and I all had the later watches so we could go straight to Trillania.

Wolfgang came to my tent as soon as we had turned in for the night. He held a small bowl, his dagger and a bandage.

'Do you want me to do it?' I didn't like the idea of cutting him, but he was doing me a favour, so if he wanted me to, I would.

'Some of the spells I have worked over the years have required me to do this. Sadly, I've become quite good at it.'

He winced as he pierced the skin till blood ran down his wrist. He held it over the bowl and watched it dribble in.

'That should do it.' He put pressure on his wrist and I picked up the bandage and wrapped it around and around the wound. I cut the end into two pieces and tied them around his wrist to keep them secure.

I stripped down to my tank top and undies so that he could access all the areas he had to. He dipped his finger into the blood and drew crosses on my third eye, either side of my throat, the depression in between my collar bones, the inside of my wrists, behind my knees and the inside of my ankles. I wasn't sure if it were my imagination or not, but as he drew the last cross I felt all ten points tingle.

'I'd better get to sleep,' I said. 'They'll be wondering what I'm up to.'

Careful not to rub the crosses on the backs of my knees off, I lay down and closed my eyes.

Wolfgang paused in the process of getting up. 'Do you want some help?' he asked.

I nodded my head without opening my eyes and he started to sing the sleep song. Within moments I was sound asleep.

***

Thanks to Wolfgang's sleep spell I made it to Trillania well before the boys. Wilfred arrived not long afterwards.

'What took you so long?'

'What is on your head?'

'I have no idea what you're talking about,' I said. 'Where's Aethan?'

'Apparently Ebony had a nightmare. He's calming her down.'

'I *bet* she did,' I said.

'Something about animals with swirling, yellow eyes. She sounded really freaked out.'

Swirling yellow eyes? I shuddered and wrapped my arms around myself. Great, now *I* was freaked out.

'Probably just her hagon's eyes getting to her.' Retchers weren't the only animals with twirling eyes.

'They're not yellow.'

'They could be, if it got sick with liver failure.'

He was still laughing when Aethan arrived.

'What's so funny?'

'Your girlfriend's funny.'

The words poured out of his big, fat mouth and there was nothing I could do to stop them. His eyes widened as he realised what he'd said and he tried to cover up his slip of the tongue.

'Cause you know Izzy is a girl and she's your friend, so that makes her your girlfriend. She's my girlfriend as well. Aren't you Izzy?' He reached over and punched me on the shoulder.

'Shut up Will,' I hissed. *Kill me. Just kill me now.*

Aethan's head swivelled between Wilfred and me before finally settling on me. 'What's on your head?'

'I'm trying out a new look. What do you think?'

If the expression on his face hadn't been confused a second ago, now it was *stupefied.* He gaped at me and then, obviously considering that both those topics were better left alone, shook his head and said, 'Right. Let's go find Rako.'

He held out his hands to grasp ours and closed his eyes.

I punched Wilfred in the shoulder as hard as I could before joining hands with him.

The world around us shimmered and when it settled again we were standing in the middle of a battle. All around us, goblins fought Border Guards. I shrieked and ducked as a spear passed through the air where my head had been.

I conjured up a sword and turned so my back was to Aethan and Wilfred. I could feel them do the same. We were on the edge of the forest near Isilvitania.

'Blimey,' one of the other Guards yelled. 'Where'd you come from?'

'We're looking for Rako,' Aethan said.

A goblin roared as it charged me, his spear ready to turn me into a shish kebab. I brought my sword down on the spear, shattering it, and then drove the palm of my hand upwards into the goblin's face. His head flicked back and I spun with my sword, slicing through his exposed neck.

'He was over that way,' the Guard said.

I didn't get to see which way he indicated because another goblin took the place of the first. That was the problem with goblins. They were notoriously lazy and if an easy kill presented itself they would take it. Unfortunately for me, as a woman I looked like an easy kill. Unfortunately for them, I wasn't.

'Where are you from?' Wilfred yelled. I felt his back push against mine for a second and I shifted to give him more room. That was one of the problems with fighting this way, movements that you might use normally, like dodging and ducking, could get your wingman killed.

'Australia,' the Guard said in a broad accent. 'Pretty quiet down where we are. You guys definitely get the pointy end of the spear.'

This goblin was more cautious than the last. He feinted towards me a couple of times, pulling back out of range before I could strike. I rolled my eyes and changed my sword to a loaded crossbow. His eyes widened as I pressed the trigger and the bolt slammed into his chest.

'You snooze, you lose,' I said.

'This way Isadora.' Aethan tugged on my arm and as a unit the three of us started to move towards where Rako was.

The fighting lightened up after we had moved about ten metres. It seemed we had landed in the thick of it. The Australian contingent of Border Guards closed rank behind us and we trotted over to where Rako stood, directing the fight.

'What's going on?' Aethan asked.

He looked towards us and swore. 'I seemed to remember telling you two you were not to come here. And you,' he pointed at Wilfred, 'what in the Dark Sky are *you* doing here?'

Wilfred gave him a grin. 'Turns out I accidentally forgot to put my armband away.'

'Accidentally forgot my arse,' Rako growled. 'All right, you're here now. What do you have to report?'

'Our mission up to this point has been successful. The night faeries have agreed that a union would be beneficial and we are on our way home with Princess Ebony.'

'Ebony.' Rako let out a low whistle. 'Well done. How far away are you?'

'We are swinging around the bottom of goblin territory. I expect we'll hit our border in about five days.'

'Sir,' Wilfred said, 'what's going on here?'

I tried to hide my smirk. Wilfred only called Rako 'Sir' when he knew he was in deep poo-poo.

Rako gave him a long look and for a moment I thought he wouldn't answer. 'Not that this is any of your concern, but the goblins have been throwing everything they've got at the castle for the last few nights.'

It was a given that the Guard would protect the castle down to the last man standing. When the Royal Family dreamt, their initial entry point to Trillania would be in their bedroom. From there they would disappear to wherever their dreams took them.

Not for the first time I felt frustrated that we couldn't tell them the truth and shield them from coming. But there were two main problems with that. Firstly, the average person would not be able to handle the truth of what danger they were possibly in when they slept. While large areas of Trillania were considered safe, animals that lived off the souls of dreamers did exist. And of course there were the goblins and others of their ilk who trespassed the Land of Dreams. But they normally left the average person alone.

And the second reason that we couldn't stop them from coming was that they needed to dream. Everybody needed to dream at least once in a while as a release for their subconscious mind. People who didn't dream, eventually lost their grip on reality and went mad.

'What's Galanta up to?' I didn't really expect an answer.

'We don't know. We haven't been able to locate her. It's as if she doesn't come here any more. Now you three need to get back to wherever you are.' He looked back at the battle and shook his head. 'Now the orcs have joined in.' He pulled his sword and trotted down to join the fight.

'Come on.' Aethan grabbed my hand and a second later we were standing outside our tents.

'Wait,' I said. 'Aren't you curious as to what Galanta is up to?'

'You heard him,' Wilfred said, 'they can't find her.'

'Oh she's here all right.' I could feel her faintly, a long way south.

'Surely a little peek couldn't hurt,' Wilfred said.

Aethan crossed his arms and for a second I thought he was going to refuse. But then he said, 'Fine. But we stay out of sight.'

'No problemo,' I said, crossing my fingers and hoping that Wolfgang's blood did the trick. I grabbed their hands and concentrated on the feel of her, making sure that I placed us a good half a mile away. We could walk in from there.

We appeared on a grassy plain that stretched as far as the eye could see. Drums sounded in the night and a large bonfire glowed in the distance. I was glad I'd added the extra distance because I had been expecting to end up in a forest. I'd never encountered her in the open before.

We paused for a few seconds to check all around us before we started walking towards the fire. A few minutes later we were close enough to see the enemy massing on the far side of the bonfire. Whatever was going down tonight was big.

'Great Dark Sky,' Aethan whispered. 'Goblins, dwarves, trolls, orcs, giants and who is that at the back?'

'I think it's the vulpines.'

'Vulpines?' Not being full faery my eyes weren't as good as theirs.

'A tribe of Bedouin fighters from the Middle East. They ride these kick-arse birds.'

'Great. Airpower.'

The drum beat increased in tempo and a group of goblins shuffled around the fire, chanting and waving their arms.

'I'm thinking that the fighting at the castle is a diversion,' I said. 'To make sure that none of us stumbled onto this.'

'You could be right,' Aethan said.

'Is that Galanta?' Wilfred pointed at a platform to the left of the fire.

I pushed out with my senses to pinpoint her location. 'That's her,' I said.

As we watched, she rose and slashed her hands to the side. The drum beat and chanting stopped instantly.

'We need to get closer,' Aethan whispered.

We dropped to our bellies and started to crawl. Hopefully, with them all staring towards the fire no-one would notice the grass shaking.

'Welcome,' Galanta yelled. 'You are all here because you have heard the rumours. Rumours that the Dark One walks amongst us again.'

A cheer broke out amongst the watchers and the goblins beat the butts of their spears on the ground.

'Now is the dawning of a new age. Our age. Too long have we been repressed. Too long have the faeries and witches held us at bay.'

She stopped as another bout of cheering broke out.

'We will rule this land and all who live in it. We will enslave the weakling humans and we will take what is ours.'

Her words sent shivers of fear down my spine. It was everything I had feared. The sheer number of chanting and cheering enemy made my blood run cold. Even with the night faeries we would be outnumbered. We would have to recruit the humans to help, and for them, without a trace of magic, or faery blood to give them strength and speed, it would be a suicide mission.

A battle field filled with human corpses was not my idea of a good time.

'What's that?' Wilfred pointed to the end of the platform where dark air was massing.

'Santanas.' I pressed myself down into the grass.

As we watched, the darkness pulsed and whirled, pulling up until a man stood next to Galanta. I'd thought the throng had been excited before, but that was nothing to what they were now. Shrieking and hissing and cheering filled the night. The goblins' spears beat the ground so hard and fast that the low vibration reached us where we lay.

He put his hands in the air and the noise died down. 'I welcome you all to my fire. It is good to see so many who have held to the faith. Welcome vulpines, welcome friend dwarves. It has been too long since I have seen you. And you, friend giants, your shadows grace the land. Welcome troll brothers and orcs. May your spears stay strong and true. Welcome goblins, highest of all, for you never gave up the search for me.'

The goblins jumped to their feet, hollering and banging their spears and a drum beat madly for a second.

Santanas waited till their noise had died down before continuing. 'There is one more amongst us tonight. One more dear to my heart.' My blood turned to ice as he turned toward where the three of us lay hiding in the grass. 'Welcome daughter,' he said. 'Won't you join me?'

I couldn't move, I couldn't think. His gaze pinned me to the ground. He leapt off the top of the platform, black smoke swirling like a colony of bats as he flew towards me.

A thousand spiders running over me, a hundred snakes wrapped around my limbs, I would have taken them all and gladly, rather than lie frozen, waiting for him to pounce.

Aethan rolled on top of me, breaking the hold of Santanas's stare. I closed my eyes and he took me with him, back to the campsite and into my body. I woke with a start, sitting bold upright in bed, but all I could see were Santanas's eyes.

Chapter Eleven

Monsters, Monsters Everywhere

It didn't take them long to get to my tent. I had my arms wrapped tight about my middle and my teeth were chattering when Aethan threw up the flap.

'What,' he said, 'in the name of the Dark Sky was that?'

Wilfred followed him in and said, 'Daughter?'

'I'm not,' I said. 'I'm his niece, that's all.'

'Well would you care to explain why he thinks you're his daughter.' I hadn't seen Aethan look this pissed off since I'd broken his nose that last time.

'Because I released him from the rock. He thinks I must be his daughter. It's not true though. There must have been a flaw in the binding spell.' I had come up with that theory all by myself, but I didn't tell *them* that.

'What is going on in here?' Isla stuck her head in through the open tent flap. 'Some of us are trying to keep a watch for bad people. Speaking of which,' she pointed a finger at me, 'you're up.'

I pulled my vest over my tank top while Aethan and Wilfred left the tent. 'Stay here boy.' I patted Scruffy on the head and he snuggled back into the blanket.

'What is that on your head?' Isla peered at me as I wiggled past her to get out.

'I had a pimple. Apparently blood's good for them.'

'You seemed to have quite a few.' The look on her face told me she knew I was lying.

'Heat rash's a bitch.'

She shook her head. 'Whatever.'

I felt bad for not telling her the truth, but I knew what would happen if I tried.

I made my way out through the trees and settled back against a trunk. Letting my eyes relax as I stared out away from the camp. The new moon wasn't throwing out much light. I was going to have to rely on my sense of hearing as well as my eyes.

The next few hours passed too slowly, giving me far too much time to think.

He couldn't be my father. Could he?

I stared at a shadow. Was that someone moving? I crept towards it to discover a leaf blowing in the breeze.

No. It was ridiculous. I mean, surely Mum would have known.

Something scraped softly at the trunk of a tree. I froze and stared towards the source of the noise. It scraped again and I slunk from tree-to-tree, slowly getting closer to the source of the noise; a badger, digging for grubs.

Why hadn't Wolfgang's blood worked against Santanas? Galanta had certainly been surprised we were there.

A hand closed over my shoulder and I let out a low yelp and spun around. Wilfred stood there with a huge grin on his face.

'You walk like a little girl,' I whispered, shaking his hand off my arm.

'Sorry.' He didn't look at all sorry. 'Forgot you'd probably be a bit freaked out after this evening's events.'

'Freaked out? I'm not freaked out.' Much.

'Anything going on?'

'There's a badger over there.' I pointed in the direction of the nocturnal hunter and for the briefest of seconds two yellow eyes gleamed at me. I shuddered. What was it with the yellow eyes?

'Cool, I love badgers. Might go check him out.' He moved off soundlessly towards where I had pointed.

I turned to head back to my tent and walked smack bang into Aethan. His hand wrapped over my mouth in time to muffle my shriek. I took a deep breath as I stared wide-eyed at him. What was it with those two tonight? Were they trying to make me wake everybody up?

My poor heart was still tap dancing when he removed his hand. 'Anything out there?' he asked.

'A big, red bear bothering a badger.'

The night's shadows made him look dark and mysterious. I stared at his lips, remembering the feel of them on mine, and I realised we were standing only inches apart.

Danger, danger. I was only inches away from making a fool of myself.

But it wasn't me that closed the gap. It wasn't me that reached my hands towards his face. I gazed up at him as his lips descended towards mine. And then I closed my eyes and arched my back and… Ebony let out a shriek that would have woken the dead.

'Buzznuckle.' Aethan let go of me and turned, racing towards Ebony's tent.

Samuel was with her by the time we got there. Light from the candle he had lit danced on the walls of the tent. 'She's okay,' he said, looking out the flap at us. 'It was another nightmare.'

'A beast.' She shuddered and started crying. 'It had yellow eyes, and they spun around and around and it looked like an animal, and then next second it was different.' Her terrified words tumbled over each other.

Aethan crouched and moved into the tent. I stayed frozen where I was, my shallow breathing matching hers.

'Get out boy,' she snapped at Samuel. 'There's not enough room in here for you.'

He pushed out past Aethan and met my eyes. We both knew what she was talking about.

I had trouble getting back to sleep. Terror had taken an icy grip on me and I couldn't push it off. Every time I closed my eyes I saw the retcher or Santanas. Each was as bad as the other.

In the end I sat up, lit a candle, and pulled out the little book I had stolen from the library. It probably wasn't the best time to read it, with only Scruffy for company and me already scared. But I figured if the animals in it were real, I needed to know about them. And besides, I couldn't get any more scared than I already was.

Half an hour later I had to concede that I had been wrong about that last bit. Instead, now I had a whole heap more things to be scared of.

Snugalofs that flew through the evening skies, descending to sever your head with their blade-like wings.

Chameleon-like Brolontas that can stand right next to you without you seeing them. They killed by ripping out your throat with their teeth.

The six-toed gurantha that moved like a sloth, unless they were on the hunt. Then they flung themselves from tree-to-tree, faster than a horse could run. They jumped onto their victims' backs and used their teeth to snap spinal cords.

The list went on-and-on, each page bringing a new type of death. I was still awake when the sun came up, happier than ever to see the gentle rays of light.

'You look like shit,' Isla said when I crawled out of my tent. She was obviously still pissed about the night before.

'Look like shit, feel like shit,' I mumbled, staggering past her.

Brent took one look at my face and handed me a coffee. I thanked him and sat on a log with my eyes closed while I sipped the bitter brew. Maybe I could sleep while riding Lily. I doubted I would ever sleep at night again.

A shadow blocked the warmth of the sun's rays and I opened my eyes to see Aethan watching me. He met my eyes and then turned away, running his hands through his hair. He did that when he was agitated. Was he regretting nearly kissing me last night?

I sighed and closed my eyes again. It was one more thing I would spend the day trying not to think about.

'How far are we travelling today?' Ebony, for all her days in the saddle and a night of broken sleep, still looked perfect. How did she do it?

'We need to get to the other side of the Thorn Forest.'

'We can't camp in it?'

'We most certainly cannot.'

I opened my eyes and stared at Aethan. It was unlike him to speak so sternly, *especially* when she hadn't even started getting annoying.

'It is imperative we make it out the other side before sunset.'

'What happens if we don't?'

There was a beat of silence during which Isla, Ebony and I all stared at him while the others busied themselves with departure preparations. It looked like the girls were the only ones not in the know.

'Ghouls,' he finally said.

Ghouls? I wracked my brain for what the book had said about them. Wraith-like creatures that emerged from the ground after dark. Their merest touch would rip your soul from your body.

And then the true horror of what his words meant hit me and I had to stop myself from gibbering in terror. I already knew that retchers were real. So if ghouls existed as well, then the probability that every damned creature in that book was real had just increased.

'You don't look so good.' Luke handed me a hard biscuit.

I sighed, and tapped it against my metal mug. We had run out of fresh food the night before. 'Didn't sleep well.'

I gave Scruffy his portion of the beef jerky as well as my own. He chewed contentedly while I folded down the tent and packed my things onto Lily.

'Come on boy.' I picked him up and swung into the saddle, settling him on Lily's rump behind me.

'How far till we get out of Thorn Forest?' Isla's face showed the tension I'm sure mine did.

'We haven't reached it yet,' Aethan said. 'By my calculations we're still about an hour from the start.'

We rode for the next hour and then another before we could see the trees thickening at the foot of the next hill.

'Thorn Forest,' Aethan said when Ebony pointed a dainty hand at it.

It took us another thirty minutes to get to the start of it. We halted and rested and watered the horses.

'Maybe we should wait,' Aethan said. The sun had only risen a couple of hand spans above the horizon.

'I'll die of boredom if we have to stay here all day.' Ebony tossed her braid back behind her shoulders and put her hands on her hips. The movement made her breasts bulge over the top of her dress.

'You'll die if we end up in there after dark.'

She pouted and then chewed on her bottom lip, worry shadowing her brilliant eyes.

'Do we have enough food to stay the day here?' Brent asked.

'We'll have to decrease our rations.'

An arrow thudded into a tree trunk a foot from Wilfred's head. 'Take cover,' he yelled, diving to the other side of the tree.

Wild cackling came from the same direction as the arrow. A wiry man wearing only a loin cloth flicked the end of his beard over his shoulder and sighted along another arrow.

This one landed next to Aethan's foot. He swept Ebony up and threw her onto her hagon. Then he tossed the reins up to where Samuel already sat on his brown mare. Samuel wheeled his horse and dragged Ebony's hagon into the forest behind him.

'Stop that,' Wilfred yelled, aiming an arrow at the old man.

'Or what?' The man laughed as he capered from bare-foot-to-bare-foot. 'You'll shoot me?'

'Too right I will.' Wilfred released the arrow.

It flew true towards the man but at the last second he shimmered and it passed right through him. He waved his hand and the arrow curved back towards us. It split into two, then four, then six arrows.

Shrieking, I threw myself to the ground over Scruffy as one of the arrows whizzed through where I had been standing. I looked around and saw everyone else, except Wolfgang, in the same position I was. He had a shield held in front of him.

'Bugger off,' the man yelled. 'I live here.'

'Good sir,' Wolfgang called out, 'you are obviously a wizard of great strength and talent. We do not tarry because we want to live here. We wish to enter Thorn Forest with a whole day of travel ahead of us.'

'I don't care.' He giggled as he talked. 'This is my home. And what I say goes.'

'As crazy as a really, really crazy person,' Wilfred muttered clambering back to his feet.

'Just one night,' Wolfgang said, 'that is all that we ask.'

'I said no and I mean no.' The little man stomped his foot. 'No, **No, NOOOO.'**

He threw his hands out on the last no and a wall of flame raced towards us. We threw ourselves at our horses and galloped them towards the edge of the forest. I held Scruffy firmly tucked into the crook of my left elbow until we reached the trees. I was really hoping the flames would stop at the edge of the forest. They did. An impenetrable line of fire stretched as far as we could see.

'Can we...?' Aethan looked at Wolfgang.

'Went straight through my shield.'

'So that's a no. What about Isadora?' He turned to look at me and I slumped down in my saddle. I didn't feel like taking my untrained skills up against that madman.

'I don't know how she would go up against human magic, and I don't think we can afford to waste more time.'

'You're right.' He turned Adare away from the flames. 'We must ride hard if we are to make it through.'

After the first few miles the foliage thinned a little, enabling us to go faster than a walk. We alternatively trotted and walked our mounts, trying to keep them rested as well as make the best time we could.

All too soon the sun's rays were overhead and then descending from the other side. Conversation became halted and then stopped all together as long shadows stretched out beside us.

'How far?' Isla's voice was a rough whisper.

'Not long,' Aethan said. But worry was evident in his voice.

The light shifted from yellow to orange as the sun started to set and we all pushed out mounts from a trot to a canter.

'Aethan,' Luke said.

'Can you do anything Wolfgang?' Aethan's voice was strung tight with tension.

'With ghouls?' Wolfgang shook his head.

'Right,' Aethan said. 'Listen up everyone, our presence will stimulate them. They will come out of the ground where we have ridden, so spread out and don't ride behind each other.'

As we stretched out into a long line, Aethan moved his mount over to Ebony and lifted her onto the saddle in front of him. I managed to control my stab of envy.

Samuel shot him a look but didn't say anything. He was no doubt wondering why Aethan didn't trust him to look after her. But if she had been speaking to me the way she had to him for the last few days, *I* couldn't have been trusted not to push her into the path of a ghoul.

I knew the exact moment that the sun disappeared; firstly, because the lingering remnants of the sun's rays that were filtering through the trees disappeared. Secondly, because Aethan leant over Ebony, gripping the reins in his hands and yelled, 'Run.' And thirdly, I knew it because as soon as the light blinked out, moans started resonating around us.

I pulled Scruffy around in front of me and kicked my heels into Lily's sides. She didn't need any encouragement to run.

Samuel, now leading the hagon and the packhorse, appeared by my side. 'Spread out further,' he said, spearing away to my right.

I watched in horrified fascination as an ink-black shadow slithered out of the ground where Samuel's horse had passed. It was the shape of a person, seemingly made from smoke, but two dimensional – like a cardboard cut-out. And it didn't walk; it floated towards me.

'Isadora,' Samuel yelled, breaking me from my fascinated observation of my impending death.

I hadn't realised that I had slowed Lily to a walk. I kicked my heels into her again and she leapt away from the ghoul, racing to catch up to the rest of the line. Ghouls were rising as far as I could see.

I threw up an arm in reflex as a ghoul appeared right next to me. A shield formed and it drifted in the other direction. I could see Aethan with Ebony, and Wilfred and Isla on either side.

A ghoul appeared in between Samuel and me, reaching out an arm towards Lily. I yelled in anger and flicked my hand at it, shattering the ghoul into a million stinging insects. They swarmed around the two of us as we raced through the trees.

'Whizbang,' I screeched as the insects banged into me, tearing tiny chunks from my neck and arms. I could hear Samuel's cries of pain, as he crouched low over his mount's neck.

They harassed us for a minute more while we slapped at them and swore, and then they disappeared.

'Please don't do that again,' Samuel grunted from beside me, his upper body covered with spots of blood.

'I promise.' I was pretty sure I looked just as gruesome.

'Nearly there,' Aethan called out.

I squinted into the distance and saw that he was right. Ahead the darkness of the trees stopped and only the night's presence held sway.

I looked across at the rest of them, a relieved grin starting to play on my lips. And then Luke let out a yell. One minute he was riding, and the next he was falling, like a puppet whose strings had been cut.

His horse rode on without him, leaving him lying on the ground with a ghoul hovering over him as it sucked out his soul.

I let out a sob as I rode. There was nothing we could do but I still felt like a traitor as we left him behind. And then we were bursting from the tree line, running into the night, away from the ghouls, away from Thorn Forest and away from Luke's body.

***

We pulled up beyond the tree line. None of us speaking, all of us staring at the ghouls standing at the edge of the forest.

'Can they...,' Isla's voice trailed off as she let out a sob.

'No. They can't leave the forest.' Aethan's voice was flat.

'Shall we camp here?' I asked. I didn't want to stay that close to the forest, but Luke's body was there.

'The horses need resting,' Wolfgang said. His mare's head was down and her sides bellowed as she tried to regain her breath. 'And then tomorrow we can....'

Nobody wanted to say it. Because that would make it real.

We didn't speak as we set up camp. Brent handed out the food and we ate in silence, all of us no doubt trying not to think about the one thing we couldn't stop thinking about.

All, that is, except Ebony. She kept up her normal verbal abuse of Samuel, her trill voice intruding on our sorrow as she bullied and bossed him around.

When she was finally in her tent he came to where we sat and bowed low. 'I am deeply sorry for your loss,' he said. 'I did not know him well, but what I knew of him was good.'

'Thank you,' Aethan said, his voice thick with sorrow.

Wilfred reached out and squeezed Samuel's arm as he headed back to his position by Ebony's tent.

'I'll take first watch,' I said, placing Scruffy on the ground and standing. 'Unless someone else wants to.'

'I'll join you.' Wilfred stood and checked himself over for his weapons.

We walked a few hundred metres from the camp and stared off into the dark. The forest had opened up onto a plain. It was too dark to see how far it stretched. With the forest behind us we only had to watch the front. There wouldn't be anyone attacking from the rear tonight.

'One hell of a day,' Wilfred said.

I reached out and put an arm around his waist, pulling him into a quick hug. Luke and he had been close.

'I didn't even see what happened,' he said. 'I didn't realise he was gone till the end.'

I held onto his big hand. 'You couldn't have saved him. The ghoul came up under his horse. He didn't even know it happened.'

He took a deep breath and let out a sigh, wiping at his eyes with the back of his free arm. I stared straight ahead and pretended I hadn't noticed.

'We should spread out,' he said. 'In case more badgers turn up.'

I snorted. 'He was a cutie wasn't he?'

He stared at me for a second. 'You were serious about the badger?'

'Of course. It was still there when I left. I saw him.'

'Nothing there babe.' He tapped his head and then twirled his finger around indicating I was crazy.

'But I saw its eyes.' My voice trailed off weakly remembering what I'd seen. Yellow eyes staring at me. I shivered and wrapped my arms around myself. I was *so* not reading that book tonight.

My watch passed uneventfully and I went to wake Isla. She hugged me and then disappeared into the dark.

I cuddled up with Scruffy, feeling relieved and guilty that we had made it through the day alive. It could have happened to any of us. But it shouldn't have happened at all.

The sound of digging woke me the next morning. The sun was just peeping over the horizon when I crawled out of my tent. A quick peep at the forest showed the line of ghouls had disappeared. In the early light I could see that the plain extended to the horizon. There would be nowhere to hide today.

Aethan, Brent and Wilfred were digging a hole. I took a deep breath and corrected myself. They were digging a grave. A grave for Luke.

I lit the fire and got the coffee brewing while Isla sorted out the food. When they had finished digging they washed their hands and then drank their coffee, staring wordlessly into the fire.

How many times had they done this? How many times had they buried a friend? The answer to that was too many. Even one friend was too many.

After we had eaten, they went to collect Luke's body, returning a few minutes later with him hanging limply between them.

They placed him on the ground and Isla and I washed his face and his hands and feet in what Wolfgang had told me was the faery tradition. We brushed his hair and straightened his clothes, and then we kissed him on his forehead – for his mother, his cheeks – for the rest of his family, and his lips – for his lover. Our falling tears mingled with each other's as we rose, backing away to let the men place him in his resting place.

Faery funerals were a short affair and as soon as Luke was positioned within the hole, the dirt was replaced where it had come from until a mound rose over him. Then we packed our things up and continued on our way.

Initially I thought it was Luke's death affecting me, but as the day progressed I realised it wasn't that. Something else felt wrong. I rose up in my stirrups and swivelled in my saddle, examining the plain as far as I could see. There was nothing there except grass and the occasional lonely shrub.

I shook myself. I was being silly. The last couple of days had been particularly stressful, you couldn't blame me for being jumpy. But into the afternoon, more and more, I noticed the others doing the same thing.

'Do you see anything?' I asked Brent.

'No, there's nothing there.' He pivoted his head again and then sank back into his saddle. 'But I feel like something is watching me.'

That was the scary part about it. It did feel like *something* was watching, as opposed to someone. And it didn't feel at all friendly.

The feeling continued to grow like a storm of ominousness on the horizon. Even the horses could feel it as they flicked their tails from side-to-side and whinnied nervously. There was something coming and it wasn't going to be good.

'No tents tonight,' Aethan said when we finally dismounted. 'Double watch and sleep ready to ride. The horses as well.'

I removed Lily's saddle and brushed her thoroughly, going through the evening ritual of checking her hooves and legs. When I was sure she was healthy I put her feedbag on and then replaced her saddle. 'Sorry girl,' I said. 'Boss's orders.'

All I removed from the saddle bags was my blanket. There was coolness in the air that hadn't been there the night before.

I drew second watch, so after dinner I curled up in a ball next to Isla and pulled my blanket over Scruffy and me.

'What do you think it is?' she whispered to me.

'I don't know.' I was managing to resist the urge to pull my blanket over my head, put my thumb in my mouth and rock myself while I cried for my Mummy. Thinking about what it might be could shatter my delicate self-control.

I closed my eyes, but every little night noise had me snapping them open and staring wildly around. Eventually exhaustion took me and I managed to sleep between my mini panic attacks.

Isla's gasp woke me. I rolled towards her and opened my eyes. She lay flat on her back, staring straight up at the retcher whose tongue was in her mouth. I screamed and pulled my sword out from beside me, slashing through the retcher's smoky body. And then Samuel was there, ripping the tongue from Isla's throat.

She let out a scream and rolled to the side, vomiting onto the grass.

Aethan and Wilfred bounded into the circle as Samuel danced in front of the retcher, his blade twirling so fast it was a blur. The creature let out a shrill cry and disappeared into the dark. We had a few seconds to breathe before the next attack came.

We spread out, facing into the dark. Isla grabbed her bow and sprang to her feet, nocking an arrow. Ebony crouched on the ground by Samuel's feet. I couldn't be sure, but it looked like she was crying.

A whirring sound came from our left and a shadow flicked by, barely illuminated in the moonlight.

'Wolfgang,' Aethan growled. 'We need light.'

Wolfgang pointed at a nearby shrub and the plant burst into light. I squinted my eyes and stared out onto the plain and my heart tried to clamber out of my chest and run away.

Yellow eyes stared back. Many, many sets of yellow eyes.

'Dark Sky,' Isla said, 'what *are* they?'

The whirring increased in volume as if the creature had turned and was coming back towards us. Suddenly, I knew at least what *it* was.

'Get down,' I yelled, throwing myself to the ground.

The snugalof dropped from the sky, its cruel wings held in front of its body in a cross. Brent ducked and rolled as the snugalof snapped its wings back out to the side.

It missed Brent's neck by a hair. If he had responded to my yell one second later it would have been all-over-red-rover.

While most of my brain ran around inside my head shrieking in horror, a tiny, analytical portion thought, 'Oh, so *that's* how they cut people's heads off.'

'To the horses,' Aethan yelled.

He was right. There were too many of whatever-the-fuck-they-were out there for us to fight. We had to outdistance them.

Isla fired off arrows at the creatures as we sprinted for our horses. Since Wolfgang lit the fire, they had kept their distance, but as they saw us mounting they lunged towards us, eating up the distance between us far too quickly.

Suddenly I wasn't so sure we *would* be able to outrun them.

Lily let out a snort of fear and leapt forwards without my urging. I snuggled Scruffy into my chest and wrapped my arms to either side as I lay low over Lily's neck. I wasn't keen on having my head hacked off by an overzealous snugalof.

A glance over my shoulder showed the yellow eyes dropping back a little, but with their eight legs they were able to maintain their pace with ease. Long tails stood up in the air above them, and hard beaks clacked open and closed.

I recognised the creatures from Cedric's book. Yaffas. If they caught us, those beaks would hack off our limbs.

Whirring came from two different directions.

'Down,' Aethan yelled.

Hugging Scruffy to my chest, I rolled to the side as the snugalofs dived. Sharp pain lanced as the tip of a wing sliced into my back. A quick feel with my fingers showed me it was just a shallow wound – *this* time.

'What are they? What *are* they?' Ebony shrieked.

'Snugalofs,' I yelled. 'Keep down if you like your head where it is.'

I had to give her credit, for all her hysteria she urged her hagon on with her knees and kept as low as she could.

A low yipping started to our right, growing in volume as more and more voices joined in.

'This way.' Samuel urged his mount to the front and then veered left.

With no better plan, we all followed.

The next time a snugalof attacked I rolled and, at the same time, stuck my sword above my body. Metal clanged on metal as my sword met its wings, but the animal let out a shriek and pivoted to the side. I heard the faint sound of its body smacking into the ground. Hopefully that was the last we'd see of *that* one.

The yipping off to our right got louder. Another quick glance over my shoulder showed the yaffa keeping pace. Snugalofs were lining up to divebomb us. We were *so* screwed.

Isla let out a yell and rapidly fired arrows to our right. I'd expected the yippers to be small and doglike. I couldn't have been more wrong. Think elephants crossed with baboons and you'd almost have it. If Cedric were correct, I was seeing my first egibany.

Running on two legs they raced towards us, their long trunks holding huge rocks. The lead one swung back its trunk and hurled its rock high into the sky. I lost sight of it in the dark but I knew it was heading our way.

'Izzy,' Wolfgang yelled.

'Got it.' I threw my arms up, believing that somehow my magic would stop the rock. For once, I wasn't disappointed. There was a loud thud and then the rock exploded, shattering into a million pieces of shrapnel. My shield protected us, but the snugalofs weren't so lucky.

Two of them screamed and plummeted from the air, their bodies limp before they contacted the ground.

'Two snugalofs with one stone.' Wilfred had a huge grin on his face.

I shook my head at my berserker friend and turned just in time to see Wolfgang hurling fireballs at the egibanies. A few more managed to throw their rocks before they were struck by the fiery tornados that raced amongst them.

I deflected my shield up and backwards, so that this time, the shrapnel flew towards the yaffas. I heard a couple of yelps and for a second the clacking beaks stilled, but then they were back, a few less in their pack, but just as determined to catch us.

The scent of burning flesh scoured my nostrils as the egibanies ran like living torches towards us. Most collapsed but a few kept coming, the urge to destroy us so great that even as the muscle was burnt off their bones, they attacked.

'Bleaurrrr,' I shrieked as the first one swept its trunk towards Brent. He chopped his sword down, severing the limb and the egibany sat down, as if realising for the first time that it was dying.

Samuel urged his horse even further to the left and we followed. The plain had changed around us and now we ran through a woodland area. The trees were far enough apart that we could keep our pace, but in the dim light we had to be careful. If we ran into one of them it would be the last thing we did.

'Trees,' Wilfred said. 'Excellent. Maybe we can lose them.'

I doubted very much we were going to lose the yaffas no matter what we did, but the trees would certainly make it more difficult for the snugalofs to attack.

Something niggled at the back of my mind. Something about trees.

'Almost there,' Samuel called.

'Almost where?' Aethan yelled.

'A safe place.'

A safe place? Here? I felt like I would never be safe again. Not while retchers and snugalofs and yaffas lived in this world. What would be next? The six-toed gurantha?

Suddenly, I knew what was bothering me.

'Watch out for the trees,' I shrieked. 'The trees.'

I was too late.

The gurantha jumped onto Wilfred's back. It pulled back its head and opened its mouth and I screamed as it bit into Wilfred's neck. It tore at skin and flesh and spinal cord, and then it sprang back up into a tree.

Wilfred slumped forward over his mount's neck. His arms hung limp by his side.

I screamed again and lightning shot from my hand, piercing the gurantha's chest. But that wasn't enough. I hurled bolt after bolt at the yaffas, the lightning slamming into the ground amongst them. Some died by direct hit, and others from the shockwaves, their bodies flinging into the air to land in a crumpled heap.

Isla screamed as well, firing arrow-after-arrow while tears streamed down her face.

'Quickly.' It was Samuel. 'Just a few more metres.'

I let him lead Lily towards his safe place, knowing in my heart it was all too late.

Wilfred was gone.

Tears blurred my vision as I stumbled down from Lily. I placed Scruffy on the ground and crawled to where Wilfred lay.

'Wolfgang,' I shrieked. 'We have to heal him.'

Isla was beside me, smoothing her fingers through Wilfred's hair. Blood pooled beneath his neck.

'Wolfgang. We have to hurry. Quick, before it's too late.'

'Child.' Wolfgang's cool fingers touched the side of my face. 'It's already too late.'

'No,' I said, shaking my head. 'No, it can't be. Not Wilfred. Not Wilfred.'

Isla pressed her face up against Wilfred's and let out a howl of grief. Her arms wrapped around him, pulling him to her.

Not Wilfred. No, no, no, it couldn't be.

I took his hand in mine and bent my head over it, sobs taking control of my body.

'No,' I cried. 'Please, no.'

I refused to believe it, I refused to give in. Even though his skin was already cooling, even though no breath came from his body. I couldn't give him up. Not my big brother.

Isla's crying slowed and she lay down, resting her head on his chest and pulling his arm around her. I reached out and stroked the back of her head and she looked up at me through tear-swollen eyes.

'I loved him,' she whispered.

'I know,' I said.

'We need to move him,' Samuel said. 'If you want to save him.'

Isla turned to him, rage distorting her features. '*He's dead*,' she shrieked. 'Can't you leave us alone to mourn?'

'Please,' he said, 'you have to believe me.'

I looked past him and for the first time saw where we were. Buildings, ravaged by time, lay in tumbled ruins around us. A soft glow hummed from the stones.

'Isla. Look.' I pointed to a squat structure that glowed more brightly than the rest. Wide steps led up to a platform. In the middle of the platform a stone carving stood. It thrummed and throbbed with power.

'Where are we?' Isla's voice was tinged with hope.

'The Oracle of Ulandes. Bring him quickly or it will be too late.'

Samuel sprinted towards the platform and Brent and Aethan picked up Wilfred, struggling to carry the big man up the steps. I tried not to look at the blood pooling where he had lain. No-one could come back from that.

Samuel was on his knees in front of the carving, his arms pressed against the ground as he mumbled out a low prayer.

'Lay him there.' He looked up and pointed to the other side of the carving. 'Where she can see him.'

He went back to his praying and I realised he wasn't mumbling, he was speaking a different language.

Wolfgang helped Brent and Aethan manoeuvre Wilfred around the statue. They placed him gently on the ground. Aethan straightened Wilfred's clothing and then bowed his head over him, tears falling onto Wilfred's chest.

Wilfred had been Aethan's lifelong friend. His best friend. He would be lost without him.

He ran back down the stairs, coming back with Wilfred's sword which he placed carefully on Wilfred's chest. Then he wrapped his friend's hands on the pommel and stepped back to where I knelt with Scruffy by my side. He glanced down at me and then knelt beside me, taking my hand in his.

We knelt in a row. Isla, Wolfgang, Brent, Aethan and I, and we held hands and prayed for a miracle.

Samuel stopped praying and gasped, coming up from his knees to his feet in a single, smooth movement. The statue blazed brilliant white and then an ethereal figure stepped out of it.

'Who comes?' she said. 'Who disturbs me after all this time?'

'Mother, I do.' Samuel bowed his head.

She sucked in a breath of air. 'None have called me Mother for hundreds of years. All else called me Ulandes.' She took a step closer to him and reached out a hand. She traced over the tattoos on his arms, a wondering look on her face. 'You have returned,' she sighed. 'My people have returned.'

His face took on an apologetic look. 'It is only I, mother. For now. The rest will follow when they can.'

'I see.' She turned her head towards us. 'And who are these?'

'My travelling companions. Good people all of them. They fight against the evil in the land.'

She floated towards us and stood looking down. I met her eyes and energy flowed out of her and into me.

'And what about this one?' She turned and knelt, placing a hand on Wilfred's shoulder.

'He was the best of men,' Aethan said. 'He was my brother.'

'And mine,' I said.

'And mine,' Brent echoed.

'He was my lover,' Isla said.

'He was a warrior?' Ulandes' hand drifted over the sword.

'We are all warriors mother,' Samuel said.

She stood and faced us, her head cocked to the side as if she were listening to something else.

'I have need of warriors,' she finally said. 'Did you bring him here for me?'

'We brought him hoping you could bring him back to us.' Isla bent her head and let out a sob.

Ulandes moved to Isla's side, kneeling to lift Isla's head with her hand. Isla let out a gasp and a shudder ran through her.

'You have known pain. Great pain and treachery. And yet, your heart is still pure.' She stared into Isla's eyes for a few more moments and then moved to me and laid her palm on my cheek.

'The world lies in wait of you. Your heart must be great if we are to survive, for if you break, the dark side triumphs.'

She looked into my eyes and her voice sounded inside my head. *Never before have there been two. Only one can live, the other must die. In the end you must go alone into the dark and let love guide your hand. Only then will you triumph.*

She moved to Aethan and took his hand. 'Great hardship awaits you. You must rediscover your love if you are to survive, for she will give you the strength you need.' She held his gaze for a moment longer and moved on to Brent.

'Young lion, your heart beats strong and true. Stay true to your cause and all will be well.' His eyes met hers for a moment more and then she moved to Wolfgang.

'Magic maker, we have great need of you. Do not let the dark swallow your broken heart. It will be made whole again.' He blinked but did not look away from her.

Scruffy let out a little woof and she turned and floated back towards me. 'I do apologise,' she said, looking down at him.

He let out another woof and a little whine. She knelt and placed her hands on his fur. 'I cannot read you familiar. You come from a different place.'

He whined and pawed at her.

'Ahhh, I see,' she said, glancing towards me. 'You worry about her.'

He let out a little, growly bark and whined again.

'Fear not,' Ulandes said, 'she will find the way.'

Scruffy licked her on the hand and she stood and moved to Samuel. He knelt in front of her and she rested her hand on his head. 'Have you come to serve me?'

'I come to serve you.' His voice was made of joy.

'I accept your servitude. You will be held above all others. For you were the first.'

'Now wait a minute.' I had all but forgotten about Ebony. 'He can't serve you. He's my slave.'

I groaned and closed my eyes. Things had been going so well.

Ulandes turned towards Ebony with what looked like amusement on her face. 'You seek to thwart me child?' Yes, that was definitely a smile playing around the corners of her mouth.

'He is my slave.' Ebony stamped her foot and put her hands on her hips. 'And you cannot have him. The slave bracelets control him and cannot be removed.' She stopped short of saying, 'So there,' but every line of her body yelled the words.

'These?' Ulandes hands stroked over the bracelets and they opened and fell to the ground.

Ebony gasped as Samuel rubbed his hands over his wrists. 'That is impossible.' Her voice wasn't quite as confident as before. 'Those bracelets were spelled by our unified magic. They cannot fail while it survives.'

Apart from Samuel, only I knew that the bracelets had already failed. But I was betting that even if they hadn't, they would have fallen off when Ulandes touched them.

'The night faeries have held my people for too long. The Ubanty Tribespeople are mine, and I will have them back.' Ulandes' voice rose to a roar and Ebony scampered back down the stairs.

'Now what of him.' As if that conversation had never happened, Ulandes tapped a finger to her lips and looked at Wilfred.

'Please,' Isla said. 'Please save him.'

Ulandes floated over to us and took Isla's face in both her hands. 'Dear heart. Would you give him up to get him back?'

'Yes,' Isla said. 'Just to know he is alive is enough.'

'So be it.' Ulandes stood and moved to Wilfred's side. She placed her hand on his head, then his heart, then on the back of his neck. Light streamed out of her into him. It flowed up and down his body faster and faster before flying up into the air in a swirl of sparks. It hovered a few metres above his body and then speared back towards him, a stream of power that lanced into his heart.

His back arched as he took one choking breath after another. Isla let out a cry of joy and raced towards him but Ulandes stood in her way. 'You will give him up?'

'I promise.' Isla nodded her head. 'Please let me be there when he awakens.'

Ulandes moved to the side and Isla knelt beside Wilfred, taking his hands off the sword and wrapping them in her own. He took another breath and then his eyelids fluttered and opened. He looked up at Isla and said, 'Am I in heaven?'

'No dear heart.' She blinked and a tear trickled down her cheek.

'Why do you cry?' He reached up and wiped it away.

'Because I love you.' She let go of his hands and stood, turning to Ulandes. 'Thank you,' she whispered, bowing her head.

Wilfred looked up at the shining being that hovered above him. 'Beautiful women, angels. Well, if this ain't heaven I don't know what is.'

Ulandes smiled and held out a hand. Wilfred reached up for it and as their fingers touched, tattoos wound around his wrists and up his arms. They were identical to the ones Samuel wore.

'Cool,' he said, looking at his arms. 'I've been thinking of getting me some ink.'

He climbed to his feet and shook his head and then seemed, for the first time, to notice the rest of us kneeling there. He looked at our faces and then pivoted slowly, staring out across the ruins to the trees.

'I died didn't I.' It wasn't a question, more a meek acceptance of the fact.

'Yes child.'

He nodded his head a few times and then turned to look at Ulandes. 'Did they cry? Cause I'm going to be devastated if there wasn't some weeping.'

I let out a choked laugh and clambered to my feet. 'May I?' I asked Ulandes, waiting for her smile before I approached him. He was hers now, and as much as I hated knowing he wouldn't be in my life every day, Isla was right. After having lost him for good, knowing that somewhere Wilfred was cracking stupid jokes and generally being a goof head was enough.

'I may have shed a tear or two,' I said, wrapping my arms around him.

He lifted me up and shook me side-to-side as he hugged me. 'Sorry to scare you.'

As soon as I was free Aethan grabbed him, clasping him hard. 'Don't do that again,' he said hoarsely.

Wilfred pulled back and looked him in the face. 'I don't get to go with you, do I?'

Aethan shook his head and Wilfred turned to Ulandes. 'Will I see them again?'

'You will be there when they need you the most.'

Brent clasped his arm and then pulled him into a bear hug, clapping him on the back while saying, 'Try to keep out of trouble.'

Wolfgang wished him good luck and goodbye and then there was just Isla.

Tears glistened in her eyes, but her smile made up for them. Beatific, she glowed as she gazed up at him. 'I always knew you were destined for greater things.'

He reached out and gently stroked her face. 'Can she...?' He turned to look at Ulandes.

'No child. She cannot come where we go. She has tasks she must complete elsewhere.'

He sighed and turned back to Isla. 'You were the great love of my life.'

She balled her fist and punched him gently. 'What's with the *were?*'

He smiled and then pulled her to him, lowering his head to hers.

I turned away to give them some privacy and met Aethan's eyes. He watched my face intently for a few seconds and then looked away and ran his hands through his hair. He was having a rough night. First losing his best friend and then finding out said best friend was in love with your sister and vice versa.

All too soon Ulandes said, 'Child, we must go.'

Wilfred pulled away from Isla and went to stand with Samuel.

'What about the monsters?' Wolfgang asked.

'I have sent them back,' Ulandes said. 'It will take great power to bring them over again.'

She turned and floated back to the statue, seeping into it as easily as she had come out.

Wilfred turned to look at Samuel. 'After you,' he said, holding his hand out.

'Well,' Samuel shot him a grin, 'I *am* number one.' He walked to the statue and stepped into it.

Wilfred followed him, stopping at the base of the statue to turn and look at us. He gave us a two-finger salute and, just before he stepped into the statue, said in his best

Arnold Schwarzenegger accent, 'I'll be back.' And just like that he was gone.

We stood for a while, none of us speaking, all of us staring at the statue. It's not every day that you get to meet a deity, and it didn't seem right to break that moment with words.

One-by-one we drifted back down towards the trees where Ebony waited with the horses.

'Well,' she said, 'this is a fine mess. Who's going to get my dinner now?'

I stared at her in disbelief. After everything that had just happened, *that* was her concern.

'You'll manage,' Isla said, 'or you'll go hungry. Those are your only two options.'

We unsaddled the horses and rubbed them down, eating the travelling food as we worked. Then we pulled out our blankets and lay around a fire Wolfgang lit. For the first time in a long time we didn't post a watch. Ulandes had said we would be safe here for the night and we believed her. The weight of her presence blanketed us softly, soothing our sorrows and our fear. One-by-one we fell asleep, none of us stirring again till the sun was high in the sky.

Chapter Twelve

Home Sweet Home

'**Y**ou can't come.'

'Try to stop me.'

'It's not safe.'

'All the more reason to come.'

Aethan and I were arguing about whether or not I would accompany him to Trillania that night. It had been going on for a while and we were getting to the petty end of the discussion.

He sighed and, as if to a very 'special' child, said, 'It's not safe for *you*.'

'I can look after myself.'

He gave me a significant look that I assumed was meant to remind me of what had happened the last time we had gone. The time Santanas had known I was there.

'I was startled.' It was the only excuse I could think of for my reaction. The truth was that Santanas scared me stupid, but if I admitted that to Aethan I wasn't ever going back.

I was enjoying our argument. It reminded me of the old days, before Galanta's spell. It was also helping dull the ache in my chest. If I weren't arguing with Aethan, I would be moping about Wilfred.

I looked back to check on Isla. She was chatting to Wolfgang and Brent, an animated look on her face. Knowing that Wilfred was alive had given her a reason to live. I was sure under all that chatter she was working on a way to reunite with him.

I shook my head and turned back to Aethan, but Ebony had ridden up beside him. *Bugger.* We'd have to finish the argument later. *That* thought put a smile on my face.

I dropped back towards the others, keen to let Aethan deal with Ebony. When we had hopped up that morning she had done her best to turn one of us into her personal slave. She had finally given up when Isla had pointed out that she and Aethan were also heirs to a throne and were capable of looking after themselves.

She had muttered to herself for a while, things like, 'Wait till my father finds out about this.' But once she realised none of us cared, she even gave that up.

It turned out that she was perfectly capable of saddling her own hagon and packing up her own tent. Who would have guessed?

We were riding as hard as we could without injuring the horses, and had covered good ground during the day. Aethan estimated that after today it was only two more days till we reached the border of Isilvitania. The problem was, that those two days would be spent in goblin territory. And we all remembered how well *that* had turned out the last time.

Isla moved her mount towards me so that we could speak unheard.

'How are you?' I asked.

'Fantastic,' she said. 'You?'

'Good. So, urrmmm, you and Wilfred. How long has that been going on?'

She looked at me out of the corner of her eye. 'Diplomatically or really?'

I smiled. That was one of the things I loved about her. So many layers that nobody else suspected. 'Let's start with diplomatically and then move onto really.'

She clapped her hands together and laughed. 'Excellent, I do love leaving the best to last. Well we've known each other for a long time, but I always thought of him as my little brother's buddy. Spending time together on this trip enriched our friendship to the point that we thought it was safe to take it further.'

I pulled a face at her. 'How boring. Give me really.'

'I've fancied him for a long time. I like strong, manly men and they don't come much more manly than that.'

'Or hairy,' I added.

She grinned. 'Keeps you warm in winter.'

I gasped. 'That long? Since last winter?'

'Try winter three years ago. I seduced him on his eighteenth birthday. We've been bumping ugglies ever since.'

'Isla!' I let out a shocked laugh. 'Is that why you came on this trip?'

'Partly,' she admitted. 'I would have come anyway. I don't trust the night faeries.' She shaded her eyes with her hand and looked toward Ebony. 'And I *certainly* don't trust her.'

Following Aethan's lead, we pushed our mounts back up to a canter. Conversation became impossible over the noise of the horses' hooves and tack. It wasn't till we slowed back to a walk that Isla said, 'All right your time to spill. How long have you and Aethan been an item?'

I considered her question from every angle, making sure I wasn't going to trigger the Border Guard Secrecy Spell before I answered. 'A proper item for about a year, but I've had a thing for him since I was a small girl. It took me that long to convince him I wasn't his little sister.'

She nodded her head. 'Wilfred used to talk about you occasionally. I could never work out how you fitted in.'

I looked at her, wanting to tell her, but knowing that I couldn't. I was pretty sure she could handle the news, hell, I was more than pretty sure, but it was the verbalisation part that was the problem. 'I want to tell you everything,' I said.

'But you can't.'

'Physically, it would be impossible for me.'

She was silent for a while before she answered. 'I suspected something like that was going on. A couple of times when Wilfred and I were together he had a fit. It looked remarkably similar to what happened to you that time.'

She was smart. So smart in fact that....

'You asked me that question on purpose,' I said.

'Hmmmm?' she said, an innocent expression on her face.

'When I had that fit, it was in response to your question on what I did with my nights in the barracks.'

She smirked and sung, 'Perhaps, perhaps, perhaps.'

'There's a name for that sort of behaviour.'

'Clever cookie?'

I laughed. 'No. Entrapment.'

She shrugged a shoulder. 'No-one ever tells me anything, so over the years I've worked out ways to glean what I need.'

'Did you ever think that if you let people know just how clever you are that they might share information with you?'

She considered me seriously. 'No,' she said. 'I hadn't looked at it like that before. Besides, I kind of enjoy the challenge.'

'Well, when Aethan becomes head of the Border Guards I'm going to suggest he makes you his Spy Master.'

She clapped her hands together. 'Spy Master. Oh, what fun!'

I smiled. It was exactly that sort of behaviour that would make her perfect for the job. People wouldn't see the brilliant mind hiding under the ditsy exterior.

We turned in early that night. We would be entering goblin territory and would need our wits about us.

Brent and Wolfgang took the early watch, leaving Aethan, Isla and me to take the late one. Historically, most attacks occur in the hour before dawn. It was safer to have three of us watching then. Ebony didn't offer to help, and frankly, I don't think we would have let her even if she did.

I raced through my evening preparations, desperate to get to bed before Aethan. I had to be there waiting for him or he would go without me. I knew it.

I lay down with Scruffy, closing my eyes and slowing my breathing. Getting to sleep had been getting easier and easier. Wolfgang had told me it was a trait of dream-walkers. As I got more proficient I would be able to sleep when and where I wanted at the blink of an eye.

My problem was that Aethan was a dream-walker too. And he'd been doing it longer.

It didn't take me long to step through to Trillania. Either Aethan was already gone or I had beaten him, because he wasn't at the campsite. I would have to wait till I was sure he wasn't coming and then go looking for him.

I shivered and rubbed my hands up-and-down my arms. I hoped he'd hurry.

A few minutes later he shimmered into view. 'You're not coming.' His heart wasn't really in it though, I could tell.

'Yep. Sure am.'

'What if he comes for you?'

'What if who comes for her?' Isla's voice intruded before I could give him my well thought out argument.

'Isla?' I wasn't sure which of us was more shocked.

'What?' Aethan said.

'How?' I spluttered.

She held up her arm. Wilfred's armband lay snug around her bicep. 'He wears it on his wrist, but hey, he has big hands. And you know what they say about a man with big hands?'

'It's big feet,' I cut her off before she could make me blush.

'You can't come,' Aethan said.

'Who? Her or me?' I pointed at Isla. A part of me was secretly delighted that she had worked out our secret. I was sick of having to keep it from her. The other part had to admit that Trillania was not currently a safe place for an untrained dream-walker. Especially not if they were with me.

'Both of you.' He shoved his hands through his hair so fiercely I thought for sure he would wake with a bald patch.

'So...,' Isla spun as she spoke, 'where exactly are we?'

Unsure of whether the spell would activate if she were there with us, I let Aethan answer. I didn't feel like writhing in pain.

'It's called Trillania. It's where we go when we dream.'

'Where dream-walkers go?'

Aethan shook his head and I was tempted to conjure up a set of drums for a drumroll. 'No, where everybody goes. Dream-walkers are conscious of being here. That is the only difference.'

'But....' I could see the cogs in her brain whirling faster and faster as she contemplated all the ramifications of what Aethan has said. 'And these bring us here?' She looked at the armband.

'They bring you as a dream-walker. The dream-catcher,' he stopped and looked at her and she nodded her head to indicate that she knew what he was talking about, 'can stop anyone who has worn one of these from coming here.'

'Bad shit that goes down here?'

'Will happen to your body when you awaken.'

'*If* you awaken,' I added.

'Are we the only ones that come here?'

I shook my head.

'Goblins?'

'Orcs, giants, trolls, mudmen. They all have their own version of those.' Aethan pointed at the armband.

'I can see why you keep it secret,' she said. 'So, what are we up to tonight?'

'You can't....'

'Aethan,' I cut her off, 'let her come. You know she's going to creep around here anyway. This way we can keep an eye on her.' I turned so he couldn't see my face and winked at her. 'And besides, we could do with the extra firepower if anything happens.'

'What do we use as a weapon?' Isla asked.

'Whatever you want.' I held out my hands and a crossbow appeared in them.

She let out a delighted laugh. 'That's so cool.' A bow appeared in the air in front of her and she snatched it before it could hit the ground.

'Hold our hands and empty your mind,' Aethan said. 'We're going to find Rako.'

'Be ready,' I cautioned her. 'Bad shit can happen.' I laughed. That had been Aethan's brief to me when my witch half had her first trip to Trillania. It had seemed so insufficient at the time but now I got it. It perfectly summed up Trillania.

The world shimmered around us and when we opened our eyes we were standing in front of Isilvitania Castle.

'Home,' Isla said. 'I didn't think I'd miss it so much.'

'Get down.' Rako's voice came from the trees behind us.

We ducked and ran to where he hid with some of the other Border Guards. Isla threw a few of them an impish grin and waved.

'What's she doing here?' Rako hissed.

'She worked it out,' Aethan said.

'Yes, but why isn't Wilfred wearing that thing?'

'That's what we came to tell you Sir.' There'd been a lot of calling Rako 'Sir' lately.

'He's dead?' Rako's voice came out in a choked whisper.

'Yes, I mean no, I mean he was.'

'He was dead?'

'We were pursued by monsters last night and a Ubanty Tribesman led us to the shelter of the Oracle of Ulandes. A gurantha killed Wilfred but Ulandes brought him back.'

I had showed them Cedric's school project that morning and we had been taking turns reading it since. It was knowledge we couldn't afford to lose.

'I have no idea what most of what you just said means,' Rako said. 'So is Wilfred resting?'

I shook my head. 'Ulandes took him. It was the price to be paid for bringing him back.'

Rako stared at us while the Border Guard around us muttered angrily. 'We must get him back,' one of them said.

'You don't understand,' Isla said. 'He has gone in servitude to a Goddess. He will be back when she wills it and not before.'

Rako rubbed his fingers over his scar. 'I thought I'd heard everything.' He shook his head and then poked it back out of the trees to check the castle.

'Sir,' Aethan said, 'we lost Luke.'

I waited for Rako to ask us where we had left him, but by the look on his face he knew what Aethan meant. It was as if someone had ripped an energy rug out from underneath him. His eyes dulled and his shoulders sagged as he asked, 'How?'

'Ghouls.'

Rako scrubbed his hands across his face a few times. 'He was a good man.'

'There's something else,' Aethan said.

'Not Brent?'

'No, the rest of us are fine. It's about the last time we were here.'

I held my breath while Aethan filled Rako in on what we had seen after we had left him, only letting that breath out when I knew for sure he was going to leave out the part about Santanas and me. I fully expected an explosion of sorts but Rako was too stunned by the news to react to the fact that we had disobeyed him. Again. I guess he was getting used to it.

'How many?' he asked in a hoarse voice.

'Thousands,' Aethan said. 'Tens of thousands. They stretched toward the horizon as far as we could see.

'And it was definitely him?'

Aethan shot me a look and said, 'Pretty sure about that.'

One of the other guards let out a whistle. 'We're going to need every man we've got.

'And more,' another one said.

'Not if we can stop Galanta,' I said.

Rako nodded. 'We need to cut the head off the snake.' He froze and peered back out of the bushes, sucking in a breath at what he saw. He pulled his sword free and said, 'You three need to get back. It is more important than ever that you bring the night faery safely home.'

I peered over his shoulder. Orcs were massing near the entrance to the castle.

'We will meet you at the border the day after tomorrow.' He gestured to the other guards and they linked hands and disappeared. They re-appeared a second later right behind the orcs, their blades slicing heads from shoulders before the orcs even knew they were there. Just as fast as they appeared, they were gone.

'Where'd they go?' Isla moved some foliage to the side as if to move towards the castle.

'Not our problem,' Aethan said, grabbing our hands. 'They have their job and we have ours.'

The world shimmered and we were back at the campsite.

'Take that thing off when you wake up.' Aethan tapped the armband.

Isla's face got the whimsical look it did when she was up to no good.

'How are you going to get Wilfred back if you die here?'

She pouted. 'Oh fine.' She closed her eyes and disappeared.

'You're going to use that on her forever aren't you?' I said.

He smiled his crooked half smile I loved so much. 'Nice to finally have a way to get her to obey me.' He pulled a face. 'Not that there is anything good about what happened to Wilfred.' The smile was gone. Instead, pain creased the skin around his eyes.

'I know what you mean.' I reached out and took his hand and he squeezed my fingers.

'You know, right up to that last minute, I really thought there was something going on between you and Wilfred. I never guessed it was Isla.'

Questions started whirling around in my head. Questions I couldn't bring myself to voice. 'I told you he was like a brother to me,' I said.

'That's not technically true.' He was still holding my hand. '*He* said you were like a sister to *him*.'

I took a deep breath. 'So you thought I had a crush on him?'

He nodded.

'And now you know I don't.'

He cocked his head to the side and stared at me. I was totally aware of the feel of his fingers still grasping mine. Never had such a small area of skin dominated so much of my mind.

'No.'

'No, you don't know, or no you do?' Honestly, the man was totally infuriating. What did I have to do to get him to realise *he* was the one I crushed on?

He tugged on my hand and I took an involuntary step towards him. 'The only thing I really know,' his voice was a husky rumble, 'is that someone is trying to wake me up.' He let go of my hand, closed his eyes and was gone.

'Damn,' I said, stamping my foot with the word. 'Damn, damn, damn, damn, damn.' I got the vaguest feeling, as if someone were shaking my shadow. He was right. They were trying to wake us up. I closed my eyes and willed myself back into my body, opening my eyes to the vision of Wolfgang, with one hand on my shoulder and the other held up to his lips.

'Shhhhh,' he whispered. 'Goblins.'

***

The others were already up when I crawled out of my tent. Ebony's eyes were huge as she hugged her arms around her chest and stared off into the trees. For the first time I felt a wave of sympathy for the woman. She'd been sent alone to a strange land to marry a man she'd never met. Along the way she'd been hunted by ghouls and all sorts of other monsters, and the only person she had known from before was gone. Loneliness and fear radiated off her, yet still she had the guts to go on.

A wave of guilt swept over me. The poor thing needed a friend and I had let my jealousy blindside me.

'We're going to have to leave the tents,' Aethan whispered.

'But then they'll know for sure that we were here.' Brent ran his hands through his hair and shook his head. 'We're too far from the border to risk that.'

'Wolfgang?'

'I can hide the campsite. They'll only find it if they stumble into an object they can't see.'

Aethan nodded and said, 'It'll have to do. Get your things and mount up.'

I tugged at Brent's sleeve. 'Do they suspect we're here?'

'Don't think so. Looks like a routine patrol. But they are heading this way.'

I ducked back into the tent and threw my things into the saddle bags. By the time I got back with Scruffy, the horses were saddled. I threw my bag over Lily and secured it, then lifted Scruffy up onto her back and mounted.

By the position of the moon we couldn't have been asleep for more than a couple of hours. That was a couple more than Brent and Wolfgang had had so I stifled my yawns and tried to stay alert.

Brent led us out of the campsite in single file. When we were clear, Wolfgang waved his hands in the air. I tried to feel what he was doing but all I got were tingles running over the skin on my arms.

Little pieces of the area surrounding the campsite seemed to snow down over the tents. Bits of trunk and leaf and ground all piecing together like a gigantic jigsaw puzzle till the tents were gone. Brent swept over the ground with a leaf-covered branch, and the last signs that we had ever been there disappeared.

We walked the horses for the next hour, my nerves twisting tighter and tighter as I waited for goblins to break from the trees. I tried not to think about Cedric's book, but the monsters from it were burned into my brain. There were so many more we still hadn't encountered, and that made my stomach tighten into a knot.

'Wolfgang,' I whispered. 'Can we shield ourselves as we ride?'

'We could,' he said, 'but we would need to continuously shift the spell. It wouldn't be long before we were exhausted.'

I rode in silence while I thought about that. 'What about if we didn't try to exactly match our surroundings, but just camouflaged ourselves? That way the spell would shift with us.'

He scratched at his beard as he considered my words. 'It wouldn't be perfect.'

'But it would be better than nothing,' I said. *Anything* had to be better than walking around totally exposed.

Aethan held up his hand and we pulled our horses to a halt. An area of extra-dense trees stood off to our side. I tried hard not to think about the guranthas that could be hiding there.

'We need to get some rest,' he said. 'If we encounter goblins tomorrow with little or no sleep we won't stand a chance.'

'Brent, you and Wolfgang sleep first. You too Ebony.'

I slipped off Lily and rubbed her down, apologising as I replaced the saddle. She whinnied and pushed her head into my hands as if to demand an ear scratch as payment for the inconvenience.

Aethan and Isla had already set up watch to the north and south-east, so I moved to the south-west of the camp. A cool breeze raised goose-pimples on my arms. The warm weather was coming to an end.

'Let me know if you hear anything boy.' I bent down and scratched Scruffy behind the ears. He pushed into my hand, twisting his head from side-to-side and letting out a satisfied rumble.

I let my eyes relax as I stared off into the darkness, trying to be alert for any movement that would indicate trouble. Stamping my feet and shaking my head, I pushed away from the trunk I had been leaning against. My eyelids felt far too heavy to make myself comfortable tonight. I would never hear the end of it if Aethan found me asleep on my watch.

Or dead with my throat ripped out by a brolonta.

That thought woke me more than any other could. Part of me wished I had never found Cedric's book. But the rational part acknowledged that we would all be dead if I hadn't. That didn't help with the fatigue from the fear-derived sleepless hours the book had given me.

It seemed like forever before Brent came out and told me to hit the sack. I grabbed my blanket and dream-catcher from my saddle and headed in the direction Brent had pointed. Ebony was still asleep, her blanket wrapped tightly around her. I lay down next to her and pulled my blanket over me, closing my eyes and trying to relax.

Exhaustion claimed me more easily than I had thought it would and it felt like only moments later that the early-morning light woke me. One more day. We only had to make it one more day before we would be back in faery territory.

I sat up and rubbed at my eyes, looking around to see where everybody was.

Isla appeared before me, her skin wet and face clean. 'There's a small brook a few hundred yards that direction.' She pointed off to the north.

'Do I look that bad?' I climbed to my feet and arched my back.

'It's not so much the look.' She grinned at me. 'It's the smell.'

I poked my tongue out at her and picked up one of the empty water bottles. 'Come on boy,' I said, heading off in the direction she had pointed.

After my initial blind approach, the low murmur of the water led me the rest of the way. I knelt by the stream and filled up the water bottle, then I undid my sword belt, pulled my fur vest off over my head and started to remove my shirt. Ebony's voice stopped me.

'Oh look at you. You're so cute.'

A quick glance showed me Scruffy sitting on the bank, far enough from me that he would have advance notice if I decided he should have a bath as well. So who was she talking to? Aethan?

I pulled my shirt back down.

'Where'd you come from? Can I pat you?'

I slid my sword out of its sheath and followed the brook around to the right. I paused at the start of a bend and peered toward Ebony.

Wet hair cascaded down her bare back, finishing at the junction where her tiny waist flared into her hips. Her full breasts hung like perfect pendulums as she leant forward, extending an arm out in front of her. She was glorious in her nudity, innocent of the way the light danced over the water sprinkled across her skin.

If it had been Aethan she was talking to, I'm not sure what I would have done. But it wasn't. Instead, a fluffy animal about half the size of Scruffy, sat just beyond her reach.

'There, there,' she said. 'I won't hurt you.'

'Ebony,' I whispered. 'Stop.'

She froze in the act of moving a foot forward.

The animal started at my voice, small wings fanning out on either side of its body.

'Oh, don't be scared,' Ebony cooed as it backed away.

Huge eyes stared up at us and it trembled visibly as I moved to Ebony's side. A long tail curved around its four feet and floppy ears fell to each side of its snout. It was totally covered in black fluffy fur that just begged to have fingers plunged into it, and yet every cell in my body was screaming at me.

'It's a narathymia,' I said.

'A narawhatty?' Ebony took her eyes off the creature and turned toward me, and that was when it attacked.

It thrust its wings out as it launched itself at her, the claws on its legs extended like twenty tiny knives.

'Stop.' I threw an arm out and it froze, hanging suspended an inch from Ebony's face.

She gasped and stumbled backwards, her legs and arms cartwheeling almost comically in her attempt to get away. 'Kill it,' she gasped.

I stared into the creature's eyes and the sadness I saw there almost overwhelmed me.

'No.' I shook my head. 'It's acting under duress.'

'I don't care what it's acting under.' Ebony thrust her head through the neck of her dress and shimmied the material down her body. 'It tried to kill me.'

I watched its reaction carefully as I said the next words. 'They have her child.'

It shook its head frantically as it mewed. I wrapped my arms around her and released my spell. 'There, there,' I said as I rocked her. 'We'll get your baby back.'

She let out a high-pitched cry and buried her face under my arm as her body shook. Then she looked up at me as if seeking the truth of my words in my eyes. 'I can't promise we'll succeed,' I said. 'But I promise we will try.'

She blinked a few times, wriggling higher up my body till she was wrapped around my neck. Then she looked down at Scruffy and hissed.

'No,' I said. 'Bad narathymia.'

She licked a paw and started to clean her head as I walked back to get the rest of my things.

Ebony walked beside me as we made our way back to the others, her wet hair reminding me that I hadn't had time to wash.

'Ah Izzy, ' Wolfgang said, 'I was thinking about what you suggested last night and I… is that what I think it is?'

I bent down and grabbed my blanket. 'Ahuh. A narathymia.'

'But it's so friendly.'

'It tried to kill me,' Ebony said, 'and she saved it.'

I turned to look at her. 'You know that makes no sense right?'

'It's adorable. What's its name?' Isla put her horses hoof back on the ground and skipped over to me.

'Mia,' I said.

Isla held her hand out to Mia, letting her smell it before she proceeded to stroke her back. Mia lifted her head into the air and purred. 'I saddled Lily for you,' Isla said, scratching Mia under her chin.

Brent pushed through the thick trees into the clearing. 'Safe to go,' he said.

We mounted and followed him out in single file.

'You're really taking that *thing* with us?'

'Her name is Mia.'

Ebony pulled a face and moved her hagon away from me. 'She's dangerous, that's what she is.'

I responded by poking my tongue out at her departing back. I may have found some respect for the woman but it didn't mean I had to like her.

'Making friends?'

I jumped and turned guiltily towards Aethan. 'I never promised to be her friend.'

'I think what you said, and correct me if I'm wrong, was that you were looking forward to painting each other's nails.'

Damn the man and his bloody memory.

'I was being facetious.'

He snorted. 'Anyway I wasn't talking about Ebony.' He held out a hand toward Mia. 'Will she let me pat her?'

Mia stopped her grooming and looked at Aethan's outstretched hand. Her lips pulled back from rows of tiny, razor-sharp teeth.

'Careful.' I was never going to hear the end of it if she bit off a finger.

She pushed her nose towards his hand, tentatively sniffing. Then she looked down to where Scruffy sat nestled against my chest, growled, and jumped onto Aethan's hand, scampering up his arm to curl around his neck.

'She prefers to be a single child,' I said as she set about grooming Aethan's neck.

Isla appeared off to our left. She jogged over to where her horse trotted behind me and patted his nose. 'Brent said to head further south,' she said.

'Goblins?'

She nodded and turned, disappearing back into the trees within a few paces.

We adjusted our course and rode in silence, the four of us listening for signs of pursuit. When another ten minutes or so had gone by Wolfgang rode over to my side.

'I think we can make it work,' he said quietly.

I stared at him for a few moments and then shook my head. 'Sorry. No idea.'

'That idea you had last night, about camouflaging us, instead of shielding us.'

'Oh.' In all the excitement of the morning I had forgotten about that.

Isla reappeared just long enough to hiss, 'Further south.'

'Do you think we should try it now?' I craned my head to search the trees around us. The fear of being found was starting to wind my nerves tight.

'We could try.'

'What do we need to do?'

'Similar to what I did last night, but instead of blending ourselves into the static background and pinning it down, we make ourselves look like a piece of the landscape.'

Huh. 'I couldn't actually tell what you did last night.'

'Hold onto my hand this time. Sometimes skin-to-skin contact helps.'

I reached across and grasped his hand, closing my eyes to better feel what he was doing. I could feel the shape of us in his head like cardboard cutouts; Aethan, Ebony, Wolfgang and I riding, with the packhorses and Brent and Isla's horses trailing behind us. Isla and Brent ran ahead of us as they searched for danger.

Wolfgang reached out and it seemed like he smoothed the edges of the cutouts. Suddenly they weren't so much like cardboard, but more like Play Dough as he squished. Hard, finished edges tapered thinner and thinner until they blended into the surroundings.

I opened my eyes and looked over at Aethan. I could make him out because I knew he was there, but it looked as if tree trunks, shrubs and grasses moved through the forest.

'Cool,' I said, holding my arm up for inspection. Foliage and shadow danced across the surface of my skin.

'Yes,' Wolfgang said. 'I think that will do quite nicely.'

'Please tell me one of you did this.' Isla's voice came from beside me.

I jumped and stared in the direction of her voice.

'Wolfgang's a genius,' I said.

'Hmmm,' she didn't sound convinced. 'How are we meant to find you if we lose track of where you are? And if all hell breaks loose and we have to fight, how can I be sure I'm not going to put an arrow into one of you?'

Aethan snorted. 'She's right.'

'I'm always right.' I couldn't see the look on her face but I knew which one would be there.

'Yes, I see.' Wolfgang said. 'I will remove it at once.'

I felt him reach out and take the nicely-blended edges and tuck them back in until the cutout feel was back.

Isla pushed a loose strand of hair back behind her ear and then held her arm up for inspection. 'Much better.' She disappeared back into the forest.

We rode in silence until Brent appeared. 'You need to head north,' he said. 'There's a goblin village straight ahead.'

We adjusted our course but a few minutes later Isla reappeared. 'Where are you going? If you keep on this course you're going to run straight into a patrol.'

'Brent told us there was a village the direction we were heading.'

She swore gently. 'Well then, head further south.'

Aethan shrugged before turning Adare's head the direction she had pointed. Mia hissed and wound her way around his throat, clearly unhappy about being disturbed.

'Sorry girl.' He raised a hand and patted her head and her hisses turned to purrs.

Over the next couple of hours, Brent and Isla appeared more and more frequently. We rode in silence, every one of us affected by the stress of weaving our way through enemy territory.

The sun was heading toward the horizon when Isla burst from a thick stand of trees and sprinted towards us. Brent was right behind her.

'Do it again,' she hissed, waving an arm at us. 'Make us invisible.'

I reached out towards Wolfgang, my mind clanging into his. I felt his slight admonishment before he joined with me. Together we pushed at the cutouts in our head, smoothing the edges.

Isla and Brent reached us, vaulting into the saddles of their horses moments before we had finished.

'They're everywhere,' Brent whispered. 'Massing near the border.'

'We need to get through to warn Rako,' Aethan said.

A group of goblins trotted through the trees off to our right. They pivoted their heads from side-to-side as they searched for us. I heard Mia hiss, but apart from that we were totally silent.

I felt naked and totally exposed as their eyes passed over our group. Sweat dribbled down my face as I stared at them. It wasn't that I feared them – I knew we could easily take that small a group. It was more the fear of being totally outnumbered. Again. That hadn't been working out so well for us. The first time we had taken a swim, and the second, well... let's just say that the fear I would reach for black magic to save us, outweighed my fear of the goblins.

As the goblins turned their attention away from us and trotted into the trees, a hand the same colour as the surroundings reached out and took mine. 'It'll be okay.' Aethan's murmur was so low only I could hear him.

I stared sideways into his midnight-blue eyes.

He squeezed my hand. 'You're good.'

'How did you know?' My voice trailed off as he ran his thumb back-and-forth over the skin of my hand.

'What you were thinking?

I nodded my head.

'It would be your worst fear, wouldn't it? Becoming like him?'

'Like Santanas. Yes.' I nodded my head. 'He was good once too.'

'He crossed a line. You won't get anywhere near that line.' He squeezed my hand once before he released it.

Dodging groups of goblins, we crept towards the border. Heavily-forested hills rose around us, tapering down into a long, meandering valley. If we could just get down that valley we would be back in Isilvitania where Rako would be waiting for us.

I thought my heart would burst from the waiting and the creeping. Standing silent while goblins' eyes passed over us was harder, much harder than fighting. Sweat dribbled down my spine as I fought the urge to rip my sword out of its holster and attack.

They knew we were there and they searched, yelling to each other in their guttural language. We walked the horses, moving as slowly as possible so that our camouflage was not discovered.

One hour passed, then another as we mimicked field mice hiding from a cat. My jaw ached from clenching my teeth and my muscles trembled with nervous energy. The hills rose steeper and steeper, funnelling us down the valley. The goblin groups grew more numerous as the topography drove us together.

Walk, walk, freeze. Walk, walk, freeze.

The agony of waiting to be discovered grew till I thought I would fly apart with the suspense.

'Not much further,' Aethan whispered as we hid amongst a stand of trees. 'One more corner and then the valley flattens out.'

'Home,' Isla sighed. 'If we make it, I won't even mind Mother yelling at me.'

A goblin, taller than the rest, pointed up the sides of the hills. A score of them broke out of his group and scrambled upwards, their daggers drawn as they searched for us.

We crept through the trees, trying to keep as much foliage between us and them as possible. I hung onto Aethan's words as we went. Only one more corner. It felt like forever since we'd left and suddenly I longed to be home. I missed Sabby, I missed Grams and I wanted Mum so badly a deep ache started in my chest.

I snorted softly and shook my head. The last thing I needed to be thinking about at that moment, was sitting in the kitchen eating Mum's lemon cake. There were goblins all around and the chance of one of them bumping into us was increasing dramatically. I had to concentrate on the problem at hand – staying alive.

In single file we hugged the edge of the valley. I could feel my breathing accelerating. My heart beat a rugged dance in my chest. Around the corner we went, stopping once to avoid collision with a group of goblins. The valley narrowed even further as it curved, and then suddenly it was opening up in front of us, the mountains sweeping away from each other.

I looked out towards the plain, towards Isilvitania, towards home. Somewhere there Rako was waiting for us. There was just one problem. The goblins that had been travelling down the valley were spread out on the plain in front of us. And while the camouflage was working with the trees all around us I didn't think it was going to cut it on an open plain.

***

'How far away is Rako?' Isla murmured.

We had followed the mountain range around to the left to stay clear of the milling goblins.

'Not sure.' Aethan shook his head. 'We're going to have to wait till night and sneak around them. Rako won't have brought enough Guards to deal with this.' He gestured towards the goblins, or at least I think he did. I couldn't be entirely sure because his arm blended in with the rocks behind him.

'What are they up to?' Brent said. 'Are they planning an attack?'

Cold fear walked down my spine. Was it possible they knew that a lot of the Guard were away acting as emissaries? Until they all returned, Isilvitania was vulnerable. This in turn meant that England was. And if the goblins went through the veil after attacking Isilvitania they would end up in Eynsford. Again. But *this* time we wouldn't be there to stop them.

The afternoon shadows lengthened as we cowered against the mountain, hidden in plain sight. Night couldn't come fast enough. As more and more goblins flowed into the basin we took turns to try to sleep. I had a feeling it was going to be a very long night.

'Orcs,' Brent whispered.

I opened my eyes and sat up, peering out into the twilight.

Huge, hairy orcs were marching out of the valley. Their shaggy, orange bodies reminded me of Wilfred and suddenly I missed him with a fierceness that took my breath away.

But the orange hair was where the similarities between him and his maternal side ended. Where Wilfred had looked human, the orcs resembled Mr Potato Head gone wrong: ears not quite level, eyes that didn't match, noses that were crooked on their already crooked faces and teeth sticking out from under their lips at weird angles. I certainly wouldn't be taking one home to meet my mother.

Isla sniffed and wiped her eyes and Aethan reached over and took her hand. 'I miss the hairy bastard too,' he whispered.

The goblins, who had previously had their attention fixed on the open plain, turned toward the orcs. The two groups eyed each other warily. While they might be fighting on the same team, it didn't mean that there wasn't any infighting.

'This might be our only chance,' Aethan said. 'Let's go.'

I pulled myself back up into Lily's saddle as quietly as I could and placed Scruffy in front of me. Slowly we walked the horses out onto the plain. I'd thought riding down the valley had been nerve-wracking, but it had nothing on this.

We made our way around the edge of the goblins, keeping as much space between us and them as we could. When we were past them, we turned our horses so the goblins were behind us.

I sent out nothing-to-see-here vibes as the muscles between my shoulder blades twitched waiting for an arrow to pierce them. It took every ounce of self-control not to kick my heels into Lily's sides and gallop screaming across the plain. I could hear the orcs and goblins squabbling and I prayed to the Great Dark Sky that they would be too focused on each other to notice any irregularities between our camouflage and the surroundings.

The dying sun helped as it cast a long shadow out onto the plain. The further away from the goblins we got, the closer to normal my heart beat became. And then finally we were too far away for them to be able to see us. I sagged in my saddle, the fear oozing away with my strength.

We rode for a couple more hours before Aethan proclaimed we were back in faery territory. By then the sun had gone and a million stars twinkled above us. I felt Wolfgang playing with our outlines once more and the shadow and darkness slid off my arm, leaving my skin unmarked.

Normally we would have stopped for the evening, but this close to home, and with that many enemies behind us, there would be no stopping tonight.

'What's that?' It was the first thing Ebony had said all afternoon. 'Over there. Is it a fire?'

We all looked where she pointed. Off to our left a tiny light flickered a couple more times before disappearing. Aethan put his hands to his mouth and a nightingale carolled in the still, night air. It took me a second to realise it was coming from him.

There was a few seconds' silence and then another nightingale responded. Aethan pulled Adare's head around and the big stallion snorted and headed towards where the fire had been. Within minutes we came across Rako's camp.

'I thought you'd gotten lost.' Rako and seven of the Guard came out to meet us.

'Waylaid.' Aethan told them about the enemy that was massing at the border.

When he had finished, Rako let out a low whistle. 'Sounds like we'd better head for home.'

Ebony nudged her horse forward until she was abreast with Aethan.

He held out his hand towards her. 'Rako, this is Orion's bride-to-be, Princess Ebony.'

Ebony inclined her head a fraction as Rako swept a low bow. 'Your Majesty,' he said. 'Welcome to Isilvitania.'

The Guard behind him mirrored his bow and murmured hellos.

'Right,' Aethan said when the formalities were over, 'time to move.'

I could hear Rako and Aethan murmuring as we rode back towards the castle, words like attack and strength in numbers, words that normally would have had my ears twitching, but I was just too tired to care. I wanted to lie down in a soft bed and sleep for a week, but I knew I wouldn't be able to. Even if the goblins and orcs weren't planning an attack, there was a Royal Wedding to organise, which meant Guard duty would be continuous until Ebony and Orion were safely wed.

Hopefully I would have time to see Sabina and Mum and Grams in the chaos that was about to ensue.

The sun was breathing over the edge of the hills when Isilvitania castle came into sight. I felt myself sagging in the saddle, and to be quite honest it was only the fact that Ebony's back was still ram-rod straight that kept me upright.

We rode the horses to the front gate, where some faeries waited to welcome us. King Arwyn and Queen Eloise, dressed in formal attire, stood at the head of the group. Eloise's eyes ran across our party, the look on her face flashing schizophrenically from adoration as she viewed Aethan, to irritation as she looked at Isla. It morphed to hate as her eyes lighted on me and then just as quickly flashed to satisfaction as she looked Ebony up-and-down. Even after twenty-four hours in the saddle the damned night faery looked perfect.

We alighted and Aethan took Ebony's hand, leading her over to Arwyn and Eloise.

'Mother, Father,' he said formally. 'I have travelled to the ends of the Earth searching for the perfect bride for Orion.'

I managed to stop the cough tickling the back of my throat from escaping. I mean it wasn't like he'd had any choice in the bride he'd brought home.

'Please greet your future daughter, Ebony.' He held her hand out towards them and Arwyn reached out and took it.

'Welcome home daughter,' he said.

'Your words are balm to my soul,' Ebony murmured, looking up at them through her lashes.

Eloise looked as pleased as a squirrel with a bag full of nuts. My urge to cough had changed to an urge to stick my finger down my throat, roll my eyes and say, 'Oh pleeeeease,' but I was pretty sure that sort of behaviour would get me kicked out of the country.

I looked at the castle entry. Someone hovered in the shadow of the arch, moving from foot-to-foot as if trying to walk off a gut full of nerves. I was guessing it was Orion. Poor bastard. I wasn't sure how I would cope being introduced to my future husband like this. Unless it was Aethan.

That thought woke me up. I'd never contemplated *marrying* Aethan before. It wasn't that I didn't want to, but more that I was too young to be interested in it. Too young, and too swept up in being a Border Guard.

We had loved each other fiercely and that had been enough. I had blindly assumed we would always be together. Hunting and fighting, loving and laughing, at night, in Trillania, the world had been our oyster. But the reality was, that one day this would be happening to Aethan. One day he would need to wed and have children to carry on the Royal line.

The question was, would it be with me?

A hard knot formed in my stomach.

Did I *want* it to be with me?

The thought of him being with someone else drove me to the edge of insanity. But was I willing to give up who I was to play nice and bear his children?

I rubbed my hands up-and-down my arms thankful that the chill air gave me an excuse for the goose bumps that had formed on my skin. Up until that moment I had thought my main concern was getting Aethan back, now I realised it was much, much more.

We followed as King Arwyn led Ebony towards the steps leading up to the castle entry. Orion stepped out from the shadow of the arch, his face neutral as he prepared to meet his future.

I could tell the exact moment his eyes fell on Ebony's face. They widened, and his mouth formed a silent, 'Oh.'

Ebony kept her face demurely downcast; a suitable pose for a shy virgin. It was a shame that that wasn't exactly what Orion was getting, but he certainly didn't seem to care as his eyes greedily lapped her up. I wondered how long it would be before her tempestuous nature rose to the surface.

Arwyn reached the top step and closed the gap between himself and an extremely keen Orion. 'Princess Ebony,' Arwyn said in a formal tone, 'I present to you Prince Orion, heir to the Faery Throne.'

Ebony finally swept her eyes up to Orion's face. He stared at her searchingly as he reached out and took her hand, touching her as if she were a delicate piece of porcelain. I had been stunned by Ebony's beauty the first time I had seen her and Orion seemed no less impacted by the vision in front of him.

'My Lord,' she purred, 'forgive my disgraceful appearance. We have been in the saddle since yesterday morning.'

I probably looked disgraceful, I mean even Isla was looking a little worse for wear. But somehow Ebony appeared as fresh as a daisy. Her long, dark hair undulated down her back in perfect waves, her alabaster skin glowed as if she had had a good night's sleep, and her clothes appeared freshly washed and pressed. If I hadn't hated her before, I certainly did at that moment. It was unfair that one woman could be so glorious.

'You are perfect,' Orion said, his tone that of a love-struck boy.

Her face broke into a radiant smile and together they turned and entered the building.

'Well,' Isla said, 'that was gag-worthy. Come on, you can sleep with me.'

I yawned so widely that the muscles in the back of my neck protested. 'Sounds good.' I followed her into the castle and up a winding set of stairs to her suite.

The hot water of her shower felt amazing but I was too tired to linger long. I changed into the clothes she had given me and gratefully lay down on the far side of her bed.

She was sitting cross-legged on top of the sheets with her head bowed. Her lips moved but no sound came out of her mouth. I wanted to ask her what she was doing, but my eyes slid shut of their own accord and I was sound asleep before she had finished.

Chapter Thirteen

Rise Of The Dark Lord

'Izzy. You need to wake up.' Isla's voice reached into the deep, dark void of my sleep and dragged me back to the surface. I felt like I'd only lain down a few minutes ago, but from the angle of the sun coming through her window, I must have been asleep for hours.

'Goblins?' I jumped out of bed and looked around for my sword. Scruffy snorted in annoyance and turned around and around, snuggling into the blanket where I had been lying.

'Not even close.' She had a bemused look on her face. 'They're holding steady where we left them. Rako thinks it may just be a meeting with the orcs.'

'Strengthening their position.' It made sense. We were doing the same.

I pulled my clothes back on and followed her from the room. 'So what's the emergency?'

'You wouldn't believe me if I told you.'

I hated it when she was right.

Scruffy trotted beside me as she led me up to the top floor and down the corridor to the room Orion used for his study. The door was open and Rako and Aethan sat at the long table. Mia was curled around the back of Aethan's neck, balanced along the top of his vest so that her coat blended with the soft fur. Arwyn and Orion were nowhere to be seen, but a man and a woman stood with their backs to the door facing Rako and Aethan.

Isla pressed herself against the wall so that she couldn't be seen from inside the room and motioned for me to do the same. She put a finger to her lips and then touched her ear.

The woman was speaking. 'Lieutenant Leighton returning from undercover ops. I'd like to be re-instated for duty Sir.'

I *so* knew that voice.

'Lieutenant Leighton?' Rako said. I could hear the sound of fingers drumming the table. I was guessing they were his. 'I seem to recall that name, but surely you can't be the same woman. You were reported dead years ago.'

The woman bowed her head. 'I regret my decision to go AWOL.'

I risked a quick glance around the door frame at the woman.

'It seemed necessary at the time.'

Same python around her shoulders, same naughty voice.

'In retrospect perhaps it wasn't the best decision.'

'You think?' Rako stopped drumming his fingers. 'So what happened? You were sent in to spy on him and then you disappeared.'

There was dead silence for a few heart beats and then she said, 'I found out I was pregnant.'

'To Santanas?' There was resigned horror in Aethan's voice.

'To Santanas.'

I could hear roaring in my ears as the room started to spin.

'I couldn't let him know,' she whispered. 'So I faked my death and fled through the veil. I found a deserted witching house in Eynsford and slept on the porch till it accepted me as its own.'

Isla's fingers were like a vice on my arm.

'I looked for the signs when Prunella was born. But there were none. I thought we were safe.'

I could feel hysterical laughter bubbling up inside. Mum was going to be royally pissed when she found out who her real father was.

'And Isadora?' Aethan's voice was a bare murmur, as if he were scared of the answer he was going to get. 'Were the signs there when she was born?'

Scruffy pressed into my legs as if to comfort me. I wet my lips and opened my mouth but no sound came out.

'There was a full eclipse that day.'

'Not totally conclusive.' Rako's voice was tense.

What were they talking about?

'Isadora Margarita Gabrielle was born on a day of a super moon. At the precise moment of her birth the world turned totally black. It stayed that way till she took her first breath.'

I pushed off the wall and stood in the doorway.

'A total solar eclipse,' Rako said. 'There's one of them every one to two years.'

'Yes, but do wild animals gather around your house whenever one occurs? Never seen the likes of it. Rabbits, deer, mice and badgers sitting calmly next to foxes and wildcats; all of them staring up at the bedroom where Isadora was born.'

What did that mean? I felt my knees go weak. I was sure the answer, when I got it, was not going to be to my liking.

Rako slumped back in his seat and shook his head. 'So it's true then. She is.'

'Two of them.' Aethan shook his head. 'That's never happened before.'

'Two of what?' I said.

Grams spun towards me and for the first time I realised it was Lionel standing on her other side. If nothing else about this conversation had freaked me out, the expression on his face would have. I'd never seen him look so grave.

'Oh Izzy,' Grams said.

I strode towards her – no mean feat when your legs are trembling. 'Two of what?' I insisted. 'What am I?'

Glass smashed and splintered as a window caved in. Legs, followed by the rest of the goblin flew through the now-open window. He slumped to the floor as blood gushed out of a deep cut on his leg, but the next goblin through was uninjured. A second window smashed then a third and a fourth. I wrapped a shield around Scruffy and tossed him high in the air. This fight was no place for my fluffy familiar.

'They're on the roof,' Aethan roared. He drew his sword and vaulted over the table. Mia jumped from his shoulder, her little wings stretched out as she glided across the room. She wrapped herself around the face of a goblin, ripping at his eyes with her claws. As the goblin reached up to grab her, Aethan ran him through with a sword. She snarled and leapt back to Aethan's shoulder before propelling herself off again.

Before I could even draw my sword Grams had whipped out her wand. She and Lionel stood back-to-back as they fired spells into the mass of goblins. I launched myself at the far end of the room where the latest window had just been broken. Isla was right behind me.

I leapt into the air, dropping down onto the first of the goblins through the hole. The tip of my sword plunged into his neck and through his spine as gravity retook control of my body. He collapsed to the ground. I pulled my sword free and turned back to the window.

Even as we fought them one thing became clear. They were not interested in us. They fought to get past us to the open door. So if it wasn't *us* they wanted, who was it?

The thought must have occurred to Aethan at the same time. 'Orion,' he yelled. 'To Orion.' Mia leapt back to his shoulder and then he turned and charged out of the room.

'Go,' Grams said. 'Lionel and I will hold them here.'

I released Scruffy from the shield and then Rako, Isla and I took off after Aethan, sprinting down the hallway and turning down the first left passageway we came to. We could hear fighting coming from other parts of the castle.

The door ahead of us was shut. Aethan raced towards it, twisting the handle and barging it with his shoulder at the same time. It was locked. He swore in frustration and lifted his leg to kick it.

'Back up,' I yelled, waiting only long enough for him to move away from the door before I let my will loose on it.

Shards of wood exploded as my power smacked into the door. Aethan was pushing past the broken bits before they'd even finished settling. The voluptuous velvet drapes that had once dressed the windows were ripped into shreds by broken glass. Furniture was strewn across the room amongst the bodies of goblins and Orion's personal guard.

'Orion,' Aethan roared. He hacked and chopped his way through the goblins between him and his brother. Orion was backed up against the far wall of the room. The lone survivor, he still fought, but slowly, as if injured. As we battled towards him, his sword was knocked from his hand.

'Noooooooo.' Aethan beheaded a goblin that Mia had blinded and then he pushed the corpse out of the way.

A towering goblin seized Orion's throat and shoved him up against the wall. He pushed him higher and higher till Orion hung from those hands like a thief in the gallows. His feet beat ineffectively at the wall and his face turned red, then blue.

'Isadora. Help him.' Aethan's face was a frenzy of tangled emotions, fear and anger warring with each other for dominance.

Even though we fought as hard as we could we weren't going to make it to Orion in time. I couldn't hurl lightning, not with Orion there. I would kill him as well as the goblin.

The answer was quite simple. I could stop the goblin's heart. I could stop all their hearts. Surely just this once wouldn't hurt. To save Orion, the heir to the throne. Surely he was important enough.

I reached a hand out towards the goblin holding Orion but Aethan grabbed it. 'No.'

'Just this once.'

'Until the next time.' The battle raged around us as eyes the deepest blue bored into mine. 'Every time seems necessary. Every time gets easier. Like a seduction it will take you over until eventually, that's all you do. All you know. There has to be another way.'

'And if there's not?'

'Then so be it. I'll not have you throw away your soul.'

I ripped my eyes away from his. He might not be about to let me throw away my soul but I sure as hell wasn't going to let his brother die. 'Stay,' I said to Scruffy, and then I ran towards the goblin line that Rako and Isla were holding back and jumped. The goblins were so startled as I flew over the top of them, that not one took advantage of my exposed stomach.

I reached them as Orion's eyes were rolling up into his head. With a scream of pure rage I struck at the goblin, my sword catching him in the side of the neck. It lodged in his collarbone and ripped from my grip as he slumped to the floor. Orion slid down the wall and I pulled the dead goblin's hands from his throat.

'Breathe,' I said. 'Come on Orion, breathe, damn you.' I lay him down on the floor and was about to press my lips to his when he let out a low moan and a cough.

I had made it in time, and I hadn't used black magic. I wasn't sure which of those two things I was more relieved about.

Orion opened his eyes and stared up at me. 'Thank you.' He pulled a face as his voice squeaked.

Before I could respond, a hand grabbed the back of my head. I yelped as I was dragged along the ground by my braid. A goblin's foot buried itself into the side of my ribs. I curled into a ball as pain exploded through my chest, utterly helpless to do anything as the goblin lifted a curved dagger above me.

'Izzy.' Aethan's voice was a shriek of despair.

The irony of him finally calling me Izzy when I was only seconds away from death was not lost on me. *Bloody typical.*

The three of them were finishing off the last of the goblins, but there would be no saving me from this blow.

Would it hurt a lot or a little? I was betting on a lot. I closed my eyes and prayed to the Great Dark Sky that the end would be swift.

The goblin's laugh turned to a gurgle and the killing blow never came. As I opened my eyes he fell to the side, Orion's sword piercing him from behind.

Orion gave me a crooked smile and then slumped back to the ground.

Scruffy was the first to reach me, licking and whining and crying all at the same time, but Aethan wasn't far behind him.

'Izzy.' His hands ran over my body checking me for injuries. 'You're safe, you're alive.' He stroked my face as he stared into my eyes. 'I thought I'd lost you.'

'You remember,' I said. 'You remember me.'

The corners of his mouth curled up. 'I don't need my memories to know that I love you.'

Fireworks exploded inside my head as he bent his face and captured my mouth with his own. Finally, finally he was kissing me the way he used to. With surety and totality, as if he would die without my mouth against his. I curled my arms around his neck and dived deeper into the kiss.

It was Orion who pulled us back from the brink of inappropriate passion.

'Legas,' he croaked. 'They took Legas.'

Aethan broke our kiss and I stared up into his face as I tried to re-order my thoughts. I knew Orion's words held dire importance, but I couldn't remember why.

Rako swore and rushed from the room and Isla stopped in the process of examining Orion's throat and let out a hiss. 'Legas was here?'

'We were discussing … crop rotations.'

I was guessing by his blush that they'd been discussing a certain night faery, *not* crop rotations.

I pushed myself up into a seated position. 'Who's Legas?'

Aethan reached out and tucked a strand of hair behind my ear. 'Orion's best friend. One of our cousins. '

The import of the words smacked into me. Galanta needed a donor body for Santanas's soul. Legas was of royal blood, just as Santanas had been.

'Buzznuckle.' I leapt to my feet. 'We have to stop them.'

'I'm coming.' Orion pushed himself up.

'It's too dangerous.' Aethan's voice left no room for argument but Orion's face took on a stubborn look I knew too well. If I hadn't known that he and Aethan were brothers before, I most certainly would now.

'You can't even talk properly.' Isla patted him on the arm as if to soothe him, but the pat was too hard and too fast to do that. It was the first time I had seen her rattled.

'I don't need a voice to kill goblins.'

I winced at the high-pitched wheeze that came out of him. His throat must have been excruciating.

'Too dangerous,' Aethan said again, shaking his head.

'If we don't get Legas back it won't matter if I'm alive or not,' Orion whispered.

He had a good point. I watched as Aethan's face wavered between uncertainty and defiance.

'It was just a small force,' Rako said from the doorway, 'not the group you saw last night. I've sent trackers after them.'

As if that had settled the argument, Orion retrieved his sword from the dead goblin, wiping the blade on a ruined curtain before sliding it back into its sheath. 'I'm going and that is that.' He strode past us towards the door.

'I can't believe he's being so stupid,' Aethan muttered. He shook his head and then dragged his hands back through his dark hair. 'It's too dangerous.'

'If anything happened to Legas he would never forgive himself,' Isla said.

'Not the point.' He started to move towards the door. 'We are his arm. The *Guard* is his arm. He rules and we protect. That's how it's done. How it's *always* been done, and Orion knows that.'

We trotted down the stairs and out a side door towards the stables. 'He's in love,' Isla said. 'That does strange things to a man's head.'

Aethan let out a snort, but his eyes flicked towards me and I had to resist the urge to take him to the ground and cover his mouth with mine.

'And women's heads,' Isla said, smirking at me.

I stuck my tongue out at her, but wisely said nothing.

The rest of the Guard stationed at the castle were already there and saddling their horses. I found Lily in a stable towards the back with Wolfgang's horse. It only took a few minutes to get the saddle on her back and the bridle in her mouth, but by the time I had finished, most of the Guard were already waiting. I grabbed a travelling pack stocked with food and water from the front of the stable as I led Lily out.

'They're heading west,' Rako said as he pulled himself up into his saddle.

'Why west? That's orc country.' Isla's perfect face puckered and I knew she was thinking about Wilfred.

I placed Scruffy on Lily's back and shrugged. 'Where's Wolfgang?' We were really going to need him.

Rako scrunched his eyes and rubbed a hand over his face. 'He went back out with the Guard to keep an eye on the goblins.'

'You mean he's not coming?'

'I've sent a message but we don't have time to wait.' The look on his face matched what I felt. Despair.

'Izzy.' Grams rounded the side of the castle and trotted towards me.

'You're hurt.' I reached out towards the streak of blood on her cheek.

'Not mine,' she said.

'Lionel?' Oh Dark Sky, If he were injured…

'Talking to King Arwyn. We're going to stay here to help protect the castle.'

'Oh, well, that's probably for the best.' My heart had been in my throat the whole time she had been fighting. I didn't think I could go through it again.

'Let's move out,' Rako called.

I pulled Grams to me, dwarfing her as I hugged her, and then I pushed her away and stared into her face. I wanted to ask her the significance of the conversation I had overheard but I was too scared of the answer.

She stared into my eyes and then nodded her head. 'Later,' she said as if reading my mind, 'we can talk about it later.'

'I love you,' I said as I swung up into the saddle.

She pressed her fingers to her lips and waved them at me as I trotted after the rest of the Guard.

We pushed the horses hard in our attempts to catch the goblins. Thought bubbles, floating back to us from the trackers, reported that the goblins continued to head west and that we were narrowing the gap, but the longer we rode without sight of them, the more tense I became. The only consolation was that if Galanta wanted Legas for what we suspected she did, then he was still alive.

'We need to rest,' Aethan said to Rako. 'The horses need to rest.'

Rako scrubbed a hand down his face and swore. 'I was hoping we would have caught them by now.' He held up a hand and we dropped from a canter to a walk and then stopped. The sun had set hours before and only adrenaline coursing through my body kept me awake.

'Why are we stopping?' Orion's voice was not improving with time.

'We need to rest.'

'They're getting away.'

Aethan laid a hand on Orion's arm. 'If we keep going, the horses will fail, and then they *will* get away.'

Orion swore and strode away. Aethan watched him with a small frown on his face.

I took his hand in mine, savouring the ability to touch him again. 'What's up?'

'He seems…,' he paused for a second, 'unhinged.'

'Legas must be a good friend to him. I know I'd be unhinged if they had taken you.'

He traced a hand down the side of my face. 'As I would be if it were you.'

'What about me?' Isla bumped me with her arm. 'Would you be unhinged if something happened to me?'

'I'd be *crazy*,' I said, realising as the joking words left my mouth that they were true. The last few weeks had bonded us beyond mere friends.

'Awww, shucks.' She gave me her cheekiest grin. 'Now if you've finished going all gushy on me, we should get some rest.'

After a couple of hours, half of which was spent in broken sleep and the other on sentry duty, we pushed on again. I tried not to think about how much further the goblins had gone while we slept and instead thought about what we were going to do when we caught them. It was going to be messy.

A couple of hours later, as the pre-dawn sky started to lighten, one of the faery trackers galloped towards us. He pulled his mount to a halt and, as it sank its head between its front legs and pulled in lungful after lungful of air, he said, 'They've stopped.'

'How far?' Orion looked as if he would leap off his horse and start running.

'About two miles further.' The tracker cleared his throat almost nervously. 'They're at The Henge.'

'Faster,' Orion croaked, kneeing his horse in the ribs, 'we will be too late.'

'What's The Henge?' I yelled to Isla as we leaned over our horses' necks and pushed them as fast as they could go.

'Powerful ceremonial stones. You know it as Stonehenge.'

A prickle of unease ran down my spine. 'When would be the best time to harness the power from the stones?'

Her face was deadly serious. 'Sunrise.'

A few minutes later we galloped over a low rise and I could see the pillars of stone standing in the distance. I had visited Stonehenge with Mum and Grams a few years ago and the difference between the site in England and the one here behind the veil was stark. These stones were still perfect. No signs of wear or damage marked their surfaces.

'It looks so different,' I said.

'This circle still harnesses the power of the Great Dark Sky,' Isla replied. 'I don't know why we didn't think of it before. Galanta's going to need all the help she can get if she's going to make this work.'

Drum beats reverberated in the still morning air and goblins shuffled around the pillars of stone. We had to make it in time, we just had to. It seemed ridiculous that after everything we had been through, it would all be for naught if we didn't make it to that circle in time.

'*Hurry*,' Orion yelled over the beat of the drums. 'We *must hurry*.'

I didn't need his words to urge me on. I clung to my reins with white knuckles and prayed.

Isla pulled her bow from the pommel in front of her and started firing arrows into the goblins. She jumped easily from her saddle while still shooting.

'Stay here,' I said to Scruffy as I leapt from Lily's back. He let out a little ruffy bark that I hoped was a yes.

'Quick.' Orion grabbed my arm and pulled me towards the goblins. 'We must find Legas.'

The goblins roared as we ran towards them. I pulled my short swords from the sheaths crossing my back and leapt towards the closest one. I didn't need to be told twice to kill those big bastards.

The goblin lunged at me with his dagger held straight out. I slapped it away with the blade of one sword and bit deep into his neck with my other one. He roared with pain and spun away from me clutching at his throat as blood pumped through his fingers.

Orion fought like a mad person, forcing his way ahead of me so that I ended up covering his back as we made our way deeper into the group of goblins. They seemed more interested in attacking the rest of the guard than attacking Orion and me. I used that to my advantage, dodging around them as much as I engaged them. We had to find Legas and we had to find him soon. The light around us was brightening and I knew that at any moment the sun would breach the horizon.

'There.' Orion pointed to our left.

I peered past him to where a platform of stone rose into the air. A body lay on top of the platform and I didn't need to be a genius to know it was Legas.

We raced towards him as the sky brightened. Any second now that sun would rise and whatever spell Galanta was planning, would start. I jumped high into the air over the last goblins, landing on the stone platform in a crouch.

Where was Galanta? What was she doing?

'*Hurry.*' It was my turn to urge on Orion. I raced toward the unconscious figure.

Please don't let us be too late. Please let him be alive.

A blazing bright disc peeped over the horizon, shooting light across the ground towards us. 'No,' I screeched, hurling myself at his body. I didn't know how or why, but I knew with absolute knowledge that if that light got to Legas before I did, all was lost.

I landed on my knees beside him but the light got there first. It touched his face. Such a familiar face. A blonde version of the one I loved.

Not Legas. It wasn't Legas.

Instead, Orion looked almost peaceful as he lay there, his hands crossed over his chest.

'Surprise.' A strong hand grasped me from behind and a dagger plunged into my side.

I sagged back against my attacker, helpless as the blade slashed toward me again, this time biting deep into the veins at my wrist. Staring up into the face of my attacker,

I watched as Orion's facial features melted, flowing and reshaping until Galanta leered down at me.

'You,' I gasped. 'It was you all along.'

She held my wrist over Orion's still body. Blood ran freely, splattering down over him. He lay on the broken stone I had unwittingly freed Santanas from. My blood sizzled as it landed.

'So nice of you to come.' Her pointed teeth made her smile that much more malicious.

I looked toward where the Guard fought. The goblins that had let us pass so easily, now battled like demons.

I was so stupid. So desperately stupid. She had played me from the beginning and even knowing that, I had walked blindly into her trap.

For once the sunrise did nothing to warm me as it blossomed in front of my eyes. Black mist grew around the stone and I knew I was too late.

Too late to save Orion. Too late to stop Galanta. Too late to save myself.

The mist rose into the air above Orion as Galanta began to chant. Black, boiling, bubbling smoke, coalesced in a cloud as her voice rose to a shriek. I pulled against her, but a foot buried itself in my ribs and pain exploded from the stab wound. I slumped to the side as I retched, red clouding my vision.

So this is what Santanas had meant when he'd said they still needed me. They'd need my blood to complete the spell. And now they had it.

Cold crept over me with a calm that stole away my fear. The fact that I was going to die took some of the horror out of what I was witnessing. I wasn't going to live under a rule of war and chaos. I wasn't going to have to fight to maintain the basic rights of mankind. I looked toward Rako and Aethan, feeling like a coward that I was giving up so easily.

They fought like mad men as they struggled to reach me. Aethan screamed my name as he slashed and hacked, pieces of goblin flying with every strike. Mia jumped from goblin to goblin, gouging their eyes with her needle-like talons.

The black mist swirled around me, cold moisture licking my skin. Evil oozed, stroking me tenderly. I closed my mouth and shut my eyes and prayed to the Dark Sky.

Just as suddenly, it was gone. I re-opened my eyes and saw it swirling over Orion and I realised what it was doing. It was looking for its donor. I had to do something. I had to stop it, but pain owned me. Each movement sent fresh spasms travelling through me.

I heard Isla calling my name. Saw her jump into the air and leap from goblin-to-goblin, using them like giant stepping stones. She fired arrows downwards as she jumped, spearing them through the shoulder and into their hearts.

The black mist split into three individual streams. They hovered over Orion's head, spinning like mini-cyclones. If I were going to do something, it had to be *now*.

And then a small, white demon attacked Galanta. Scruffy's growl was savage as he tore at the back of her calf. She shrieked and turned toward him and with a scream of rage and pain and defiance, I tore myself from her grip. My hand hung limp from my cut wrist but I didn't need my hand as I slammed into Orion's body.

I clambered up him, spreading myself over him, trying to protect him. Galanta's voice wavered but the spell continued, wailing out of her as she fought off Scruffy.

Isla was nearly there. A path of dead goblins littered her wake. She roared with fury when she saw Orion lying there. Confusion clouded her face for only the briefest of moments. The clues fell into place more quickly for her than they had for me.

Legas had never been there. Orion was the one who had been taken. And Galanta, the shape-shifter, had replaced him. They'd orchestrated the near strangling to give a reason for her voice to be different.

If the situation hadn't been so dire, I would have been impressed. Instead, I looked up at the spinning cyclones and I screamed as they descended like spears.

Lancing pain burnt into my back as the mist struck. Once, twice, three times I felt the evil pierce me. It burrowed deep as it made its way towards Orion. It violated as it dug, and yet, a small piece of me recognised it, acknowledged it.

A small piece of me welcomed it.

I recoiled in horror, lifting myself off Orion as I screamed. I wasn't sure which was worse: the pain of the intrusion or the pain in my soul. Was this what I was? Was this what I was made of?

This evil, this sin, this filth?

For a second the burrowing stopped, the mist deciding it was home. I shook my head from side-to-side and resisted the icy tendrils as they spread out through my body. I pushed at it with all my might, forcing it out of me. Forcing it through me, and then suddenly the burrowing continued.

Three black blades emerged from my chest, flowing out and down to Orion. I rolled away from him but it was too late. He jerked as they slammed into him, one stream in each nostril and the other into his mouth. Three great snakes, they slithered out of me and into him.

'No.' My shriek cut through the air as Galanta's spell stopped.

Orion's body jerked and shuddered, like a bag full of fish. His head flopped from side-to-side as he fought the invasion.

'No.' Isla's scream echoed my own. 'Orion.' She flung herself down beside me and pressed her hands to his heart. 'Fight it,' she commanded. 'You can beat this. You're strong enough.'

Galanta's triumphant laugh belied Isla's words. 'Master,' she yelled. 'I have found you a body. Take him. Make it your own.'

I coughed weakly and rolled to my side, blood flowing out of my mouth.

'You.' Isla climbed to her feet and turned towards Galanta. 'You will die for this.'

'Perhaps,' Galanta said. 'But it won't be today.'

Orion's body rose jerkily into the air, pulling him up onto his feet. Isla gasped and reached a hand out. Higher and higher he rose, floating above us as he started to spin. Faster and faster he turned, till he was a blur, not a man. And then as suddenly as the spinning started, it stopped, and a bolt of light shot out of him. Another one followed and then another, until it seemed that a strand of light shone from each pore.

I stared as he floated back to earth. Had Orion won? Is that what the light had been?

All sounds of battle stopped as his feet touched the ground. He rolled his shoulders and flexed his head from side-to-side, and then he opened his eyes.

Where Orion's eyes had held warmth and laughter, these held only madness.

The goblins let out shouts of triumph and surrounded the members of the Guard that were still standing. They pulled swords from hands limp with shock. We had failed.

I crawled backwards like an injured crab, my damaged arm cradling the wound in my side. Isla grabbed my good arm and dragged me away as Santanas viewed the battleground.

'This is a fine welcome.' He threw back his head and laughed. 'Blood and death everywhere I look. I always said you should start as you mean to go on.'

Scruffy whimpered and grasped my leather shirt with his teeth, helping Isla haul me backwards off the stone platform.

Santanas flexed Orion's body as if trying it on for size. 'You have done well,' he said to Galanta. 'Everything seems to be in working order.'

'The wards my Lord?'

'Are exactly as they were. None may kill me except those who love me.' His eyes took on a dangerous glint. 'Do you love me Galanta?'

She bowed her head. 'No my Lord.'

He held his hand out and a dagger sprang from the hand of a dead goblin and soared through the air till it smacked into his palm. He trailed the edge of the dagger around Galanta's throat as he walked around her. 'Are you sure about that?'

'I respect and revere you, but I do not love you.' The words came out in a choking gasp.

'Very good,' he whispered in her ear. 'We do not need little complications like that getting between us.'

He spun away from her and looked out over the battlefield. 'And where is my daughter? Why isn't she here to greet me?' Santanas's head turned till he pierced me with those eyes. 'Ahh, there she is. Daughter come.' He held his hand out and I felt his compulsion press against my mind. I shook my head and growled and Isla dragged me faster.

'She is dying Great Lord,' Galanta said.

Dying? That was no surprise.

'Kill them now Lord and you cut the head off the snake.'

I let out a low moan as Isla dragged me over a rock.

'Ahh Galanta,' Santanas strode towards her, 'now where would be the fun in that?'

'Rako, my Lord, and Aethan, the elite of the Guard, I brought them all here for you.'

'Patience, patience. We have plenty of time.' He turned and looked out toward the Guard. 'I want them to bow down in fear. I want them to grovel at my feet.' His hands twisted into fists and his voice rose to a shriek. 'I want to eat their hearts and dance on their graves. But first,' he said, turning toward me, 'I would thank my daughter.' He held a hand out and my body lifted into the air, my arm stretched like a kite string as Isla maintained her grip.

He flicked his other hand at Isla and she let out a shriek as she slammed backwards into one of the upright pillars of rock. Let free of her grasp, I floated through the air and down to the ground at his feet.

Santanas stared down at me and shook his head. 'Galanta.' His voice was that of a disappointed teacher with a wayward student. 'I told you we only needed a drop of her blood.'

She bowed her head, but there was a smile in her voice when she said, 'Forgive me, Lord.'

He turned his attention back to me way too quickly. 'Daughter, will you join me?'

I tried to spit at him, but too much blood was pooling in my throat and breathing was becoming difficult.

'Ahhhhh,' he said. 'It seems I must heal you first.' Light flowed from his outstretched hand. It cascaded over me, cocooning me from head-to-foot. I braced for the pain I knew was coming. Instead though, warmth infused me. I groaned with relief as it spread through me, wiping away my pain in its wake. When it was finished, I was whole.

I climbed unsteadily to my feet and wiped the last of the blood away from my mouth. 'Father.' I inclined my head. There was no need for him to know about Mum.

'Daughter. Are you well?' From the tone of his voice I half expected him to offer me a nice cup of tea.

'Yes, thank you.' This was all very polite and totally surreal.

'Will you join me daughter?'

'I'm sorry father,' I said, 'but I can't.'

The look on his face changed to one that I'm sure before that moment, Orion's face had never worn. Twin thunderclouds gathered under lowered eyebrows.

'It seems I may need to use some... *gentle* persuasion.' He chuckled softly.

I braced, ready for whatever he threw at me. I was expecting pain, I was expecting agony. All I knew was that I was not going over to the dark side.

'She loves the faery Prince,' Galanta said.

'Does she?' He let out a wild laugh. 'How convenient.'

He chuckled as he gestured. Aethan's eyes met mine as two goblins grabbed his arms and dragged him towards us.

'I'm sorry,' I mouthed. If I had been quicker, if I had been smarter, then none of this would have happened.

The goblin forced Aethan into a kneeling position beside me. I knelt beside him and he reached out and took my hand.

'No matter what,' he said, 'you say no.' Mia, almost invisible as she snuggled against the edge of his fur vest, hissed softly. I wasn't sure how much she understood but she had been in this position herself; forced into servitude through love.

'I can't lose you,' I whispered. Not now. Not after finding him again and again.

'You say yes and *you* will be lost to *me*.'

'Let's make this even more interesting,' Santanas said.

I heard some muttered curses and a yelp as Rako and Isla were dragged towards us. A goblin ripped at Isla's braid as he shoved her onto her knees beside me. Tears ran freely, cascading down her face, but I knew she wasn't crying for herself. She stared up at Santanas and mumbled, 'Orion, oh Orion.'

Rako struggled upwards, shoving against his goblin handler as he tried to pull a dagger.

'Enough.' Santanas's hand cut through the air in time with his word and suddenly movement became impossible. My diaphragm laboured to move my chest enough to draw in air.

'Now,' Santanas said, 'which one of you wants to go first?'

Aethan's eyes bulged as he struggled to move, his face pulling into a grotesque mask. Hate emanated from every pore of his body as he glared up at the man who wore his brother's body.

I found myself wishing Wolfgang were there, but even with him I suspected we would still be in the same predicament. But without him we had only me. Only me to combat the magic of the mad War Faery. We were so screwed.

'Don't be shy. Speak up.' Santanas put his hand behind his ear and swivelled his head from side-to-side. 'Oh silly me.' He waved his hand and suddenly I could move my head.

'You... evil... bastard,' Isla spat in his direction.

'Yes.' Santanas stroked his chin. 'This is much more interesting.'

'Izzy,' Aethan whispered. 'Do something.'

'I can't,' I whispered back. What could I do against the might of Santanas. I was just a failed faery.

'Maybe I'll start with you.' Santanas grabbed Isla's braid and pulled her head back. Sweat and tears mingled on her face as he stroked the edge of his dagger up-and-down her throat. 'Would you like that?'

'You *can*,' Aethan whispered.

'He's too powerful.'

'Not for you.' He turned and looked me right in the eye. 'That's what your Grandmother was trying to tell us.'

'Or maybe I'll start with you.' Santanas let go of Isla's hair and moved to Aethan. 'You seem like a chatty fellow.

Perhaps you'd like to tell me which part of you I should cut off first.'

I struggled against the invisible bonds as Santanas laid his dagger against Aethan's throat. What had Grams been telling them? She's mentioned a total eclipse and animals. A foretelling of sorts. But foretelling what?

And then I remembered the words Ulandes had whispered into the quiet of my mind. *Never before have there been two. Only one can live, the other must die.*

Two what?

'Should I start here?' Santanas's voice was like a lover's caress as he sliced the blade gently down Aethan's cheek. Blood welled and ran in its wake.

'Izzy.' Aethan's whole body shook with his efforts to fight back.

'Or here?' Santanas pulled his arm back and put the tip of the dagger to the side of Aethan's throat.

Never before have there been two. Never before have there been two.

The tip of the dagger penetrated Aethan's skin and I went berserk.

I took all my will, all my anger, all my love and I slashed at the bonds holding us in place. They parted like butter before a hot knife and I had my answer.

I was a War Faery. The second War Faery.

Only one of us could live.

As the bonds melted, Aethan threw himself backwards from the blade. The look on Santanas's face would have been comical if our situation weren't so dire.

'Nooooooo,' I screamed as I climbed to my feet.

I held my hands out and twin bolts of lightning raced towards Santanas. He slashed his hand and they disappeared, sucked back into the air they had come from.

'My Lord,' Galanta shrieked as she threw herself in front of Santanas.

He shoved her to the side and she stumbled over a rock and fell to her knees. Isla snarled and jumped on her back, smashing her face into a rock.

Noises of battle started up again as the Guard took heart. But even though we had made a comeback, the numbers were still against us. Too many goblins still stood, too many still fought.

Vivid darkness danced around Santanas as he faced off against me. Black air crackled as he smiled a smile that reached his eyes with madness.

'And lo,' his voice thundered out across the earth, 'it has come to this. Father against daughter. Blood against blood. You know you can never win.'

'I don't know anything of the sort.' I was trying to stay positive but I didn't like my odds. He had so much more experience than I did.

'A good attitude. You sure you won't join me? Together we could rule the world.' Sparks leapt off his fingers as he flexed them. I had a feeling this was going to hurt.

'Already got a nice job thanks. Pays well, and we even get holidays.' We circled each other as we sparred verbally.

'Don't say I never did anything for you.' He hurled a black ball of fire straight at my heart.

I threw my hand up and flicked it to the side with a slice of air. It slammed into a goblin and erupted over his body, coating him in black flame.

Lightning flowed from my body as bolt-after-bolt slammed into Santanas's shield. He smiled and covered his mouth with his spare hand as if to cover a yawn. Then he wiggled a finger at a stone pillar. It rose into the air and speared towards me, straight into a shield I shaped like a wedge.

Stone shrieked as it exploded into a million tiny pieces. I flexed my shield and directed the shrapnel back at Santanas. He winced as the first fragments peppered his skin and instantly a black shield wrapped his body.

I was never going to get through that shield. He was just too good. Too experienced. Too powerful. While he looked like he'd just had a good night's sleep, I was panting and streaked with sweat.

'We need to pull back,' I said to Aethan. 'I can't best him.'

The black shield shimmered and disappeared and Santanas smiled at me. 'Now daughter. Is that a proper way to treat your father?'

As the words left his mouth I saw Mia scamper up onto Aethan's shoulder. Her lips pulled back from her teeth and she launched herself into the air. Silently she soared towards Santanas.

I held his gaze and said, 'No.' Any second, any second now. 'This is a much better way.'

Talons extended, teeth exposed she ripped into his face with a scream of defiance. This was the monster that had stolen her baby. This was the bastard that had sent her through to our world from Trillania. She was crazed with fury and she was going to make him pay.

It only took a second for her to gouge out his eyes. A second for her to do what I hadn't been able to.

He screamed and ripped her from his face, and *that* was when I struck. As blood poured out of his empty eye sockets I slammed a lightning bolt into him. It lifted him off his feet and threw him backwards into a pillar of stone.

'Nooooooo.' Galanta ripped Isla's hands off her throat and clambered towards him. 'My Lord. My Lord.'

Santanas's groan let us know he was still alive. His wards had protected him to a certain extent. Without either faery or witch magic he would be a while healing, but he would be back.

Only someone who loved him would be able to kill him.

Aethan scooped Mia up off the ground and cradled her in an arm. 'Quick,' he said. 'We must leave while we can.'

The goblins had stopped fighting, all of them staring at the macabre scene Santanas made. I could smell his burned flesh from where I was.

I grabbed Isla's hand and stumbled back the way we had come. It wouldn't be long before the goblins realised we were escaping. Scruffy ran at my heels as I followed Rako and Aethan out, threading through the stupefied goblins.

'Noooo,' Galanta's wail cut through the air. 'Kill them. Kill them all.'

The goblins around me stepped back warily as I raised my hands. 'That's it,' I said, my voice full of bravado. 'There's plenty more where that came from.'

The truth was, though, that I didn't know how much more fuel I had in the tank. I had nearly died and been through a healing and then I had fought. I was exhausted.

'Kill them,' Galanta yelled.

Rako and Aethan reached their swords and the rest of the Guard, but we were surrounded. The looks on the goblins faces told us we only had moments before they summoned the courage to attack. The horses were just too far away for us to make a getaway.

'Foiled again,' Isla muttered. She threw an arm around me to help hold me upright as I staggered against her.

'I can do this,' I said. 'I can.'

'Sure you can,' she said, but her voice held no conviction.

'Kill them or know my wrath.'

The look on the faces of the goblins around us became resolute. The first raised his dagger and charged towards us and a wall of fire slammed into him.

Isla gasped and looked at me. 'I thought you were spent.'

'Wasn't me,' I gasped.

The sound of hooves beating over the ground reached us as a fresh wave of Border Guard raced towards us. They yelled war cries as they came, and there at the front was Wolfgang. I'd never seen such a beautiful sight.

The goblins peeled back from around us and sprinted in the opposite direction. It was lucky that maths wasn't their strong point, or they would have realised that even with this fresh supply, we were still badly outnumbered. But I wasn't going to tell them the error of their ways.

'Cowards,' Galanta screamed. 'Stand and fight.'

Aethan supported my other side as we staggered towards our horses.

'Mia?' I asked.

'She's going to be fine.'

'That's one brave little girl,' Rako said as he hauled himself up onto his horse.

I tried to mount Lily but my legs wouldn't obey me. Instead I found myself staring up at the saddle wondering how I was going to stay there, *if* I managed to get there.

'I'll take Scruffy.' Isla's voice shook as if trying not to cry. 'You take Izzy.'

Aethan climbed into Adare's saddle and reached down for me, pulling me up in front of him and settling me in his arms. Mia clambered down till she was nestled in my lap. I wrapped an arm around her and closed my eyes and promptly fell asleep.

Chapter Fourteen

The Aftermath

I woke twice on the way home. Once when Aethan climbed down from the saddle with me still cradled in his arms. I stayed awake long enough for him to lay us both down and wrap one arm and a blanket over me.

The second time was when he picked me up and climbed back into the saddle. I knew I should stay awake. But I was exhausted and despondent and I didn't want to be awake in the world as it was right then.

Orion was dead and Santanas was back.

Days don't come any worse than that.

'Izzy. Oh no Izzy.' Grams' voice woke me.

I lifted my head to find we had arrived back at the castle. 'I'm fine,' I said, but my voice was garbled with exhaustion.

'She lost a lot of blood.' Aethan held my hands as I slid from the saddle. Grams wrapped me into a hug as soon as my feet were on the ground.

'I'm fine Grams.' I kissed her cheek and looked around at the chaos unfolding.

'Orion.' I winced as I heard Queen Eloise's voice. 'Where is Orion?'

Isla grasped her mother's hands and pulled her into her arms. I saw her whispering in Eloise's ear as tears streaked down her face.

'Noooooo.' Eloise's scream made the hair on my arms stand up. 'Nooooo.' She pushed Isla away. 'I don't believe you.' She raised her hand and slapped her daughter across the face.

Isla lifted a hand to her cheek as she stared at her mother.

'You,' Eloise hissed. 'You treacherous slut.' Her eyes blazed and spit flew from her lips. 'Did you plan this? Did you?' She pounced on Isla, clawing at her with her nails.

'Mother.' Aethan grabbed her arms and pulled her off Isla. 'It's not her fault.'

Bloody streaks marred Isla's cheeks.

Eloise turned towards Aethan. As she threw herself into his arms her howls were that of a wounded animal.

Isla pressed her hands to her face as fresh sobs took her. She resisted me for a second as I wrapped my arms around her, but then she sank into my embrace.

I had been kidding myself if I'd thought I hated Eloise before. Now though, feeling Isla's heart breaking as she shuddered against me, now I knew what *real* hate was.

Eloise let out another scream and flapped her hands at Aethan. 'What is it?' she screeched.

Mia arched her back and hissed, revealing shiny teeth.

'Kill it.' Eloise pointed. 'Kill it now.'

'Mia is a hero.' Aethan scooped her off his neck and held his arm out to me.

I scooted forward and Mia jumped into my arms, scampered up to my neck and hissed at Eloise again.

'You.' Eloise's eyes bulged. 'You... you....' Her face turned first red and then purple as she shook her arm at me.

'Isla, Izzy,' Rako said. 'You two get out of here. Izzy, take Isla home with you.'

I nodded as I backed away from the Queen. She seemed to be having some sort of fit.

'How did you get here?' I asked Grams.

'Your car is parked around the side.'

'Come on,' I said, grabbing Isla's arm.

She stumbled along beside me, the fight gone from her. In the space of a few days she had lost her lover and her brother. Now it looked like she had lost her mother too.

We reached my car and I helped Isla into the back. Her eyes stared at nothing as Scruffy pressed up against her leg. Lionel climbed into the front passenger seat and Grams started the engine. She backed up and drove past the front of the castle.

Ebony stood on the stairs. One hand was pressed to her mouth and the other to her stomach as King Arwyn spoke to her.

A group of faeries stood at the end of the drive. As we slowed and then stopped, two of them started to open the veil.

'Service with a smile,' I said.

Isla blinked her eyes a couple of times and looked out of the window.

'Poor Ebony.' I actually felt sorry for her; coming all this way just to have Orion killed before they were married.

'They're getting ready to close the veil,' Isla said.

'Close it?'

'It will be sealed during the official mourning period for Orion. For thirty days.' She pivoted and looked at the castle through the back window.

The veil was open in front of us and Grams put her foot on the accelerator.

'Wait,' Isla said. 'We have to stay.'

'We can't,' I said. 'Your Mum, she doesn't mean it. But she's a little crazy at the moment and you and I make it worse.'

'You don't understand.' Even in her grief her brain worked better than mine. 'Ebony came to marry the *heir* to the faery throne. Not Orion.'

As we drove through the veil I spun in my seat to stare out the back. Aethan was standing on the front stairs of the castle and Arwyn was placing Ebony's hand in his.

'Stop,' I screeched, but it was too late.

The edges of the veil started to flutter back together. The last thing I saw before the veil was sealed, was Ebony rise on her tiptoes to press a kiss to Aethan's lips.

THE END

To be continued in Faery Revenge...

Enjoying the War Faery Trilogy? Want to find out when *Faery Revenge*, the final book in the trilogy is released?

Sign up to my Fantasy Book Club to find out. I'll also be looking for a VIP group of readers to preview *Faery Revenge* before it hits the stores, so watch out for an email from me.

You can find the sign up button on the top right of my website www.donnajoyusher.com on any page BUT the home page, or go to http://eepurl.com/2IMcT to go straight to the sign up page.

If you enjoyed this book, I ask that you give me the gift of a review on the site that you bought it. Reviews are the lifeblood of any author. It doesn't have to be long or flowery, I just ask that it is honest. Without those reviews the task of marketing becomes a lot harder so I thank you in advance for your time and effort.

About Donna Joy Usher

Hi there. I'm Donna Joy Usher. I started writing my first novel when I was seven. With no idea about plot or character development (I mean I *was* only seven) my storyline quickly disintegrated into a muddled jumble of boring dialogue between two horses. Disillusioned, I gave up writing stories for quite a while after that. Instead, I concentrated on my studies, eventually graduating as a dentist.

After many years of 'drilling and filling' I turned to writing in an effort to escape the seriousness of my day job. During that time I created my first book, *The Seven Steps to Closure*, and discovered that I love nothing more than making other people laugh. Well that, and my husband and two miniature schnauzers, Chloe and Xena.

I currently live near the river in beautiful Perth. When I am not working or writing, I love to paddle board, walk on the beach and sip chai lattes at the local cafe.

You can connect with me on Twitter (@donnajoyusher), my blog site (www.donnajoyusher.com), Facebook, Goodreads, or LinkedIn.

Like a Little Chic Lit??

Try Out One of These Beauties.

Cocoa and Chanel

Book One in The Chanel Series

by Donna Joy Usher

Winner of the 2014 Next Generation Indie Book Awards - Ebook Fiction Category.

Winner of the 2014 National Indie Excellence Awards - Humor Category.

Faced with the unattractive options of an affair with her boss's husband or the unknown, Chanel Smith chooses the unknown and unwittingly traps herself into joining the New South Wales Police Force. More interested in fashion than felony, Chanel staggers through training and finds herself posted to the forces most notorious crime hot spot: Kings Cross. Against her wishes she becomes entangled in a case of the worst kind, a serial killer targeting young women in The Cross.

As she is drawn further into the seedy underworld of The Cross in her attempt to unravel the truth, Chanel makes new friends, new enemies and draws the attention of the killer. Can she solve the case in time, or will she become the killer's next victim?

Cocoa and Chanel is available for sale in print form on Amazon, CreateSpace, and other online distributors. It is also available as an eBook on Amazon, Nook, Kobo, iBooks, Oyster, Page Foundry, Scribd and Tolino.

Goons 'n' Roses

Book Two in the Chanel Series

Finalist in the 2015 Indi Excellence Awards Humor Category

It's been 3 months since Chanel's world fell apart and now she's ready for a vacation. Unfortunately, her all-expenses-paid trip to Las Vegas is not turning out as she had hoped. Within hours of arriving, her mum, Lorraine, is kidnapped. Then Trent, her boss and Lorraine's boyfriend, disappears; but not before he imparts information about an Interpol investigation into missing girls in Las Vegas.

When Chanel hooks up with local bad boy, the seriously sexy Billy, in a bid to get information, things only start to get worse. As she and Martine search for answers they are thwarted by obstacles and pursued by ruthless killers.

Who really kidnapped Lorraine? What happened to the missing girls? Can the delicious Billy be trusted? These are all questions that she needs to find the answers to, before the answers find her.

The Seven Steps to Closure

Winner of the 2012 elit Publishing Award Humor Category.

Honourable mention in the London Book Festival.

Tara Babcock awakes the morning after her 30th birthday with a hangover that could kill an elephant - and the knowledge she is still no closer to achieving closure on her marriage breakup. Things go from bad to worse when she discovers that, not only is her ex-husband engaged to her cousin - Tash, the woman he left her for - but that Jake is also running for Lord Major of Sydney.

Desperate to leave the destructive relationship behind and with nothing to lose, she decides - with encouragement from her three best friends - to follow the dubious advice from a magazine article, *Closure in Seven Easy Steps*.

The Seven Steps to Closure follows Tara on her sometimes disastrous - always hilarious - path to achieve the seemingly impossible. It is available for sale in eBook and print form on Amazon.

CPSIA information can be obtained at www.ICGtesting.com
Printed in the USA
LVOW07s1845201016

27L V00011B/806/P